# PEOPLE
# WILL TALK

# PEOPLE WILL TALK

## KIERAN SCOTT

**G**

GALLERY BOOKS

New York   London   Toronto   Sydney   New Delhi

# G

Gallery Books
An Imprint of Simon & Schuster, LLC
1230 Avenue of the Americas
New York, NY 10020

First Gallery Books trade paperback edition July 2024

GALLERY BOOKS and colophon are registered trademarks of Simon & Schuster, LLC

Simon & Schuster: Celebrating 100 Years of Publishing in 2024

For information about special discounts for bulk purchases, please contact Simon & Schuster Special Sales at 1-866-506-1949 or business@simonandschuster.com.

The Simon & Schuster Speakers Bureau can bring authors to your live event. For more information or to book an event, contact the Simon & Schuster Speakers Bureau at 1-866-248-3049 or visit our website at www.simonspeakers.com.

Interior design by Hope Herr-Cardillo

Manufactured in the United States of America

10  9  8  7  6  5  4  3  2  1

Library of Congress Cataloging-in-Publication Data is available.

ISBN 978-1-6680-3810-9
ISBN 978-1-6680-3811-6 (ebook)

*For Matt*

*Lucky #3*

# PROLOGUE

T he bride was crystal clear on one thing: she would have the most unique, the most elaborate, the most decadent chandelier money could buy as the centerpiece for her wedding. Chandeliers being the wedding trend of the season, and she being the most famous engaged socialite on the East Coast—though the engagement was a secret at the moment—this did not seem like an unreasonable ask. Yes, it was a last-minute wedding, but if she couldn't have everything her heart desired on her wedding day, well, then she'd been lied to her entire life.

The chandelier arrived encased in a large wooden crate secured to a flatbed truck and required a full-sized forklift to convey it to the wedding tent. Three prize-winning hydrangeas were removed by the landscapers to allow the forklift access to the lawn, which it summarily destroyed, requiring new sod to be put in later that evening. The wedding planners kept to the edges of the dance floor while the chandelier expert they'd hired directed his two assistants and the six movers in meticulously extracting the giant light fixture from its protective wrapping.

The piece, there was no denying it, was a work of art. Made of thousands upon thousands of handcrafted bronze leaves, twisted and soldered along delicate, metal vines to mimic lush strands of ivy, the chandelier contained four tapering tiers and one hundred and fifty bulbs. It had movement, it had life—it weighed over three hundred pounds. It was so beautiful that the wedding planners and their team members gasped in awe at the sight of it. One of them even applauded, but only for a moment, before she remembered she was a professional and clasped her hands behind her back.

The piece had been made in India by a family of craftspeople known for generations to be experts in fine metalwork. They toiled on the chandelier for over a year and were so proud of their creation, they took a family photo with it that still hangs in their workshop in a place of honor. Upon completion, the matriarch of the family barely had the heart to let it go. It was a point of pride. It was one of a kind.

It was never intended to be a murder weapon.

# CATHERINE

Peter Frank was sitting in the lobby of her beachfront hotel. What did it mean? Had he come here for her? How did he know where she was staying? And why did she have to be just emerging from an intense workout with her Lululemon capris full of ass sweat?

Catherine was about to say his name, to get his attention, but paused. The sun streamed through the wall of French doors off the high-ceilinged lobby, and a light ocean breeze swept the delicate curtains across the gleaming parquet floor. In the restaurant of the lobby, silverware clinked gently against china plates, the scents of freshly brewed coffee and maple syrup permeating the air. Outside, seagulls cawed, and in the distance were gleeful shouts of children playing in the sand.

Watching him from across the room, Catherine could almost imagine that she and Peter were here on vacation together. Down the shore for a weekend getaway from their two kids, who were back in the city with their nanny. If they had never broken up, would this be true? They could have had two kids by now. Could have been married all this time. Could have been happy.

"Catherine!" He stood up from the deep armchair in which he'd been tapping away on his cell phone and smiled the smile that had broken her heart a thousand times. His dark brown hair had been recently cut, and his skin had a just-off-the-beach sort of tan. Though she knew from his Instagram he'd spent the last few weeks in the UK, not the south of France. "Look at you!"

She smiled back, grateful that she had, at least, smoothed her hair back into a sleek ponytail in the bathroom and reapplied deodorant. Her brand-new lash extensions were intact, having been applied just yesterday by Damon DeAngelo, extension-master to the stars. She also happened to know she looked fit as hell in this particular outfit.

"Peter! What are you doing here?"

"Lucking out, it seems." He leaned in to kiss her cheek and she closed her eyes, inhaling his clean, spicy scent, which still stirred things within her—just as it had done since she was nineteen years old.

"I can't believe you're seeing me like this," she said, hoping to God her deodorant was working.

"Come on, Cat. I've seen you every which way," he said, making her blush. "I'd heard you'd RSVP'd yes, but I wasn't sure you'd make it. I know how busy your weekends are."

So, he wasn't here looking for her. She tried not to let the disappointment show on her face.

"They are, usually. But this is why I have a staff, so that I can also have a life—occasionally. You know how much I always loved your mother's *clambakes*." Some sarcasm in the word *clambake* because Camilla Talbot-Frank's midsummer soiree was much more formal than its title suggested. "Although, I was surprised to be invited. It's been a while." She hadn't been invited to one of these, in fact, since she and Peter had officially broken up twelve years ago, when they were twenty-two, but who was counting? "I was starting to think I was blackballed."

She laughed and sipped her water.

"Never," he replied, but his easy smile dimmed a bit. "I'm

actually really glad you're here," he said. "And bumping into you like this . . ." He paused and glanced at the floor for half a second, clearing his throat. "I'm just really glad you're here."

"Hey," she took a step closer and touched his wrist. "Is everything all right?"

The smile returned full force. "Yes, of course! Just having a nostalgic moment."

He looked into her eyes and her heart all but stopped. When he looked at her like that, she forgot who she was, where she was. She forgot how much time had passed since she'd last seen him. Who she'd been with since. Who *he'd* been with. When he looked at her like that, they were college freshmen again, standing in the middle of a disco-themed mixer, palms sweaty and hearts pounding, about to share their first kiss. They were twentysomethings indulging in a quickie in a forgotten closet. They were celebrating her thirtieth birthday with one night in Barbados, which to this day, she'd never told a soul about.

"Babe! Hey, babe! I ordered room service. I say we go try out that massive shower before they bring it up."

Cash Blakely, Catherine's insatiable boyfriend of the last three months, slid up next to her and wrapped his arms around her hips, pulling her into him. He had just worked out too, but somehow wasn't sweaty at all, and Catherine saw Peter take a small step back as he took Cash in. Was that jealousy she saw in his eyes?

It was a fight to bite back her grin.

She turned to kiss Cash full on the lips, then shifted in his arms so that he was behind her, arms still clasped around her.

"Cash, this is Peter Frank. Peter, this is my boyfriend, Cash Blakely."

"The famous Peter Frank," said Cash, releasing her and offering his hand. "It's nice to meet you, man."

Peter shook hands with Cash. "Likewise. And I think you're

the famous one," he said smoothly. "My mom is a big fan of your low-impact series."

"Oh, thanks," Cash said. "That's definitely one of my more popular rides, especially with ladies of a certain age. You want me to autograph something for her?"

"No, no. That's all right. Nice of you to offer, though."

Peter gave Catherine a look that was at once quizzical and wry and . . . disappointed. She knew he must be thinking that Cash was a little too eager, a little too simple, and he was being generous. But he also seemed thrown by the embodiment of perfection that was her fitness celebrity boyfriend, and her heart didn't know what to do with itself. She had to wonder, if Cash hadn't been here, where might that nostalgic moment have led?

She was a horrible person. Only Catherine Farr could be standing wrapped in the arms of the perfect man and be fantasizing about another. But this was Peter. She was always slightly less than sane around him.

Besides, she and Cash hadn't been dating that long. It wasn't like it was serious or anything.

Peter's phone beeped and he checked it. "I should go," he said. "But I'll see you both later, yes?"

"You bet," said Cash.

"Looking forward to it," Catherine added.

Peter gave her a nod. "It really is good to see you, Cat."

Then he turned and walked through the airy lobby and out onto the patio, slipping his sunglasses on against the bright summer sun.

"I thought no one got to call you Cat," Cash said, kissing her cheek.

"They don't," she said. "Peter Frank does what Peter Frank wants." She took his hand and tugged him toward the grand staircase. "Let's go test that shower."

Cash gave her a wolfish smile and she tried not to feel guilty over the fact that her current state of excitement had more to do with the surprise encounter with Peter than with him. They were halfway up the stairs when her phone vibrated. She checked the text. It was from Peter.

Meet me in my room after the announcement.

Apparently, their meeting had the same effect on him.

# MAYA

> Meet me in my room after the announcement.

When she got the text, Maya Romero was sitting in the back of the town car her agency had paid for. It was the first communication she'd had from Peter in a week. Her hands hadn't trembled when she'd saved three match points in her first ever grand slam final at Wimbledon just over a week ago, but they trembled now. She texted back, mistyping every fourth letter.

> What does that mean? Where have you been?
> I've called you a hundred times! Are you ok???

No response. Not even the three scrolling dots.

"Is there any way you can go faster?" she asked Tatiana, her driver. They had only met a few hours ago but had since been through the gauntlet of Jersey Shore traffic together and were now bonded for life. After Tatiana had bailed on the parking lot that was the Garden State Parkway around exit 129, Maya had gotten so carsick from all the twists and turns and stops and starts that they'd had to pit-stop at a Wawa for ginger ale and fresh air, where Maya had ended up signing half a dozen autographs before she finally felt well enough to get back in the car.

"Not unless you want me to commit vehicular manslaughter," joked Tatiana.

Maya looked around. It was a hot July day in Cape Crest, New Jersey, and dozens of families and couples traversed the streets, toting boogie boards, pulling beach carts, or concentrating all their attention on melting ice cream cones. Tatiana inched the car forward toward the end of the tree-lined shopping district, and Maya's fingernails curled into the leather armrest.

Her phone buzzed, but it wasn't Peter. It was her agent, Bobby Fury.

> Adidas countered. 5 years 100 mill to stay. I say we take it.

Maya's throat tightened. It was a ridiculous sum of money. Of course she should take it. But she'd always wanted Nike, and they'd come in with a strong offer. Normally she would use Peter as a sounding board on a decision like this, but until five seconds ago, Peter had been ghosting her. He hadn't called her after her *Tonight Show* appearance on Monday, hadn't shown up for their planned lunch with the Babolat people on Wednesday, hadn't even texted a smiley face when she'd made Jenna Bush Hager laugh so hard she'd spit Pimm's on the desk at the *Today* show yesterday morning. When he left London for his flight back last Sunday, she'd been sure he would be waiting at his apartment with the ring they had chosen. A pink, five-carat diamond, cushion cut, surrounded by smaller diamonds in an intricate white-gold setting. Wasn't that what they had talked about? No distractions until after Wimbledon. And if she did well, they'd get engaged. (Because if she did poorly, she'd be in no mood.)

But she'd done more than well. She'd won the whole bloody thing, as the Brits said, and beaten two top-ten players in the process. As of Monday, she was ranked number four in the world. She had the replica Venus Rosewater Dish for her mantel and a one-hundred-million-dollar offer from Adidas to keep Nike from poaching her.

All she needed now was Peter. But he hadn't been at his apartment when she'd arrived. Hadn't answered her calls or texts that night or the next morning, when she'd had to go on *The View* with more under-eye makeup than she'd ever worn in her life. The doormen didn't know where he was, and after two days she'd felt uncomfortable staying in his apartment and had moved over to the Plaza. (Her own five-bedroom villa was in Boca, and she was barely ever there anyway.) Maya had tried getting in touch with his brother, Jensen, but Jensen had notifications turned off, and there were no other mutual friends to turn to. She had his mother's phone number, but that did not seem appropriate.

Maya and Peter moved in different circles when they weren't together, and when they were together, mostly remained in the bubble of her tennis life. This whole debacle had made her realize that in the last year he'd become completely ingrained in her world, while she knew next to nothing about his. She'd always appreciated the fact that he seemed willing to assimilate into her crazy lifestyle and hadn't expected her to reciprocate, but now . . .

> Yes. Let's accept. Thanks Bobby.

He marked her text with a thumbs-up. And just like that, she was one-hundred-million-dollars richer. She sat back and waited to feel a thrill of accomplishment, but all she felt was anxiety.

> When can we announce?

> Once we're signed. You know the drill.

She did know the drill. But she also loved announcing things. Nothing felt official until it was announced. Until people could read about it on ESPN.com or tennis.com. Until her father could read about it.

Her father.

It wasn't possible, was it? That he had somehow gotten to Peter?

It wasn't the first time the sickening thought had occurred to her over the past few days. She imagined her handsome, chisel-jawed boyfriend beaten and bloodied in an alley somewhere, one leg broken, a wrist snapped. Normally her father didn't send his men after a person unless said person had crossed him, but one never knew. Perhaps Daddy Dearest imagined that simply dating his daughter amounted to a punishable offense.

But no. Of course, nothing had happened to Peter. At least nothing catastrophic. If it had, it would be all over the news. Although, that didn't mean her father hadn't gotten to him in some more subtle way. Her stomach burned just imagining it.

Peter *had* been acting a little strangely during his last week in the UK—leaving the room to take calls at random times, staring off into space distractedly. She had asked him once what was wrong, and he'd told her she was imagining things, or maybe projecting her stress about the final onto him. He'd kissed her and told her to concentrate on her tennis. So that's what she'd done, because that was what she was supposed to be doing. But what if . . .

Her fingertips curled into the leather seat at her sides. Peter wouldn't leave her. Not for a bribe. Not because of some random threat. He was stronger than that. He'd promised her that her family's history, their reputation, didn't matter. She'd left that behind. All of it. She was Maya Romero, tennis champion. A world-class athlete with a clean life. Her father couldn't touch her.

Her phone rang. She almost answered it without checking the screen, but then stopped herself.

UNKNOWN

*Shit.*

A very small part of her wanted to pick it up, just in case. Just in case it was Peter. But she knew better. This was the third one this week. That was her limit. She declined the call, then texted her assistant, Bekka London.

> Time for a new phone.

The reply came instantly.

> On it.

"Pulling up to the house now," Tatiana said.

Maya sat forward. There were broad-shouldered guards in well-cut tuxedoes at the imposing, wrought iron–and-gold gate. Tatiana rolled down the window and the hot air poured in, invading Maya's space. She could hear strains of music on the wind, the sound of crashing waves in the background.

"Good evening," said the deep-voiced guard. "Who do we have?"

"Maya Romero."

Tatiana handed over the invitation. The guard leaned in and gave an impressed frown at the sight of Maya in the back seat.

"Congratulations on Wimbledon," he said.

"Thanks," she replied, praying he wouldn't request a selfie. She wanted to ask him if he'd seen Peter. If he knew what this announcement he'd referenced was all about. People didn't normally make her feel off-kilter like this. Nothing made her feel off-kilter like this. Maya was a competitor. She was a champion. She was in control, always. It was how she had survived on her own all these years. It was all she knew.

The guard clicked something on his iPad, handed the invite back, and waved Tatiana through. "Enjoy the evening."

The gates couldn't have opened slower. The car moved forward and up the long, winding hill until the sprawling Frank estate came into view at the top of the bluffs. Built in the Victorian style favored in Cape Crest, it was all turrets and spires and gingerbread trim, the siding a deep red that made the stark white scrolling stand out against the lush grass. Beyond the home, built into the bluffs, were levels of decks and patios, all leading down to the private beach below. Maya saw waiters and waitresses in white jackets, expertly balancing trays of hors d'oeuvres and champagne.

"I thought you said this was a clambake," said Tatiana.

"The Franks don't do anything without champagne," Maya replied.

She wished this could have been a casual affair. Coolers of beer, buckets full of crab legs, wedges of lemon and corn fritters and mac and cheese. She'd literally kill for some mac and cheese. But though she'd only met Peter's mother twice in the last twelve months, Maya was aware that the way Camilla Talbot-Frank threw a party, any clams would be delivered to a white-clothed table on fine bone china. And if there was any beer on the premises, it would be poured into glasses, thank you very much.

At least Peter didn't need everything to be first class all the time. The two of them had been known to hit a dive bar in Melbourne or a corner tapas joint in Mallorca. It was what she loved most about him. For someone who could have been so spoiled and privileged, he definitely was not.

But then, could she really trust that? Seven days ago she would have said she knew Peter better than anyone else in the world.

But where had he been all week? Why was he ignoring her? He hadn't even posted on Instagram once since leaving London. The last post on his feed was an artsy photo of her on the evening of her win, standing on the balcony at the little house they'd rented in Wimbledon Village, the sun setting behind her. He'd captioned it *My girl the Champion.*

> My car is just pulling up. Come meet me.

She stared at her phone. Nothing. Her breath was beginning to grow shallow.

"Here we are," Tatiana said, easing the car to a stop at the top of the circular drive. A valet immediately popped open the door. "Have fun, Maya."

Maya smoothed the full skirt of her light-pink, two-piece dress and took a few deep breaths. Peter was here somewhere. And when she found him, she had a sinking feeling that what happened next was going to be anything but fun.

# LEANNE

"The fuck?" Leanne Gladstone said.

"Lee!" her nephew, Hudson, scolded, rolling his eyes. "You kiss your mother with that mouth?"

She shoved her phone away and smirked at his borrowing of her mother's favorite admonishment. "Sorry. Don't tell Nonna."

"Is everything okay?" He eyed her bag worriedly, his blue eyes full of concern. She ran a palm over his dark hair, which sprang right back into place, sticking up straight from his forehead. He ducked away from her touch, but halfheartedly, like he knew that's what kids his age were supposed to do, but he wasn't fully irritated by her yet. Hudson could sometimes behave very young for his age. His therapist said it was a case of arrested development, something that often happened to kids who lost a parent at a young age. But they were working on it. He'd finally stopped waking up in the middle of the night, but he did still have a bed full of stuffed animals and a Winnie the Pooh nightlight. Leanne didn't mind either of these things, though. No need to rush him into growing up too fast.

"Yes, everything's fine," she lied.

"Can I go play Spike Ball with the cousins?"

"On the beach?"

"I'll be careful, I swear."

She was about to say no—because he'd ruin his new pants, because he'd definitely end up fully submerged, because he might get sucked out to sea by a random rip current—but he so seldom saw his cousins, little assholes that they were, that she couldn't deny him some bonding time.

"Okay, *but*." She snapped her fingers at him repeatedly, because he was already running off, and he froze. "Do not. I repeat, do not. Go in the water. Do I make myself clear?"

He rolled his eyes again but smiled. "Yes, Lee."

She narrowed her own eyes to keep from smiling back. He looked so much like her sister when he did that. "Go."

As soon as Hudson was gone, Leanne plucked a flute of champagne from the tray of a passing waiter and downed half of it before fishing her phone out again. Peter Frank was ordering her to his bedroom? Was he kidding? And what announcement? This was a clambake, not a board meeting. She tossed back the rest of the champagne and shoved the flute under her arm to text back.

WTF???

No response. Shocking.

Leanne glanced around for someone to talk to, but the only people she knew at this party were waiting on the actual guests, so they were a bit busy. She spent a few minutes scrolling through food porn on Instagram—an activity that always calmed her—and then her phone rang. It was Jordan Troy, her attorney. Turning her back to the party, she answered. "Jordan? What is it? What's wrong?"

"Hello, Leanne. How are you this fine evening?"

Leanne closed her eyes, her brown curls dancing in the ocean-side breeze and itching her cheeks. She took a deep breath for patience. "I'm fine, Jordan. And you?"

"Doing well, thanks. Doing well."

"You can't be doing that well if you're calling me on a Saturday after six."

"Fair point." He chuckled. "Well, I heard from Mr. Blythe and you're not going to like it, I'm afraid."

She spoke though clenched teeth now. "What?"

"Peter still hasn't signed the papers."

"Oh, come on!" she snapped. "We've already extended the deadline twice."

"I know, I know. But he cited a family emergency."

"Oh my God." Leanne rubbed her forehead. "I'm literally standing under a tent at the family's estate in the middle of a party with three hundred other people. Unless the family emergency is that they've run out of toilet paper, there is no family emergency."

"Well, we can file a court order. Compel him to respond."

"Yes. Do that." She pushed her red-framed glasses up on her nose with her middle finger. It was something she used to do as a kid for fun—just to see if anyone would notice—but it had since become an unfortunate habit. "That's what I want to do."

It was what she'd wanted to do the first time Peter had toyed with her, but her lawyers had convinced her to give the extension instead. They'd said that the Frank family wasn't a family you wanted to piss off. Though they hadn't used those exact words. And she'd agreed. Because she wasn't an idiot. The Franks basically owned this town and everyone in it, plus half of the Upper East Side and—from what she'd heard—a chunk of southern France. But this was getting ridiculous. Hudson was about to start school— his first year in junior high. He deserved to have a stable home. He deserved to feel secure and grounded with people who loved him, who would check his homework, who would make sure he ate right and went to bed at a reasonable hour and didn't have too much screen time. He needed to live with her and Tony, full-time. He needed to know he was officially theirs.

It was what Monica would have wanted.

"All right, but just to remind you—"

"You don't have to remind me. File the court order."

"But, Leanne, I—"

"Am I paying you, or are they? File the fucking order."

She hung up the phone and dropped it on the rock wall behind her just as another waitress walked by with a tray. The woman paused. "You look like you could use one."

Leanne took two. "Thanks."

The woman winked and kept walking. Across the tent, Leanne spotted Camilla—Peter's mother and Hudson's grandmother—and for half a second she wanted to go over there and tell her where she could stick her family emergency. No doubt she had something to do with this latest delay. But then she noticed that Camilla was locked in an intense conversation with a man she'd never seen before—tall and muscular, with a shaved head, his suit a bit too tight for his taut body. He looked like a bodyguard or a bouncer. They were just outside a corner opening, and she seemed to be admonishing him for something. His thick neck was bowed, and she slapped the back of one hand against the palm of the other repeatedly. That was Camilla for you, always busting balls. Leanne slugged the first glass, and half of it dribbled down the front of her striped sundress.

"Fuck!" she snapped, earning disturbed looks from the nearest group of rich bitches.

Just then, Hudson reemerged from the crowd, pants soaked up to his knees, a spray of wet sand across his face and more embedded in his curls.

"Don't be mad."

Yes, it was definitely going to be a shit night.

# CATHERINE

Catherine hadn't seen Peter since she'd arrived at the party. It was as if he was purposefully staying hidden, keeping her in suspense. That text . . . she hadn't stopped thinking about it all day. Did he really think she was going to meet up for a booty call in the middle of his mother's beloved clambake? She had a boyfriend. Whom he'd *just* met. And *he* had a girlfriend. One with a notoriously ruthless father. Although, he hadn't posted about her in over a week. Maybe something had changed?

God. What was wrong with her? No. *No.* He had to be out of his mind if he thought she would even consider it.

"Babe! Babe! Smile!"

Cash lifted his phone and threw his arm around Catherine, leaning them both back so that he could get a selfie with the gorgeous ocean view in the background. Catherine tilted her head, showing her good side, and flashed a wide smile, displaying her newly whitened teeth. Photo accomplished, Cash leaned her back even farther and kissed her.

She had not shown Peter's text to Cash.

"This is a great party," he said as she stood up again. "Thanks for bringing me."

Catherine pulled out her lip oil for a touch-up and glanced around. They were still in the hushed mingling stage of the evening, a band of former beach bums—dressed in expensive linen garb—playing quiet yacht rock in the background. She knew from experience that as the night grew older, things would get a bit rowdier, especially down on the beach where some hot DJ Peter had hired would turn it up. But for now, it reminded her of that chiropractor's convention she'd helped coordinate in the first year of her party-planning career. Total snoozefest.

That was the thing about Cash, though. He could find the fun in anything.

"See that woman over there? She's SpinMeRightRound. In the flesh!" Cash's green eyes were wide with excitement as he pointed out a tall, impossibly toned sixty-something in a gold minidress.

"You're kidding," she said. SpinMeRightRound was Cash's biggest fan. She took every one of his strength classes live and was always the first person to comment on his Instagram posts and TikTok updates.

"Nope! She showed me her profile on her phone and everything. She's taken my classes five *thousand* times."

"Dang. I hope I look half as good at her age."

Catherine eyed the woman, who was obviously salivating after Cash like he was a carb. As the number one instructor on the number two fitness app in the country, he got this look a lot. Even if he weren't famous, he would get this look. The man was six foot four with the body of Adonis and the chiseled good looks of a classic movie star. Square chin, bright eyes, dark hair, not to mention a voice that could melt butter. She looped her arm through Cash's and turned him in the other direction.

"Let's do a lap," she said. "I want to see if I can find their staging area. I'm dying to know how they're keeping all these oysters chilled to perfection."

"Always working," Cash said, and kissed the top of her head.

He was almost a foot taller than her, even though she was wearing these ridiculous heels. "That's my girl."

Catherine smiled. Cash was the perfect boyfriend. They were equally ambitious and equally connected, and as such he completely understood her drive, her work schedule, and the fact that she was not going to be available one hundred percent of the time. They had met at the engagement party of two of his colleagues, Bea Lively and Antonio Morrow, which she had planned—she was now in the finishing stages of planning their wedding—and had hardly been apart since. And yet, this very morning, she'd been fantasizing about what a life with Peter would have looked like. Truth be told, she fantasized about this more often than she'd ever care to admit.

Peter was her college boyfriend, for God's sake. Her first love, yes, but still. Shouldn't she be over it by now? Shouldn't she be completely unaffected by random mysterious texts?

Maybe if she hadn't kept hooking up with him on and off for years. Honestly, sometimes she felt like an addict. She'd try to quit him cold turkey and then he'd somehow tempt her back. By texting her a photo when he found a store selling white chocolate KitKats (her favorite) or sending her flowers on her mom's death day or calling her after inking some deal his dad didn't think he could close because it wouldn't feel real until she knew about it.

But she was done with that now. Done. She was thirty-four years old. This was ridiculous. She pulled Cash to her and kissed all her internal frustration into him.

"Damn," Cash said under his breath. "Want to get out of here?"

Maybe they should. The farther away she was from Peter the better.

The band broke into a loud flourish—the sort that preceded a change in tone or . . . an announcement? Catherine's breath caught.

"This is it," she said.

"This is what?" asked Cash.

Catherine moved to the edge of the patio. There were half a dozen such patios arranged in a semicircle around the backyard overlooking the ocean, connected by a series of flower-lined stairways. The patio on which she and Cash stood, overlooked the band, and Catherine trailed her gaze from the stage to the immediate surrounding area, looking for Peter.

"It's just . . . Camilla," she improvised. "She makes a speech every year."

When Catherine was in college, she was obsessed with Camilla Talbot-Frank. The woman was so elegant, so at ease speaking in front of a crowd. She looked everyone in the eye and really listened when they spoke. If Catherine had never met Camilla, she wouldn't be the person she was today. Camilla had inspired her. Watching her had taught Catherine everything she knew about poise and elegance and grace under pressure. Being among the Franks had taught her how important it was to be well-connected. To follow up with people when they offered to meet for a drink or introduce her to one of their friends or colleagues. One never knew who was going to help them get what they wanted. Even though she and Peter hadn't worked out in the end, at least she'd gotten something out of the relationship.

This was part of the reason she and Cash worked so well— a natural reciprocity. Both their social media followings had exploded once they'd started posting and tagging each other. After their weekend in Aruba with his friends back in May, her voice mail had been so full of requests for meetings it had maxed out. And Cash, who had always had a following among the older set, had seen his roster of twentysomething followers swell.

Finally, there was movement down below, but it wasn't Camilla stepping out onto the dais. It was Peter. Her chest caught at the sight of him. He wore a light-pink shirt, open at the collar, a pair of dark gray slacks, and dress shoes. His dark hair was tousled by the wind, but that only added to his laid-back charm. He smiled as he approached the microphone at the center of the stage.

This was definitely it. The "announcement." Catherine's pulse picked up. Maybe he was going to declare his undying love for her and ask her to run away to the Maldives with him so they could finally be married and live happily ever after. She wondered what she'd do if that happened. What Cash would do.

Then, someone else stepped out onto the dais.

"Is that—Tilly Dansforth?" Cash said.

Something turned inside Catherine's stomach. It *was* Tilly Dansforth. The devil herself. Golden-blond hair gleaming, skin perfectly tanned, set off by her white lace cocktail dress. She could not look at Tilly without vividly recalling that night, junior year, when Tilly had flown out to visit Peter. Catherine had gone to a lecture, then come back to find them both drunk, Tilly straddling Peter in the middle of their dorm hallway, railing about how he could do so much better than Catherine. The only saving grace was that they'd both been fully clothed.

Tilly was one of the more famous socialites on the Upper East Side, and not just because she threw the most notorious parties and had been photographed with every celebrity that had ever lived. Her parents, Cookie and Daniel Dansforth, had recently died in a plane crash when their pilot had lost consciousness on a quick flight from Teterboro to Martha's Vineyard. It had been all over the news—Cookie having given more money to women-led charities than God, and Daniel having amassed more wealth than anyone in his generation. Wealth Tilly and her younger brother, Brandt, had inherited upon their parents' deaths.

"How do you know Tilly Dansforth?" she asked.

"Everyone knows Tilly Dansforth," Cash said. "Me and Misty

did a private for her a couple years ago. That woman is a beast with the core work. I couldn't even keep up."

Catherine gritted her teeth. "You hate core work."

"Truth." He punctuated the statement by clinking glasses with her, then downing the rest of his drink.

Peter and Tilly stepped up to the microphone. Together. He reached for Tilly's hand. She leaned into his arm. They both smiled.

*No.*

It was then that she noticed there were others walking onto the stage. Camilla and her husband, Tate. Peter's older brother Jensen and his wife and kids. And was that . . . Brandt? She hadn't seen him in the flesh in years, but she recognized the floppy hairstyle and the clipped blond beard from the press coverage of his parents' funeral.

"Hello, everyone! If I could have your attention, please?" Peter's voice washed over the crowd and into Catherine's chest.

A hush fell over the backyard as anyone who hadn't already noticed something was happening tuned in. The sound of the crashing waves down below intensified.

"I believe you all know Tilly Dansforth."

The crowd applauded politely, and Tilly offered an elegant wave.

"My mother has asked the two of us to do the honor of welcoming you all to the annual Frank Family Clambake!"

"Here! Here!" someone shouted, and glasses went up around the grounds.

"And we'd like to make a little announcement, if you'll indulge us!" said Tilly.

Peter leaned in to whisper something in her ear, and Tilly smiled and shook her head, pushing him playfully. Catherine thought she might actually die. Then Tilly turned toward the microphone again.

"The announcement is that this isn't *just* the Frank family clambake, this is also my wedding. *Our* wedding. Peter and I are pleased to invite you all to join us as we take our vows under the gazebo at seven thirty this evening, where he'll make me the happiest woman on earth."

A scream cut the stunned silence. Catherine's hand flew up to cover her mouth. It was only after she took a breath that she realized the scream hadn't come from her.

# MAYA

It took a moment for Maya to recover.

Okay. Several moments.

Shaking like a tiny dog on the Fourth of July, she found the nearest bathroom. Tears leaked from her eyes. This had to be a nightmare. Peter wouldn't do this to her. He couldn't. He loved her. She knew he loved her. They had made plans. Said things to each other that they had never said to anyone else. She had never even *heard* of this Tilly person.

She wrestled her phone out of the stupid, pointless, tiny purse she'd bought in London to match her dress and dropped it on the bathroom floor with a clatter. *Shit.* When was she going to wake up? Now? Now? *Now?*

"Okay. You're okay," she said to herself, scrabbling the phone off the floor. "Everything's okay."

Except it so very much wasn't. She sat on the closed toilet and called Peter. It went straight to voice mail. She released a string of expletives she'd never said before—at least not in that order—and called Shawn Groff. If ever Shawn was going to earn his paycheck, this was it. The love of her life, the man she'd picked out an engagement ring with less than two months ago, was marrying someone else. This was the reason the occupation of "life coach" had been invented.

Shawn was in his forties, gay, an avid golfer, and had degrees in psychology, ancient history, and library science. He was the most well-read person Maya had ever met or likely would meet, and he was basically her best friend. He was also paid a ridiculous salary.

"Hi Maya," Shawn said into the phone. "Have you seen Peter? Did he explain why he went dark?"

"Shawn. OhmyGod." She bent forward at the waist, her free arm clamped across her stomach. "Peter just announced his wedding."

"Congratulations!"

"Not *our* wedding!" She dug her teeth into her bottom lip. "*His* wedding. To someone named Tilly Dansforth."

"The canola oil heiress?"

"Is that what she is?"

"Wait. No. Maybe it's plastics . . ."

"Shawn!"

"I don't understand."

"Exactly! *I* don't understand! He . . . well, *she* just announced to the entire party that we're all here for their surprise wedding!" Maya kept her voice down, glancing at the locked door. There were voices in the hallway. "And even better, he texted me telling me to meet him in his room after the announcement. Like I'm going to come running? When he didn't even bother to dump me before proposing to someone else? How could he do this to me? He said he loved me. He said . . . he said . . ."

"Maya, I'm so sorry. But honey, you need to breathe."

"I *am* breathing!" she shrieked.

"No, I don't think you are."

He talked her through a few breathing exercises, counting for her as she inhaled and exhaled. She did as she was told, closing her eyes, breathing deeply, listening to the soothing sound of Shawn's voice. Gradually, her pulse began to calm. She leaned hard into the porcelain sink, the coolness a relief.

"Listen to me," Shawn said. "Are you listening?"

Maya took a breath. "Yes. I'm listening."

"Good. What do you want?"

"To murder someone," she said.

"What do you actually want? Out of Peter? Out of this situation?"

*I want this* situation *to not be happening.*

"I want an explanation," she said evenly, opening her eyes. "I want him to tell me this is all a joke. And if it's not, I want . . . I want the opportunity to get his head examined. Or at least to talk him out of it. He loves me, Shawn. I know he does. *You* know he does."

"I know," he said softly.

"So what happened?"

"I don't know."

An image of Peter, under the white sheets at the apartment in Wimbledon, smiling wolfishly after going down on her. It was just over a week ago. That look in his eye. Like he could spend the rest of his life in that bed just making her happy. He was her person. The only living soul outside of her team whom she trusted. Literally the only person she trusted in the world who wasn't on her payroll.

"Listen, if you go to his room, as he requested—"

"As he *ordered*."

"If you go to his room, will you get what you want?"

Maya considered. She hated the idea of doing what he'd told her to do. Especially in this moment. Of being at his beck and call. He'd just humiliated her in front of hundreds of people. He'd broken her heart. He'd treated her like she didn't even exist.

But yes, if she went to his room, there was a possibility she would get what she wanted. Once he saw her, he'd set this right. He'd have to.

She stood up straight in front of the mirror, looking herself in the eye. She could do this. She could. She was in control. "I'll let you know how it goes."

"That's my girl."

Maya hung up the phone. Her skin was flushed hot, even with the air-conditioning in this place set at subzero temperatures, so she raised her arms over her head, closed her eyes and brought them together down to heart center. She breathed in and out, repeating her prematch mantra to herself—the one Shawn had taught her. What would she do without him?

*Calm around me. Calm within me. Calm around me. Calm within me.*

She did this until her internal temperature cooled and her temples ceased their throbbing. Then she went to find Peter.

The house was huge and lofty, with four floors and a zillion bedrooms decorated in beachy tones of blue and beige, and by the time she located Peter's bedroom, she had second-guessed herself a dozen times. She was also not the first to arrive, and Peter was not even there. When she opened the door, she found two women facing off with Tilly Dansforth, who, close-up, reminded Maya of Anya Tabakova, that psycho bitch from Belarus who had once tried to take Maya's head off with a crosscourt forehand after the point had been called dead. She was toned, tan, sinewy, and her teeth were too big for her face. She was blond, like Maya. But unlike Maya's natural, sun-kissed blond, Tilly's was clearly salon-enhanced.

The women were sniping at one another, but stopped when Maya walked in.

"Ah. Here she is."

The look on Tilly's face told Maya that she expected her to react the same way these other two had—whoever the hell they were—and freak out. So she did the exact opposite.

"Hello, I'm Maya Romero," she said, turning to the two other women and extending her hand with a confident smile.

"Catherine Farr," said the first, who had impeccably smooth, long dark hair and wore an expensive, sleeveless trapeze dress with a high collar and tons of crystals in an intricate pattern. Too much makeup, false eyelashes, possibly Botox. But she had a good, firm handshake.

"We know who you are," said the other woman, ignoring the offered hand. She had a slight Jersey accent, wild curls, and rage emanating from her eyeballs. "What we don't know is what the fuck is going on. Where's Peter?"

"He'll be along in a minute," Tilly said with a dismissive wave of her hand. "I'm the one who invited you here."

"Wait, that text was from *you*?" said Catherine.

"What text?" Maya asked.

The woman with the curly hair took out her phone and showed the screen to Maya.

> Meet me in my room after the announcement.

Maya suddenly felt very, very played. She had never attended a traditional high school and she wondered if this was what it was like. Fake texts sent by the bitchy queen bee from your boyfriend's phone. She'd always been glad she missed it and it made her even angrier that she was experiencing it now. And at the hands of this woman who had to be at least a decade older than her. So much for maturity coming with age.

"Yes, it was from me. Apologies for the theatrics, but I wanted to get this all over with at one time." Tilly clasped her hands lightly in front of her.

"Get what over with?" Maya asked.

Just then, a door at the far end of the room opened, and Peter stepped in. Maya felt a physical pull toward him that was practically impossible to resist. He was here. In the flesh. After all these days of ignoring her. It was almost as if she was watching a fictional character come to life. He was wearing a perfectly cut tuxedo now, pressed and pristine, and he tugged down on the shirt cuffs as he entered. His shave, after growing an attractive scruff while in the UK, was sharp as a knife. He looked completely at ease until he glanced up and saw Maya. Then all the color drained from his face.

It was somehow extremely gratifying.

"Peter," Maya said calmly, though her heart fluttered around like a drunken bird. "What is going on?"

His Adam's apple bobbed as he took in the other two women. He cleared his throat, stepping over to stand next to Tilly. "That's what I'd like to know."

Every inch of Maya ached. Her fight or flight instinct was all fight. She wanted to launch herself at Tilly, to rip her throat out with her bare hands, but she remained still.

"What's going on is, Peter and I are getting married. And we intend our marriage to be a partnership in every sense of the word. So, I've called you all here to tell you the following."

Peter reached for Tilly's hand. "Tilly—"

"Shh!" she said, batting his fingers away. "I need to do this."

Maya's vision went hazy and she blinked until she could refocus. She watched Peter as Tilly spoke. He kept his eyes trained on the floor, his jaw working.

*Look at me*, she pleaded silently. *Look at me!*

"Catherine, Peter will no longer be investing in your little party planning venture," Tilly said. The air quotes around *party planning venture* were visible from space.

Catherine snorted and started to speak, but Tilly cut her off.

"And Leanne, I'll be adopting Hudson as my son, so your bid to steal him away from his father is officially done."

"*Steal* him. Steal him? Who the fuck do you think you are? Peter! You can't—"

"And Maya. Sweetie."

Maya's gaze flicked to Tilly. Forget her throat. She wanted to rip this woman's face off with her fingernails.

"Your relationship with Peter is now over."

She looked *so* smug. She was clearly waiting for Maya to run from the room in tears. Obviously Tilly knew nothing about her. Maya was not one for public histrionics or outbursts of any kind. At least none that anyone knew about. Her last name was Romero, yes, but she was nothing like her father, who had singlehandedly made that name so infamous. That scream earlier? That was an anomaly. And no one had seen her do it anyway.

"I think it's up to Peter whether or not our relationship is over."

She returned her attention to her boyfriend, her partner, her would-be fiancé, until he finally, finally looked at her. There was a flash of something in his eyes—the briefest hint of emotion.

"Peter?" she said. *It's me. Remember me? The person who held a cold washcloth to your neck when you were throwing up from food poisoning in Monte Carlo? The one you baked a birthday cake for from scratch in your previously untouched oven? The one you were cuddled up in bed with just a few days ago, sipping champagne and watching the movie* Wimbledon *at Wimbledon because it felt so ironic it was almost unironic?* "Say something."

He swallowed. "I'm in love with Tilly. Our families are very old friends. I'm making the wise decision for once in my life." He cleared his throat and put his arm around Tilly's waist. "I'm sorry to have led you on, Maya."

"*Led me on?*"

Maya looked into his eyes, searching for something, anything, to cling to. A little spark, a touch of irony, a glimmer that said he was still Peter—still hers. There was nothing.

"Yes. I really am sorry."

Tilly grinned at her. "But congratulations on winning Wimbledon!"

# CATHERINE

Catherine knew Leanne was talking—ranting—but all she could hear was a low, whooshing sound that seemed to emanate from somewhere in the back of her skull. The sun seared her eyes and sweat pooled on her upper lip. She had no idea how they'd gotten outside. Didn't remember leaving the room or walking downstairs or any of it. Peter really was getting married. To Tilly. Conceited, blond, skinny bitch Tilly. Catherine could still see her at the age of eighteen in her baby-pink hot pants and bandeau top sucking on a ring pop on the hood of some asshole's Bentley, trying to get Peter to notice her. Like an Upper East Side Lolita with a fake nose ring. Tilly had *always* wanted Peter. She'd basically acted like he was her birthright. And now she had him.

Why? Why Tilly of all people?

Peter had been through plenty of girlfriends since he and Catherine had broken up. He'd fathered a child. But he and Catherine had always stayed connected. They called each other when they were lonely. They checked in with each other for advice on relationships and family and business decisions. She was Peter's best friend, and he was hers. A best friend with occasional benefits.

But that was all over now. She'd always known it would eventually have to end. That one or both of them would get married. That some other man or woman would come between them.

But why did it have to be Tilly?

Leanne was still talking, now into a cell phone. Shouting something about a court order and telling someone off for being "slow as fuck." Catherine looked up at the house, looming against what now seemed like a psychotically blue sky.

She needed to talk some sense into Peter. There was something more going on here. She could feel it. Why else would he trap himself in a loveless marriage? Not just loveless—torturous. That's what it would be for him to be married to a domineering, self-centered, prima donna like Tilly. Torture. Besides, he hadn't let himself be trapped the first time, when Leanne's sister, Monica, had wanted to marry him. She'd had the baby single and they'd worked it out and it had been fine. Well. For a few years, anyway.

The whooshing sound suddenly stopped, like slamming a door closed on a room of rowdy children. She needed to text Peter and tell him to meet her somewhere. But where? Guests were already moving toward the gazebo to witness the vows. And what if Tilly still had his phone? The very idea of that stuck-up bitch receiving her texts to Peter made her intestines clench. Forget the phone. She was going to have to do this the old-fashioned way. Catherine started back inside, but Leanne grabbed her wrist.

"Where are you going?" Leanne asked.

"I have to talk to him. I have to talk him out of this." A stiff breeze blew Catherine's hair across her face and into her mouth. She swiped it back out ungracefully.

"You can't do that," Leanne said.

"Why not? He'll listen to me."

"Peter Frank doesn't listen to anyone. He doesn't *care* about anyone."

"That's not true," said Catherine. "You don't know him."

Leanne's scoff somehow held the weight of the world. "I know he wouldn't even look at you in there. Or me. Or even Maya. Tilly's got his balls in a vise." Her phone beeped and she looked down at it, typing a response as she continued. "Besides, they've got thumbheads stationed at every door. Look."

Catherine turned. Two giant security guards flanked the French doors they'd just come through. Maybe she should try to get past them. If she caused enough of a commotion, Peter would be called and then he'd have to talk to her.

The door suddenly flung open and out walked, not Peter or Tilly, but Brandt—Tilly's younger brother. He seemed agitated, but his eyes instantly fell on Catherine, so she lifted her hand in the start of a wave. Instead of coming toward her, though, he took a hard right and stormed off, flaps of his suit jacket whipping around. Face burning, Catherine turned her wave into a hair smoothing and cleared her throat. It *had* been years since they'd seen each other. Not everyone had a talent for remembering everyone they'd ever met like she did.

"Good cover," Leanne said, patting her arm.

"Whatever. I'm going to find Peter. I'm doing this for all of us, okay? Do you really want Tilly to be Hudson's mother?"

Leanne went rigid. "Of course not. I'm surprised she could even say the word *mother* without her brain literally imploding."

There was an image.

"See? Then I have to try. For Hudson's sake."

It was a low blow, using the name of the kid she had cursed the existence of dozens of times over the last twelve years. Using Hudson against Leanne in particular, given everything that had happened with Monica. But desperate times . . .

"Fine," Leanne said. "Your social media funeral."

Catherine paused. Shit. Leanne was right. If she caused any drama, it would definitely be caught on video, and she and Cash would be tagged all over it. Half the people here followed one or both of them already. Causing a social media storm by breaking up her ex-boyfriend's wedding could mean career suicide, and it would definitely mean relationship suicide.

Meanwhile, she'd utterly forgotten about Cash. He was here somewhere, looking for her, no doubt. She'd said she was going to the bathroom. How long ago was that? Ten minutes? An hour? A year? It felt like a year.

Tilly didn't understand that she'd leveled the wrong threat at Catherine. Farr and Away Events wasn't a "little party planning venture," and she didn't need Peter's investment anymore. Sure, maybe his seed money had gotten her going in the beginning, but now Catherine was one of the top five wedding planners on the East Coast. Someone even Tilly herself might have hired—if she wasn't marrying Catherine's ex. If Tilly and Catherine hadn't gotten into a bona fide cat fight over Peter some fifteen years ago in this very yard. (Not her finest moment.) But what Tilly didn't know, it seemed, was that Catherine had a slew of investors, more revenue than she'd ever dreamed of, and a wait list twenty-four-months long for her services.

So no, she didn't need Peter anymore. Not the way Tilly thought she did. She just liked having him on her books. It made her feel closer to him, gave her an excuse to stay in touch, and kept him invested in seeing her succeed. Literally.

"Are you going to stay for this shit show?" Leanne asked, shoving her phone in her bag.

She shouldn't. The healthy thing to do would be to find Cash and get the hell out of here. She had nothing to gain from watching Peter and Tilly walk down the aisle, other than fodder for her nightmares. Maybe they could still make that gallery opening one of her former clients had invited them to.

"Oh. My. God! It really *is* you!"

A plus-sized girl in a tasteful black dress approached Catherine, practically shaking. She wore flat shoes, neutral makeup, and gorgeous false eyelashes, her white-blond hair dyed pink at the roots. Catherine pegged her as a member of the party-planning staff, as she herself had worn this basic uniform to events hundreds of times in her career, the dress to blend into the background, the flats for comfort during hours upon hours on her feet. The woman's eyes were red, as if she'd been crying or smoking up recently, and her eyeliner was a bit smudged at the corners—not in a purposeful way.

"Catherine Farr, right? I'm your biggest fan."

She sniffled through a wobbly smile, and Catherine knew it had been tears and not pot. This softened her.

"It's so nice to meet you . . . ?"

"Oh, I'm Farrah. Farrah Cox? My mom, Felicia, is a party planner and I work for her. We actually planned . . . this." She waved her hand in the air vaguely and her smile wobbled again. "Do you think I could get a selfie?"

Catherine's spirits lifted a bit, like they always did when someone asked for a selfie.

"Sure!"

"I could just take it for you," Leanne offered, grudgingly. "Hi Farrah. Thanks for not hiring me to do the cake."

"Oh, hi Leanne." Farrah's cheeks went pink as she handed over her phone. "My mom thought about it, but she was worried you . . . well . . . you know the family so well, and—"

"She was worried I'd spit in the frosting?" Leanne said, and shrugged one shoulder. "Fair."

Farrah stepped up next to Catherine, and Catherine moved in, striking her most flattering pose, hand to hip, knee crooked, head slightly thrown back.

"Say *screw the bride!*" Leanne trilled.

Farrah giggled nervously. Catherine's smile grew stiff.

"Well, you did a lovely job with the party," Catherine told Farrah as they broke apart. "It can't be easy keeping a secret wedding secret." Bile rose on the word *wedding*, but she swallowed it down. "Especially one involving people with such a high profile."

"Oh, I didn't even know about that until it was announced," said Farrah. She took the phone back from Leanne and scrolled through the photos as she spoke. "My mom is, like, a vault. But anyway, I'm sure you could do *so* much better."

For half a second Catherine thought Farrah meant she could do better than *Peter*. But then realized she meant better planning the party. Catherine was really starting to like this girl. She hadn't even thought about Peter in, oh, ten seconds.

Maybe he'd leave Tilly at the altar. That would be something to see.

"You know, Leanne, I think I *will* stay." She looped her arm around Farrah's. "Farrah, I'm sort of dying to see your staging area. Do you think I could get a backstage tour?"

"Oh my God, of course! And you *have* to see the chandelier. The thing's been a total nightmare to get hung, but it's to die for."

# LEANNE

It wasn't going to happen. That was all there was to it. She just would not let it happen.

Hudson lived with her. She was the one who got him out of bed at five in the morning and into that ridiculous private school uniform and onto the bus with food in his belly and finished homework in his bag. She was the one who brought healthy snacks to his soccer games and attended his back-to-school nights and took his temperature when he was sick. She was the one who had been fighting for full custody for the last year while Peter flitted around with his tennis ace girlfriend from country to country, forgetting birthdays and missing Zoom calls and hardly ever apologizing.

Okay. That was unfair. Peter was actually pretty good at apologizing. He was a good father—when he was present. She had always been honest with herself about that. She shouldn't have told Catherine he didn't care about anyone, because he *did* care about Hudson. But he was so seldom present. And now, suddenly, sole custody? Monica was definitely turning over in her grave.

Tilly would take Hudson away from her over her dead body. And while her lawyer had told her to wait, she knew that she couldn't survive the night without doing something. Without at least trying.

By the time the vows had been recited and everyone had flocked to the tent for the cocktail hour, Leanne knew exactly what she was going to say. She crossed the sparsely occupied dance floor and approached the bride from behind.

"Excuse me, Tilly, I don't believe we've officially been introduced."

Leanne kept her voice as level as possible, speaking loudly enough to be heard over the music and the laughter and the joyous conversation, quietly enough to not sound threatening. It was very difficult to avoid sounding threatening.

Tilly turned at the sound of Leanne's voice, a champagne flute held elegantly in her left hand, a massive diamond sparkling on her finger, next to her brand-new wedding ring. Her expression was a picture of condescension, and in that moment, Leanne understood what it was like to want to do violence to another person. It was a hot, crawling, pulsing feeling within her chest and a burning behind her eyes. It was blurring at the edges of her vision. If anyone had so much as touched her, she would have bitten their hand off.

Tilly took a sip of her champagne, the diamonds in the wedding ring catching the light thrown off by the monstrous chandelier overhead. The vows had been short and sweet, the kiss perfunctory. All of it stunk of something rotten. Leanne wondered what this snake of a woman had on Peter Frank, and whether or not it was true.

It was probably true.

"I really don't think you want to do this here."

"I'm Leanne Gladstone." She thrust out her hand determinedly. "My sister was Hudson's mother. She wanted to be Peter's wife. She died in an accident I'm ninety-nine-percent certain he caused, and I've been caring for his son ever since. And you are?"

The older couple Tilly had been conversing with made a discreet getaway. Tilly's lips pursed in an expression that was somewhere between amusement and disgust. "I'm the woman Peter *chose* to marry."

Leanne lowered her hand. This fucking bitch.

"And however you've inflated your importance in Hudson's and Peter's lives, I'm sorry to tell you that particular version of the story you've made up for yourself has run its course."

Leanne didn't know she'd moved until she felt the pain in the back of her hand. She'd batted the champagne glass out of Tilly's fingers so violently, it shattered against the back of a vacant chair. Someone nearby screeched as champagne and glass splattered everywhere. She hadn't known she was going to do it until it was done. And once it was done, she wasn't sorry. The frisson of fear that crossed through Tilly's overly made-up eyes was worth it.

"Tilly? Are you all right? What happened?"

Tilly's brother, Brandt, appeared at her side. Leanne recognized him from the wedding party, and because of the fact that he was his sister's carbon copy, aside from a slightly crooked nose. If she had to guess, he'd either broken it playing polo or falling down a flight of stairs at some hedonist-themed frat party.

"She's patently insane!" Tilly said, shaking out her ringed hand.

"You're not taking Hudson from me," Leanne said, trembling.

"I think when the authorities interview all the witnesses to what you just did, we definitely will be," Tilly said.

Leanne looked around. At least two dozen people were staring at them, clearly horrified. She couldn't have cared less. Let them tell the cops. As far as she was concerned, all she'd just done was proven how far she would go to keep Hudson.

And then she saw him. Hudson himself. Standing between two other guests. Her heart sank. He looked . . . scared. His big blue eyes had taken in everything. He looked from Leanne to Tilly, then back to Leanne. He had clearly heard Tilly say she was going to take Hudson away.

She plastered a smile on her face. "Hey Hudson!" said Leanne. "It's okay. We were just—"

Hudson turned on his heel, shoved a middle-aged man aside, and ran.

"Hudson!" Leanne moved to go after him, but a strong hand clamped her upper arm. It was Peter, appearing as if from nowhere.

"I'll go," he said.

"No, I—"

"Leanne, I understand why you're upset," Peter said quietly, moving his hand to the top of her shoulder and looking her in the eye. "Trust me. We'll figure this out. Right now, Hudson needs his father."

Leanne swallowed. She hated when Peter did this. Took charge. Acted maturely. Made her believe in him. Or, at the very least, in his love for his kid. She nodded mutely, not trusting herself to get anything other than a sob past the lump in her throat.

"Call Tony and go home," he said. "Hudson can stay here tonight. I'll call you tomorrow and we'll talk."

There was a barely perceptible shift in his eyes, toward Tilly. Leanne's heart rate calmed ever so slightly. He was telling her that he didn't agree with Tilly. He was telling her it was going to be okay. She nodded, not trusting herself to speak.

Peter moved sideways through the crowd to go after his son. Leanne found she couldn't move. Her knees were liquid and her vision blurred. When she pulled out her phone to call her husband, she could hardly even see the screen.

She believed Peter, but should she really leave Hudson here for the night after what Tilly had said upstairs?

"You heard my husband," said Tilly. "It's time for you to go."

When Leanne turned to face her, two security guards were standing at her side.

# CATHERINE

"I think it's time to go, Cat."

Catherine turned abruptly. The pad of her foot landed on a sharp pebble and she grabbed it, hopping on the other. Where was her shoe? What had happened to her shoe?

"Ow! Ow! Ow!"

She latched onto Cash's thick arm for support and nearly went down sideways anyway. He had to hold her around the waist to stop her from falling.

"When did you get this drunk?" he asked.

He sounded so judgy. No, not judgy. He sounded pissed. Maybe both? But it had been a long night. The announcement and the Tilly threats and the vows and the dancing and the food and the party and the *open bar*. If you weren't going to get drunk at an open bar with top-shelf everything, when were you going to get drunk?

"You can't be mad at me! It's a party!"

"Yeah, and you disappeared for like half of it!"

"Oh, poor famous baby can't take care of himself at a party. How many women came on to you? Twenty? Forty? Where's what's her butt? Spinfortits?"

"Oh my God. Let's just go."

"We can't go. I have to find Peter."

"Peter? Are you fucking kidding me? We said goodbye to Peter and Tilly fifteen minutes ago."

Catherine waved her hands in front of her and shook her head. Not a good combination. She was immediately dizzy. She sat down hard on the pavement, and this time Cash didn't move to catch her.

"No, no, no. I have to *talk* to Peter. I have to tell him. He *can't marry Tilly.*"

She was staring at Cash's shoes. They had red soles. Was her boyfriend wearing Louboutins?

"He already *did* marry Tilly."

"I know!" she snapped her head up and nearly puked. "But he can't *be* married to her. It's just wrong."

"What the hell is it with this guy, Catherine? You two broke up over ten years ago! Are you really still carrying a torch for him?"

Catherine cracked up laughing. "What, me? No. No! I don't carry a torch for him. But you know what they say, you always love your first love."

Cash backed up a step, his beautiful shoes making a horrible scratching sound on the pavement. "So you *are* carrying a torch for him."

"No! You don't get it. Peter and me. We're . . . connected." She mashed her fingers together, trying to weave them, but it didn't work. So she tried again. And again. She seemed to have four hands. "Like, forever. You wouldn't understand."

"No, I guess I wouldn't," Cash said. He pulled out his phone and turned away from her.

"What're you doing?" She tried to push herself up, but her knee hit something sharp. The same damn pebble? This was very unlike the Franks. Normally everything was pristine. She really should complain to the groundskeeper.

"Booking you an Uber back to the hotel. I'm going home.

I'm sure the love of your life won't mind you leaving your car here while you sleep it off."

"No, wait," she reached for his hand, but he backed farther away.

"I'll call you tomorrow," he said.

She squinted at his broad back as he stormed off. "Wait, Cash! Cash!"

He stopped to sign an autograph, then disappeared behind a hedge.

Somehow, through sheer force of will, Catherine managed to find her way to her feet. Her phone pinged with a text. The Uber information. Candi in a red Toyota was coming for her in fifteen minutes. Catherine couldn't believe Cash had left her. She couldn't believe she was alone. She couldn't believe she'd lost a shoe.

Lurching forward, Catherine decided it would be a good idea to take off the other shoe. Noticing there was blood on one of the straps, she chucked it into the bushes. Still stumbling, but more balanced, Catherine took in her surroundings, trying to figure out where the exit was. She'd need to know after she talked to Peter.

There were fewer people around now. She could hear shouting and laughing coming from one of the balconies somewhere in the distance, but the tent was darker, lit only by flickering candles. A couple of stragglers clung to their parting gifts, and each other, as they made their way toward the front drive. Catherine fished her phone out to text Peter when she heard a crash.

She squinted. Someone was in the tent. Tilly. Catherine could just make out the blond hair. The long white dress. But something was wrong. She was struggling with someone. Someone had a hold of her arm, and she was trying to back away.

"Tilly!"

Catherine rushed forward. She wasn't sure why. She hated Tilly. Who cared if someone was trying to hurt her? Maybe somewhere deep inside Catherine was, simply put, selfless. A hero. She'd help a damsel in distress even if she wished said damsel had never been born.

"Tilly! Are you okay?"

What happened next happened so fast, it was a blur. Tilly broke free of her captor, who disappeared into the darkness of the tent. She whirled around and, with no control over her own force, slammed her now freed arm directly into Catherine's stomach. Catherine, wind knocked out of her, grabbed Tilly's shoulder, tore the delicate strap of her dress, and then threw up all over Tilly's open-toed, crystal-lined shoes.

Even with all of this considered, it was Tilly's solid, uppercut right to her jaw that was the most surprising moment, before Catherine completely blacked out.

# MAYA

After two hours of wallowing in her suite at the Plaza, Maya couldn't take it anymore. She turned her phone back on.

She had a hundred and twenty-seven texts. Most of them from Peter.

> I can explain

> Everything is a mess

> You were the only good thing I had

Well, that and his Manhattan penthouse and his apartment in Milan and his villa in the south of France and his fancy new wife.

She should check social media. See if anyone from the party had posted about the wedding yet. According to Peter, his mother usually had her parties on lock, but there was no way this wouldn't get out. The press would have a field day. Maya Romero, the good girl of the WTA tour, had not just been cheated on by her very public boyfriend—he'd *married someone else*. It would be all anyone would be talking about on social media and on Tennis Channel. Shit, ESPN might even pick it up. How could he do this to her? Why? Why *now*, when they should be talking about her meteoric rise from number fifty-two in the world last year, to this year's Wimbledon champ?

Wrapped in the hotel's fleece robe with a half-empty bottle of champagne in her lap—something she'd fished out of one of the many congratulatory gift baskets she'd had messengered over from his apartment—she kept scrolling the texts. It was all the same. All ridiculous. If he cared one iota, why hadn't he warned her? At least given her a chance to control the narrative. Focusing on the ramifications to her career and her image allowed her to not focus on the fact that her heart was, quite excruciatingly, broken. He'd shattered her. Not just that, he'd left her out here all alone.

Was this why he'd been so distracted at Wimbledon? Had he been planning his wedding behind her back?

Can I call you???

I need to explain

I was not leading you on. I don't know why I said that. You know I love you.

She should just delete them all. Stop torturing herself.

But then, just as she was about to hit the delete button, two new texts came through in quick succession.

COME BACK

THIS ISN'T OVER

And these texts were not from Peter.

# CATHERINE

At some point, she fell out of bed and crawled to the bathroom. At some point, she threw up again, mostly in the toilet, then broke a mirror reaching for a toothbrush.

At some point there was a buzzing sound, long and low and consistent, and she wasn't sure if it was coming from her mouth, her head, or the window.

At some point she finally passed out again and dreamed she was in a hammock on a canoe with Peter, being circled by buzzing sharks.

---

The screams woke Catherine like an ice pick to her temple. Her first thought was of Peter.

Peter.

Why Peter?

Catherine sat up straight and her brain slammed into the front of her skull. The pain was like nothing she had felt before. When she tried to peel her eyes open, heart now pounding, bile rising in her throat, she found they were glued to her eyeballs. The screaming continued.

She moaned, which made her head throb worse. She swallowed once. Twice. The third time her throat burned with the effort. Her fists grasped the sheets at her sides, recognizing immediately that they were not her own, and she concentrated on opening first her right eye, then her left. Her right hand stung and she winced.

There was blood on her hands. The screaming stopped.

The blood was also all over the sheets. In this room that she did not recognize. Gold wallpaper. Floral sheets. Crystal lamps on antique tables.

Finally, she remembered. She was at Peter Frank's home in Cape Crest. The annual Frank family clambake on their private beach. She remembered Peter dancing with Tilly, huge smiles on their faces as they twirled and posed for photos. Hers was perfectly genuine—pure joy. His was strained. She remembered wanting to talk to him about it. Had she? She remembered fighting with Cash, and watching as he turned his back on her to storm off. She remembered flowers and confetti and clarified butter. Champagne, torn silk, a spray of crystal sequins in the grass.

She couldn't remember every detail, but she knew it had been a disaster. Why had she come here? What was she thinking?

Her jaw was killing her.

There were shouts in the distance. Another scream. Catherine forced herself up and over to the window. Her mouth tasted like the bottom of a trash bin. The day was overcast, but the brightness of the white clouds was still intense, assaulting her eyes, and tears streamed down her face as she blinked and blinked. Below was the parking area, brick pavers lined with gorgeous, blooming hydrangeas in purples and pinks and blues.

In the center, a car—Peter's black McLaren—was parked diagonally with a scrawl of red paint directly across the now dented hood. *LIAR* spelled out in haphazard letters. The windshield was smashed in three places.

Footsteps pounded beyond the closed door.

"Where's Peter?" someone shouted.

"Peter!"

Catherine stumbled over, flinching as she gripped the door handle with her bloodied hand. She was cut, she noticed for the first time, straight across her palm. It took two attempts to get the door open, her eyes unfocused, her hand slick. When it finally swung wide, Peter's brother, Jensen, stood in the center of the shadowed hall, disheveled in his suit pants and shirt from last night, dark hair soaked with sweat.

"What is it?" she said, her voice a croak. "Is Peter okay?"

"It's not him. I can't find him. It's—"

An odd, choking sob emitted from his throat. He bit on a fist to stop it.

"Jensen!" Catherine blurted, panic rising in her chest. "What?"

"It's Tilly," he said, eyes wild. "Tilly's dead."

# CATHERINE

Catherine knew exactly where to find Peter. She waited until Jensen was gone, then went to the en suite bathroom and almost hurled. There was vomit in the toilet and splashed on the seat, a broken stand mirror on the floor, and a smear of blood on the sink. She could tell this was not how she'd cut her hand—all the glass was still in the mirror frame—so she assumed she'd cut it before going to bed, if the blood had made its way in here. She cleaned it all up with hand towels from the closet, then shoved the towels in the garbage can. Then she washed her cut hand with the cat-shaped soap in the soap dish and fixed her face to the best of her ability. At least the Franks always stocked their guest rooms with high-end products, so she was able to wash, remove her eye makeup, and moisturize. She combed her hair back into a high ponytail and she found a pair of new slippers at the bottom of the closet. Then she swiped on some deodorant, wrapped her hand in an obscenely soft towel that would never be the same again, and checked herself out in the mirror. Passable. She hated going anywhere without a full face of makeup, but her dress had held up well overnight, and desperate times called for desperate measures. She headed for the beach.

She didn't know until that moment that it was possible to feel horrified and exhilarated all at once. Tilly was dead. She should feel sad. But she had to bite back her smile. It was as if last night had been some kind of alternate universe and she'd just woken up, returned to the correct timeline. Where Peter was not married, and everything was possible.

Jensen hadn't told her what happened. How Tilly had died. Had there been someone with her? If not, who had found her? She hoped it hadn't been Peter. Couldn't imagine what that would do to him. Yes, he was a strong, solid, devil-may-care guy, but that wasn't all he was. Peter felt things. Deeply. And he'd already been through so much.

Her head radiated pain outward, sharp like an ax against the inside of her skull as she raced down the first set of patio stairs. The humidity. Goddamn the humidity. Making it hard to breathe, hard to focus. And she could only imagine what it was doing to her hair.

Halfway down the hill, Catherine could see the crowd near the wedding tent. That girl from yesterday—Farrah—was there, still in her party uniform, blubbering into the arms of an EMT. Catherine saw a few other emergency workers, as well as Camilla, who wore light-pink silk pajamas and a black robe with little pink cats all over it, talking urgently into a cell phone. Catherine had forgotten about Camilla's cat obsession. She loved cats, but was allergic, so she surrounded herself with decorative cats. Little porcelain cats on windowsills and cat motifs etched into mirror frames. Cat statues near doorways and at the foot of the stairs. They were all expensive, handmade, imported cats, of course—no crocheted pillows or tea towels here. But still. Catherine had always found it an odd affectation. Although it did make the formidable Camilla seem more human.

She watched as Camilla handed the phone to Peter's father, Tate, then walked back toward the tent. Was that where they had found Tilly? In the wedding tent? It seemed so impossible. Just a few hours ago, the woman had been resplendent in a wedding gown, twirling across the dance floor in Peter's arms.

A sudden flash of a memory hit her. Tilly punching her in the stomach? Had she ripped Tilly's wedding gown?

Catherine tasted sour champagne in the back of her throat. She pressed her good hand into one of the brick planters that ran alongside the pathway and tried to focus. But the memory was gone. And she felt someone standing right behind her.

She turned quickly, head spinning, but no one was there. A woman in landscaper gear stood a few yards away, watching her.

Catherine jogged off, dipping down the hill and out of view, the slippers slapping against her heels. She pulled them off when she hit the sand, cool beneath her bare feet. It occurred to her that she had no clue where her shoes were. Damn. She really loved those heels. She raced along the sand, ducking into the reeds and up the dune on the hidden path that only a handful of people in the world knew existed. After an excruciatingly steep climb—Cash was always telling her she had to work more on her cardio—she came to the base of the rocky outcropping that hid a cozy circle of soft sand. It was big enough to lay out a few blankets and stash a cooler, and it was where Peter and his friends used to get stoned and do shrooms in college, staring up at the stars for hours until they sobered up or came down or passed out.

And there he was.

"Peter?"

He startled, looking up with wild eyes. His head had been held between his hands and tucked between his knees, and now his hair stuck up on both sides like two little devil horns. He stared at her.

"I know, I'm a mess." She blushed, embarrassed, running a hand over her hair to push back the flyaways. "I just woke up and heard what happened and—"

"Cat?" His voice cracked and her heart basically died.

"Are you okay?"

She moved across the little clearing and sat next to him on the flat stretch of rock, pulling her knees up under her chin. Peter stared out across the small clearing, where the reeds whispered against one another in the morning breeze.

"She's dead."

"I know. Peter . . . what happened?"

Maybe Tilly had some sort of condition that no one had known about. It was possible that Peter had partially married her out of pity. A heart problem? Some sort of weird, insidious cancer? Maybe he'd known she wouldn't be around much longer and that's why he'd agreed to the marriage. Or maybe she'd dropped acid last night and it had gone badly. Done some bad cocaine? Tilly always had believed she was better than everyone else. She probably thought the things that felled the common folk could never take her down.

Peter picked up a glass Catherine hadn't noticed. Whiskey. He downed what was left in one gulp, then sniffled mightily. His bottom lip quivered.

"I fucked it all up, Cat. I fucked it all up."

She reached across and cupped his biceps with her uninjured hand. She could feel the warmth of his skin through the cool, smooth fabric of his shirt. "Peter, no. This isn't your fault. Whatever happened, it's not your fault."

With every fiber of her being, she wanted to hold him. To pull him to her and let him cry. To kiss him and tell him everything was going to be all right. That she was here. That they were together. And that as long as they were together, there was nothing they couldn't handle. Hadn't they proven that time and time again?

"What happened to your hand?" he asked, staring down at the bloody towel between them.

"Oh." She let him go and lifted it. "I have no idea. But I may have left one of the guest rooms a bloody mess. You know me. Walking disaster zone."

Except she wasn't. At least, not anymore. But her impulse for self-deprecation around him would never go away.

Peter stared at the bloodstain for a very long time. For half a second Catherine thought he had zoned out. Maybe *he* was on drugs? Then he shifted his weight, reaching over to gently take her injured hand in his. He lifted it to his face and kissed it. Tears welled up in his eyes and he closed them. She couldn't tell if he was breathing.

"Thank you for caring enough to come find me."

"It was nothing. Anyone would have done the same."

"But no one did." He looked into her eyes, full of gratitude. "Just you."

"I mean . . . of course," she said, her heart swelling. "Whatever I can do."

Ten minutes later, when they emerged onto the beach, two police officers were walking toward them from the direction of the house. They looked relieved when they first saw Peter, then turned all business.

"Peter Frank? We've been looking everywhere for you."

"And here I am," said Peter, in his usual congenial voice. The one-eighty would have startled most people, but not Catherine. Peter was never not "on" in the face of authority.

"And who's this?" asked the shorter of the two cops. She was struggling for breath, but Catherine couldn't blame her. It couldn't have been easy walking on the beach in those heavy, boxy shoes.

"I'm Catherine Farr," she said. "Peter and I are old friends."

"Oh, good. We were looking for you, too," the cop said.

Catherine blinked. "You were?"

"We need to establish a timeline for last night," said the other cop, who was taller and fitter and older than the woman. "If you'll both come with us."

A timeline? Why would they need to establish a timeline? What did that even mean?

Peter and Catherine exchanged a confused look. "I get why you need to talk to me, but why Catherine? She barely even spoke to Tilly last night."

Beads and crystals on the floor. Vomit on a white shoe.

"Because we're treating Ms. Dansforth's death as suspicious," said the tall cop. "And apparently Miss Farr got into a wicked argument with your wife last night and was one of the last people to see her alive."

# LEANNE

The second Leanne awoke the morning after the wedding, she understood she'd made a huge tactical error. She never should have left Hudson at the Frank compound. Tilly had been completely out of control, what with her declaration and then having Leanne physically hauled off the property. What if she ordered security to keep her out indefinitely? What if Peter, Tilly, and Hudson were, at this very moment, jetting off on a private plane to some undisclosed location where Leanne and her lawyers couldn't touch them? What if she never saw her nephew again?

Logically, she knew, it wasn't as if the two newlyweds were super focused on a custody battle this morning. They were probably still asleep. Which was why she had to get her ass over there.

She rolled out of bed at seven a.m., pulled on a Yankees baseball cap and texted her husband, who was already out on his trawler, that she was going to get Hudson. He responded with a thumbs-up emoji.

When she arrived at the Frank home, she was surprised to find the gates yawning open and a police officer stationed at the driveway, rather than the normal security detail. She pulled up next to him and put her window down.

"Hey, Bill. Everything okay?"

"Hey, Leanne." Bill Polaski looked a tad pale. "Not really."

"Why? What happened? Is everyone okay?" Her pulse fluttered like a trapped moth inside her wrist.

"Not sure I can say. Do you have business here this morning?"

"I just came to pick up Hudson," she said. "Bill, what's going on?"

He looked left and right, though there were no other cars in sight, then leaned closer to her window. "It's Tilly Dansforth. They found her dead this morning in the wedding tent. Crushed under the chandelier."

Her hand flew up to cover her mouth. "Jesus, Bill. What the hell happened?"

He shrugged. "No one knows. They found her a coupla hours ago. Donnie said it was not pretty."

"Oh my God."

Leanne floored it up the drive, her mind racing. She had to get Hudson out of here. She hoped he hadn't seen anything. She tried calling Samantha Parker, her best friend, who was the Franks' head landscaper, because maybe she knew something, but it just rang out. The man who answered the door was not the usual butler, but he wore the uniform of crisp brown khakis, white shirt, and blue blazer. He seemed familiar. Tall, bald, broad, mid-forties. Then she remembered she'd seen him with Camilla at the party, getting scolded.

"Can I help you?" he asked, posture ramrod straight.

"Yes, I'm Hudson's mother—uh, aunt. I'm here to get him." She started past the man, but he blocked her path. She took a steadying breath. "You're new. There's a lot going on. I get it. But I'm on the list."

"It's okay, Liam," Peter's voice called out. "That's Leanne Gladstone."

The man's expression changed slightly, recognition dawning. "Ah. Mrs. Gladstone. Of course. My apologies."

Leanne strode inside and over to Peter, throwing her arms

around him. He hugged her back, briefly, before they both realized simultaneously that this was weird.

"What happened? Are you okay?"

He smelled like alcohol and sweat and had clearly pulled on the first clothes he'd seen—a pair of athletic shorts and a wrinkled polo. He was barefoot, which she thought was odd, and he looked like death warmed over.

"What a shit show, Leanne. There are cops all over the place, interviewing everyone. . . . My mom is not happy, and my dad has basically locked himself in the study."

"I'm . . . so sorry. What about your brother? Is he—"

"Jensen used his kids as an excuse to go back to the city." Peter scoffed in the way people do about their lucky siblings. "Plus, he used to have a massive crush on Tilly, so he's acting like he's been personally affected. He's no help."

"Speaking of kids . . . let me get Hudson out of here. I don't think he should be around any of this."

Peter pulled back slightly. "Hudson's not here."

"What do you mean, *Hudson's not here*? You told me last night you thought he should stay over."

"Yeah, but then he and I talked and he said he wanted to go home with you. He said he had a soccer game today and he'd never get to sleep if he was here with the party going on all night. Which, to be honest, kind of impressed me. I mean, what eleven-year-old is that responsible and self-aware? Guess that's all your influence."

Even in the midst of her impending panic, Leanne was pitifully grateful for the acknowledgment.

"Peter, Hudson did not come home with me last night. Tilly threw me out right after I . . . we . . ." She paused at the pained look on his face. "Whatever. He's not at my place. I put his laundry in his room before I came over here, and his bed had not been touched."

"Okay. Okay. Don't panic." He reached out and squeezed her

shoulder, his palm warm and his grip strong. "I'm sure that means he decided to stay after all. He's probably up in his bedroom. I'll go check."

"No, I'll go. You go check the game room."

Peter nodded, and they both took off in opposite directions.

*Please*, Leanne thought as she nearly tripped over one of Camilla's stupid cat statues and took the plushy carpeted stairs two at a time. *Please, please, please, please be here.* She shut her eyes for a moment, outside the closed door of Hudson's room, imagining him asleep in the double bed, facing the ocean. Imagining the moment of pure joy and relief she was about to experience at finding him safe and sound.

She opened the door. The room was empty.

# CATHERINE

"I honestly don't remember much. I wish I could help more. I don't usually drink like that."

Catherine was starting to regret not calling a lawyer. Every time she watched a TV show that involved crime and punishment, she balked when one of the suspects talked to the cops without representation. *How stupid are you?* she'd think. *How hard is it to get a lawyer?*

But now she understood. When you were innocent, you saw no harm in talking to the police. You even thought they might respect and appreciate you for being so helpful and upfront about everything. You thought that maybe you'd even be the person to reveal some important bit of information that everyone else had overlooked that might help them figure out what had really happened.

Because whatever had happened—and she hadn't yet learned how Tilly had died—it had to have been an accident. Murder was something that happened on TNT. Or on those true crime podcasts everyone was always listening to. It was something that happened to people in other parts of the country. It wasn't something that happened to her. Or to people she knew, even if she loathed them. Probably the cops in this tiny, tony town were just bored—looking for a crime where there wasn't one. Because if you were a police officer whose primary job was to stop kids from skateboarding in the town square, wouldn't you be excited to have a murder to solve? So, really, did she need to start trying to find a criminal lawyer in the middle of a summer Sunday morning? Hardly.

And then the police started asking questions. And they all revolved around accounts of her argument with Cash. Of how "volatile" people said she'd been. How angry and upset. And then she'd supposedly "attacked" Tilly? That was not something she would do. At least not today. Maybe when she was twenty, but not today. But then why did she keep having these random flashes of memory that involved, well, fighting with Tilly?

Then it occurred to her that she couldn't even clearly remember this argument with Cash or what they'd fought about or who might have witnessed it. That she had no idea how she'd gotten to the room she'd woken up in—the room with the broken glass and the bloody sheets, which, of course, she didn't mention. And before long, all she could think about were the many, many times she had yelled at the TV screen, "Lawyer up, you moron! They're going to trap you!"

"Okay, since you seem to be having such a difficult time recalling your actions last night," the officer said, pencil hovering over his small notepad. He was a tall man, mostly bald, with a band of gray hair clipped tight around his ears. His nose was long and broad, with a pair of glasses pushed down so low it was a miracle they hadn't slipped off. He gazed at her over them with sharp, brown eyes. His name tag read VIRGIL. First name or last, she had no idea. He hadn't introduced himself. "What about this morning. What were you doing alone on the beach with the husband of the deceased?"

"Seriously? His bride just died! I wanted to see if he was okay! I thought he might need a friend. Is there something wrong with that?"

Virgil glanced briefly at his partner, name tag MAGRIN, who took a sip from a pink smoothie the chef had made for her and glanced at her notes.

"Is that what the two of you are?" Virgil said. "Friends?"

Catherine felt a rush of what could only be called satisfaction. She clicked her teeth together to keep herself from smiling. "Yes. We've been friends for years. Why? Did someone say something?"

Maybe Peter had said something. Maybe he'd said she was the love of his life and he only wished he'd married her years ago, because then he wouldn't be in this situation. Tilly would be alive and well and living in St. Tropez, and he and Catherine would have a house in Connecticut and another in the Hamptons and they would have been at a spa in Sag Harbor this weekend instead of here being interrogated by the police.

Officer Virgil turned to a new page in his notebook. "What room did you sleep in last night? I understand you don't remember choosing it, but certainly you remember waking up this morning?"

"Honestly? I'm not sure. There must be a hundred guest rooms in this house."

"There are seven," the officer corrected. His partner slurped her drink. "But no matter. Our men are conducting a thorough search right now. I'm sure they'll figure it out."

Catherine gave a stiff smile. She had to get the hell away from these people and find a way to eighty-six those sheets. Because if they didn't think she was a suspect now, they certainly would once they found the room she'd stayed in drenched in blood.

"Great. Can I go now?"

The officers looked at each other again, communicating silently. "Yes," said Virgil, who had asked all the questions. Catherine was fairly certain she'd yet to hear Magrin speak. He produced a business card from a shirt pocket. "But if you think of anything else, please call."

"Will do."

Catherine got up and walked quickly toward the front hall, but instead of hooking a left toward the door, she turned right and ran upstairs as fast as her slippered feet would carry her. She knew exactly which guest room she'd stayed in, and she found it quickly, with no sign of the police anywhere. She threw the door open and stopped in her tracks.

The bed had already been stripped and remade, and the scent of bleach hung in the air. Clearly, the staff hadn't been given the day off for the death of the favorite son's wife. All she could do now was hope that the cleaning crew had thrown the sheets away in some nondescript garbage bag with the rest of the wedding refuse, adhering to their usual level of Pentagon-worthy discretion.

From down the hall, raised voices caught her attention. She closed the door quietly and moved toward the sound.

"And you want full custody? What a joke! This is pure negligence, Leanne."

"Well, technically, *Peter*, you currently have full custody, so if anyone was negligent here it was you."

Catherine paused at the top of the stairs. At the other end of the long hall, Leanne pounded furiously away on her cell phone while Peter paced, shoving his hands through his hair. Neither of them noticed her.

"Did you try all his friends?"

"That's what I'm doing now," Leanne said. "Did you check everywhere?"

"Liam and the rest of the staff are on it."

"You mean the personality-free Gollum at the front door? Where the hell did he come from, anyway? What happened to Felipe?"

"Is that really what you're going to focus on right now? The fact that my mom got a new butler? And he's not a Gollum. He's an ex-marine medic, for God's sake."

"Wait. An ex-marine? Why? For protection? Is there something I should know? Has your family been getting death threats?" Leanne demanded.

"Okay, now you're just being insane. You know she was in the hospital back in June. She thought it would be good to have someone medically trained around at all times."

"Um, I don't think it's insane to ask. Your new wife just died in a freak accident and now our kid—"

"They're going to find him. They said they'd text me when they found him." His voice grew louder with every word. He slid his phone out of his pocket and checked it. "I can't believe this is happening. Where *is* he?"

"Where's who?"

The voice came from directly behind Catherine, startling her so thoroughly, she jumped. Peter and Leanne both looked over, noticing her for the first time. It was Maya Romero. She'd come up the stairs so quietly, Catherine hadn't noticed her approach. Now she stood there in white silk pants and a dark green tank top, her hair pulled up in a high ponytail. She looked gorgeous. Fresh-faced. Young. She even smelled young, like fresh-cut grass and wildflowers.

"What're you doing here?" Catherine said before she could stop herself. She ran her hands over her hair and smoothed her dress.

"You came back," Peter said.

"It's Hudson," Leanne snapped. "He's missing."

# MAYA

"So, Catherine, how do you know Peter again?"

Maya stepped into the library with the other two women, trying her best to act normal. But inside, her heart was slamming around in her chest like a hornet, frantic to be released from the glass under which it had been trapped. Peter looked like shit. Was it because Tilly was actually his one true love all this time and now she was dead? Or was it because he was up all night texting Maya and now he was dealing with cops and an investigation and a missing kid? It had to be the latter, she told herself. If Tilly was his one true love, then why had he spent his wedding night texting Maya instead of being with Tilly? Why had he taken his eyes off her long enough for her to go and . . . die?

Catherine, who also looked like shit, paused in the center of the air-conditioned room. Clearly, this woman meant something to Peter, or Tilly wouldn't have invited her to her little prenuptial power play. Maya had never heard of her, but Peter had been chock-full of surprises lately—he'd never once mentioned Tilly, either. Maya wanted to know what she was dealing with in Catherine.

"We were together. In college," Catherine said, speaking in a skeptical tone, as if it was difficult for her to believe that Maya didn't know this already. The look on her face was almost proprietary.

But Peter was in his thirties. Why would he bother telling Maya about his college girlfriend? "And he's an investor in my business, Farr and Away Events."

"Oh. Wait, I've heard of you!" Maya said. "Didn't you do Valentina's New York baby shower?"

Catherine's entire face lit up. She looked a lot younger without her makeup. Maya preferred her this way. She never understood why people spent so much of their precious time in front of the mirror only to make themselves look older or more artificial. "Yes! That was one of my first celeb events."

"I heard it was amazing," Maya said. "I was sorry I couldn't be there."

In truth, Maya couldn't stand Valentina Vielo, the former number one in the world, and had skipped the shower to train. She was secretly happy when Valentina decided not to come back to the game after having her twins. The woman was always such a diva in the locker room that other players, coaches, and trainers would scurry out of her way when she walked in. Her nose was always in the air and she literally looked down it at everyone. When Maya got to number one, she would behave exactly as she always had. Polite, deferential, kind, inclusive.

"But I remember you sent a lovely gift," Catherine said. "Valentina adored the matching cashmere onesies."

"Wow, good memory."

"Well, you know, it's part of the job," Catherine explained, blushing. Though Maya couldn't see how remembering every gift was part of the job months after the event was over.

Peter stepped in behind them and closed the doors. The entire time they'd been speaking, Leanne had been over by the windows, making hushed, panicked phone calls and shooting off texts.

"Look, this is probably obvious, but if the cops talk to any of you, I wouldn't mention that meeting Tilly called last night after the announcement," Peter said. "I've already deleted the texts from my phone, and I think we should all just keep it to ourselves."

Maya felt uneasy at the idea of being interviewed by the cops. As far as she knew, the news of the wedding and the death hadn't broken yet, but it would. If she was interviewed by the police, she could only imagine what the headlines might say. It had been bad enough when Peter married another woman, but this? Maya's image was squeaky clean, but there was no doubt people would start dragging out her father and his past exploits and start musing about whether or not the apple hadn't fallen so far from the tree.

She had to be ready for that. She knew this. But that didn't mean she didn't hate it.

"Peter, one thing I don't understand," Catherine said. "I got that text yesterday just seconds after we bumped into each other at the hotel, and I saw you with your phone. How could Tilly have sent it?"

When the hell had these two bumped into each other? After everything that had happened yesterday, Maya had imagined that Tilly had somehow kept Peter under lock and key, or at least under close watch for the past week, and that's why she hadn't heard from him. But somehow he was out and about? Bumping into ex-girlfriends?

"She figured out a way to duplicate my phone." Peter glanced at Maya. "She always was a whiz with tech. She hacked it so any texts I sent for the last week didn't go out. I was also having trouble making calls, but I figured it was just the crappy service here."

"She hacked your phone?" Maya didn't know how to feel. Did that mean he hadn't gotten *any* of her texts this last week? That Tilly had been reading them all? The thought made her blush, and she sat on the nearest chair, covering her face with both hands.

"Are you okay?" Peter asked, coming to her side.

"Don't," she said, in a tone that made him instantly back off. She wanted to both strangle him and kiss him. Tell him to jump off a cliff and take her to bed. This was not her. She was never this indecisive. She knew what she wanted, and she went out and got it.

*So what do you want?* Shawn's voice said in her mind.

She wanted Peter to explain. Needed to know when he'd decided to get married, exactly, and why. She needed to know why he hadn't told her. Whatever the reason, it had to be bad. She hadn't just imagined the last year of her life with him. Something had gone sideways and she needed to hear from him what it was. If only she could get him alone.

"I'm sorry, why do you want us to keep Tilly's little meeting a secret?" Leanne asked. "Wouldn't it be better for the police to know how narcissistic and controlling she was?"

"Way to not speak ill of the dead," Catherine said.

"Like you didn't hate her guts," Leanne shot back.

"Listen to yourselves. This is why," Peter said. "All she did in that conversation was give each of you concrete motives to murder her."

Silence. Maya looked up at Leanne and Catherine, all three of them obviously freaked. Peter wasn't wrong. Tilly had yanked the rug out from under the relationship Maya had exposed her heart for. She'd threatened to take Hudson away from Leanne, when Leanne clearly thought of Hudson as her own son. And she'd told Catherine she was going to take money out of her business, which was thriving.

"Wow," Leanne said finally. "It's so incredible how you care *so much* about us, Peter. Now can we get back to trying to find our kid?"

Maya turned over Peter's words in her mind. Yes, Tilly had given her a motive in front of witnesses, but she'd left before the vows. She had a record of a car service taking her back to the city. She'd ordered room service. She'd rented her comfort movie, *She's the Man*, on demand. She had a rock-solid alibi.

But still. Her family was her family. And if what Tilly had said got out, her father would definitely be at the top of the suspect list. That was the last thing she needed.

"Peter's right," Maya said.

"Of course he's right," Catherine said. "We all have motives. God, it's almost like Tilly knew she was going to die and she purposely set us all up."

"That's dark," Leanne said.

"But still," Maya said. "I think we should all make an agreement. A pact. Here and now. We don't mention that conversation to anyone. Ever."

"A pact? What is this, second grade?" Leanne said.

Maya blushed at the clear dig at her age.

"I'm in," Catherine said, hands on hips. "It's a deal. A pact. Whatever."

"Same," said Maya.

"Me too," Peter added.

They all looked at Leanne, who rolled her eyes in a grandiose way. "Fine. It's a pact. We're bonded for life in our little obstruction of justice club. *Now* can we get back to finding Hudson? I can't believe you didn't check on him last night, Peter."

"Not that I'm in any mood to defend what went on here yesterday," Maya said. "But it was his . . . wedding." Her vision grayed slightly as she said the word. "Don't you have a nanny or some staff who should be taking care of that when there's an event going on?"

Peter gave Maya a grateful look, from which she immediately turned away.

"*Take care of that*?" Leanne said sarcastically. "You're talking about a living, breathing child. Peter's and my flesh and blood."

"You know what I mean. Take care of bedtime. Or, I don't know. Tell him a story or something?"

"He's eleven. You really know nothing about kids, do you?" said Leanne.

"Okay, there's no reason to attack her. We all want to find Hudson. Can we just—"

The double doors to the library opened and a tall, fit man in the household uniform cleared his throat.

"Liam," Peter said. "Anything?"

"No, sir. We've searched the entire property," the man said in a clipped tone. "I'm afraid there's no sign of your son anywhere."

# CATHERINE

Leanne, Catherine, and Maya exchanged phone numbers so they could keep in touch in case the police reached out to any of them, then Leanne and Peter disappeared together. They wanted to try to get one of the police officers on-site to put out a missing person report for Hudson, and left Catherine alone with Maya, whom he'd asked to stay. "Don't go anywhere. Please. We need to talk," he'd said, in such an earnest voice that Catherine had to look away.

For half a second, Catherine thought it would be awkward, the two of them alone, but then Maya got a call and left the library as well. Catherine knew she should check out of the hotel and go home, but she didn't want to leave until she knew Peter was all right. Though how he could ever be all right with everything he was going through, she had no idea. She went to the bathroom, smoothed her hair back again as best she could after her trek on the beach—using a mirror framed by gilt cats, still weird—splashed cold water on her face, and went downstairs to wait in her dress and slippers.

She really wished she had some shoes.

Sitting on a settee in the lounge, Catherine avoided eye contact with anyone who walked through the room by pretending to be fixated on her phone. In truth, she was absently scrolling through her and Cash's Instagram feeds from the night before. There were dozens of photos of the two of them dancing, drinking, eating, selfie-ing. All of the photos had thousands of likes and hundreds of comments. Some of them she had no recollection of taking. There was even one of her pressed up against some woman she didn't know and couldn't recall the name of, dancing like a pair of sorority girls on spring break. She also noticed that she hadn't taken a single shot of the bride or the wedding ceremony, a big miss for a wedding influencer like herself. Her followers would have eaten up the details of this particular A-list wedding, especially now that it had also turned into a murder mystery.

How sick was that?

She glanced at her texts to see if Cash had apologized for stranding her in Jersey. Nothing. But shockingly, it wasn't even nine a.m. He was probably still asleep, while she felt like she'd lived through three lifetimes.

Back on Insta, her eye caught on a headline and her heart froze.

### HEIRESS DIES HOURS AFTER SURPRISE WEDDING

There was a photo of Tilly in a slinky silver dress, probably taken outside some charity event or club opening. She scanned the article, phrases jumping out at her.

*Married Peter Frank, most recently linked to tennis star Maya Romero . . .*

*Found early this morning . . .*

*Details not released . . .*

*Family had no comment . . .*

*Brother Brandt Dansforth now stands to inherit the full estate . . .*

*This is a developing story . . .*

Peter strode into the room, eyes trained on his phone, a flurry of voices sounding behind him. Whoever he'd been talking to was now barking out orders, and people were shouting to one another, sounding very on-the-case. Leanne was nowhere to be seen. Catherine shoved her phone away, stood and cleared her throat.

"Oh, Cat. Hey. You're still here." Peter shoved his phone into his pocket. "Do you need a car?" he asked.

"No, I drove here last night, actually. But . . . I just wanted to . . . check you're okay."

Peter looked her in the eye and the creases in his forehead seemed to smooth away. "Of course you did. You're always looking out for me."

She smiled. "Someone has to."

Peter held her gaze, long enough that something stirred deep within her. He reached for her hand and held it, lightly, and it almost made her melt. "Thank you, honestly. I don't know what I'd do without you. I definitely wouldn't have made it through this morning."

"Well, you still have a few hours left before you can claim you've done that," she joked, amazed at how calm and collected she sounded. "Peter, when was the last time you ate something?"

He tilted his head back to look at the high ceiling, still holding her hand. "God, honestly? I don't know. Wedding cake?"

Ugh, how sad. How surreal. "I saw some of the staff bringing trays to the officers. I'm sure if you went down to the kitchen you could get some fruit and probably pastries, knowing this place."

"True. I should do that. It's going to be a long day."

"And take a shower. You'll feel better if you do."

Peter smiled at her, a tired, grateful, intimate smile. "Thanks, Cat. Do you want to come with me?"

"To shower?" she teased.

He laughed. "Uh, no. Although, in any other situation, I wouldn't mind that."

Catherine blushed from her scalp to her toes.

"I meant, do you want some food?"

Did she ever. But she felt gross and exhausted and she really had to get back to her room at the hotel and figure out what to do about Cash. There was also work to do today. She needed to finalize a few things for the wedding she was planning for the end of August, and it was getting down to the wire.

"No, thank you, though. I should go. I've got some calls to make."

"That's my Cat. Hardest worker I know."

She smiled. *My Cat.*

"You're probably exhausted. Let me get you that car. Someone can drive yours over later." He took out his phone again. "Leonard can take you."

"It's really not necessary."

"No, I insist. It's the least I can do."

Catherine finally capitulated, enjoying the feeling of being taken care of by Peter and looking forward to a quiet ride home in the back of a freshly cleaned and vacuumed town car instead of navigating the streets full of tourists herself. Peter gave her a quick kiss on the cheek before going in search of some food—she wondered if he even remembered Maya was waiting upstairs for him—and Catherine went outside to wait for Leonard to bring the car around.

In the parking area, a pair of men argued over the hood of Peter's spray-painted car, debating how best to handle the mess, while a police officer paced with his cell phone to his ear, free hand pinching the bridge of his nose. From down the hill, there was a single whoop of siren, and suddenly an ambulance appeared, lights flashing. Catherine's smile slowly dropped away as she realized this ambulance was likely here to remove the body. Tilly's body.

She glanced around and saw the officer was Officer Virgil, the man who had interviewed her earlier, and he was now standing near the bottom of the wide stairs, staring up at her. She couldn't quite read the look on his face—he had sunglasses on now—but it seemed pretty close to a glower. Had he seen her smiling? Shit, what was wrong with her? Even if she hadn't hurt anyone, she *had* just been flirting with the husband of the deceased. The man whose son was also missing.

Turning away from him, she pulled out her phone and quickly texted Cash.

> Did you get home okay? I'm sorry for last night. You won't believe what happened. Call me when you wake up.

Then she slipped on her sunglasses and hurried into the back seat of Leonard's car, grateful he'd pulled up as far away from the cop as possible.

# LEANNE

"I'll have the crew go out and check the docks. You and Sam hit the playgrounds. I put out word to all the downtown businesses through the chamber of commerce, and Jace is keeping his eye out at the train station. We'll find him somewhere."

Tony's deep, resonant voice filled Leanne's car through its speakers, taking a slight edge off her terror. Her husband had an uncanny ability to calm her down in any and all situations with a mere word or a touch. It was one of her favorite things about him, since she tended to get stressed and anxious easily. But this . . . this was beyond his superpower.

"What if something happened to him?" she said, her own voice a croak. "What if someone . . . took him?"

Yes, Leanne's imagination had taken her to some wild places over the last few hours. Like what if Tilly's death was somehow connected to Hudson going missing? What if someone had committed a double crime? Murdered Tilly and kidnapped Hudson as a way to get to the Franks and their massive wealth? Hadn't anyone around here ever read a cozy mystery?

She'd floated this idea to the police back at Peter's, and the officer she'd spoken to had tried *not* to be condescending as he'd told her that the chances Tilly's death and Hudson's disappearing act were linked somehow were slim to none. For one, if someone wanted to kidnap Hudson, they would do it from somewhere less secure than the Frank estate, which had more cameras than the VMAs. Secondly, if a kidnapper was going to murder an adult—and they weren't officially saying it was murder, but *hypothetically*—if they were going to murder an adult to get to a kid, they would have murdered the kid's caretaker.

Of course they were right. Death by chandelier was kind of . . . messy for a murder, wasn't it? And it would have to have been premeditated. What kind of sicko crushed a woman under a ginormous chandelier?

Someone who really fucking hated her, that's who.

Leanne shook her head, trying not to think what the body must have looked like. She had to focus.

Third, there were the child's mindset and emotional state to consider. Had anyone thought to talk to him about the fact that his father was getting married and asked him how he felt about it?

No, actually. Peter hadn't even bothered to check in with his son before the surprise announcement of his wedding. Hudson had been totally blindsided by the whole damn thing. And then he'd seen his aunt attack his new stepmom.

*A-plus behavior there, Leanne.*

Finally, there was no ransom note. No call. No text. Kids didn't get kidnapped for no reason. If someone took a child from a family like the Franks, the motivation was money, one thousand percent of the time.

With all this in mind, their theory was that Hudson had simply taken off either to be alone or to make a point or to get attention, and then he would be back as soon as he was hungry enough or his phone needed a charge. In the meantime, though, they'd put out the word to local businesses to keep an eye out for him.

None of this made Leanne feel any better. Though she definitely needed to call Rita over at the FroYoYo. Hudson lived for her toppings bar.

"I'm sure he's just hanging out at a friend's or at Fred's Diner," Tony said. "He'll be back in his bed, safe and sound, by tonight."

"And we'll ground him for life," Leanne said.

"And we'll ground him for life," Tony confirmed.

They hung up just as Leanne was pulling into the driveway of Samantha's home. Sam was already waiting in the garden with a thermos and a bag from Beachside Bagels. Leanne's stomach grumbled at the sight. She'd never been one of those people who couldn't eat during a crisis. Crises just made her pound carbs.

"Hey. Anything?" Sam said, dropping into the passenger seat of Leanne's car. She pulled out a pumpernickel bagel with about a half a pound of butter on it and handed it over.

"Nothing yet. And bless you," said Leanne as she tore off a massive bite.

Sam curled the brim of her Yankees cap with one hand and slouched down in her seat, pressing her shins into the dashboard as Leanne pulled right back out onto the road. "I say we start on the northside first, at Roosevelt Park. It has those little play storefronts. Perfect for crashing overnight."

"See, this is why I called you. I need your logical brain right now."

Leanne drove to the outskirts of town, away from the tourists who were just starting to crowd all the favorite pancake joints and coffee bars. Her own business, My Sister's Bakery, had already been open for two hours, but her manager had it covered. Liberty Kellor had been working for Leanne since she was in high school and now she had two kids of her own and two jobs as well. There was no one Leanne trusted more to hold down the fort.

Ten minutes later they pulled into the parking lot of Roosevelt

Park, where an exhausted father pushed a squealing toddler in a baby swing, yawning as he stared at the iPhone in his free hand. Leanne and Samantha each took one of the play structures. There was no sign of Hudson.

"It's okay. It's just the first one," said Samantha.

But he wasn't at Beachwood Park, either. Or at Waterside. Or at the gazebo near the pickleball and tennis courts. They tried the skate park, the basketball courts, and even the arcade, which had some old-school, coin-operated kiddie rides outside that a child might be able to sleep in. Nothing.

Parked outside the clapboard toy store, with a statue of a giant Lego man grinning out the window at her and brightly colored "We're Open" flags whipping in the wind, Leanne rested her forehead on the steering wheel and held back tears.

"We need to try to think like Hudson. Let's say your dad just got married out of nowhere, you don't even know this person who's supposed to be your new mom, your aunt had a fight with the new bride. Where would you go?"

"Francesca's," Leanne said flatly. She had the pizza place one town over on speed dial.

"Right, so what's *Hudson's* happy place?"

"Minecraft?"

Sam snorted a laugh. "Are you *sure* Peter's staff checked the entire property? Did they look in my shed?"

Samantha was the head landscaper for the Franks and kept a ton of equipment on the premises for convenience. Leanne happened to know that Sam and Peter used to have the occasional tryst in said garden shed, though, and the very idea that Hudson might be hiding there made her itchy.

Then, out of nowhere, it hit her.

"Oh my God! The hideout!"

Her tires squealed on the pavement as she peeled out.

"Where are you going?"

"To your house. We're going to need your truck."

———

Twenty minutes later, Leanne held her breath under a tarp in the bed of Samantha's pickup as Sam talked to a guard at the service gate of the Franks' property. On a normal day, Sam simply drove up to this slightly camouflaged secondary gate and put in the security code, coming and going as needed, but today was not a normal day.

"The police really don't want us to let anyone in, Sam."

"I know, Trev, but if I don't get that lawnmower fixed today, I'm not going to be able to trim their lawn tomorrow and you know how Mrs. Frank is when the grass gets above three quarters of an inch. I've gotta get in there and get it. I'll stick to the service drive, I swear."

There was a long beat. Then the telltale sound of the gate scrolling open.

"Thank you! I won't be long."

Sam parked the truck near the edge of the property, then came around to whip the tarp off Leanne, who took a deep breath of warm air and scuttled out of the back.

"Where the hell is this hideout and how have I never seen it?" Sam asked, swiping her palms on her denim shorts.

"Because it's in the reeds. Follow me."

At the top of the dunes to the south of the Franks' property was a swampy field of reeds that grew anywhere from four to six feet tall. In any other part of town, they would have been clear cut, new earth carted in, and condos built on top of it, but the Franks owned this land and they valued their privacy. What they didn't know—what no one but she and Hudson knew, was that somewhere in the middle of these reeds was an old, run-down shed. One that, once Hudson had told her he'd found it, she had forbidden him from going back to. Because who knew what sort of shape it was in, whether there were rusty nails sticking out everywhere, if there were rabid animals nesting there? Hudson had promised, and she had all but forgotten about it.

What better place for him to hide out from the world?

Luckily, there was a semi-beaten path, so Leanne followed it, hoping it had been beaten by her nephew.

"Hudson!" she called out. "Hudson, buddy! Are you out here?"

Nothing but birds chirping and the wind clicking the reeds together.

"It's kinda creepy out here," Sam whispered behind her.

"Thanks for pointing that out," Leanne replied. "It makes me feel so much better." Sam rolled her eyes. "Hudson!"

Nothing. They kept walking. Around a bend in the path, Leanne paused. They'd found the shed. And it wasn't actually that broken down. But it did look like the sort of place a serial killer might bring his victims. The two small windows were boarded up, rust holes perforated the metal walls, and there was a big ass hole in the roof.

The door creaked on its hinges, swaying back and forth in the breeze. She almost hoped she wouldn't find him here. Except that, after this, she was all out of options.

"Hudson?" Leanne called. Nothing. She glanced over her shoulder at Sam. "Let's go."

"I'm not going in there," Sam said, shaking her head.

"Sam! My son could be in there!"

"So go get him!"

"Unbelievable. Didn't you once spear a poisonous snake with a pitchfork?"

Sam shrugged. Leanne trudged forward and pulled open the door. "Hudson?"

Leanne stepped inside slowly, to the sound of crackling paper.

Littering the floor were dozens of pastry wrappers and doilies, the detritus from so many wedding treats. There were a couple of crushed soda cans and a remote charger lying on the floor. The beanbag chair in the corner was empty and a long coil of rope was haphazardly piled near the dusty shelving, which held rusty cans of old paint thinner and turpentine. Definitely not the ideal hangout for a child.

Sam had finally come up behind her, having waited long enough to not hear a scream.

"Well, the little bugger was definitely here. And he definitely snuck back into the wedding tent to grab dessert," Leanne said, picking up a wrapper that still had some chocolate stuck to it.

Sam looked around, tongue pressed into her cheek, hands on hips. "But where the hell is he now?"

# CATHERINE

"**M**urphy, I don't understand. We've done this a thousand times. There's no reason customs should be causing problems. Did you fill out the form properly?"

Catherine had showered, changed, and gone out to grab an acai bowl so she could hunker down and get a little work done before going back to the city. Cash had requested a late checkout when they'd booked their room—he slept late on Sundays when he didn't have any live classes to teach—for which she was now very grateful. She knew when she got back to the city she was going to have to deal with him and the emotional fallout from last night, and she really needed to get some work done before then.

Unfortunately, she wasn't even back in her room yet and work was already falling apart. Her assistant had just informed her that the shipment of Tag Heuer watches, the primary component for Bea and Ant's wedding gift bags, might be held up indefinitely by US customs. The wedding was only six weeks away, and she and Murphy were supposed to be flying down there in three weeks' time to walk the site and make sure all t's were crossed and i's dotted. She didn't need any hiccups right now. This was the biggest event of her career.

"I have it right here," Murphy said, his voice veering toward a whine as it always did when he was stressed out. "Every field is filled out. The valuation is correct. I don't get it."

"Take a photo of it and send it to me. I'll call a guy I know in Newark and see if he can give us some advice."

She pulled her ponytail over her shoulder before yanking open the door and striding into the air-conditioned lobby of her hotel. This was going to be a long morning. Actually, it had already been a long morning. And her head still hurt from whatever she'd gotten up to last night. Her jaw, too, she'd noticed when brushing her teeth earlier. It hurt when she opened her mouth too wide and it was tender when she touched the left side. Had someone elbowed her on the dance floor or something?

"Miss Farr?"

Catherine froze. The two cops from earlier were standing at the front desk.

"What are you doing here? Is Peter okay?"

They glanced at each other, Magrin's eyebrow arching as she popped a peanut in her mouth from a small package she was holding. She actually had lovely brows, Catherine noticed. She wondered if she got them threaded somewhere in town. She'd have to ask later. It was always good to know the best local stylists in a resort town for future wedding-planning purposes.

"Why are you looking at me like that?" Catherine demanded. Virgil had a narrow-eyed, confused expression on his face.

"It's just you look completely different from earlier."

"It's called a shower and makeup," Catherine said. She actually looked human now, thank you very much.

"Mr. Frank is fine," Magrin put in, her tone placating. "We have a few more questions for you."

Catherine looked around the crowded lobby. Their conversation had caught the attention of a few people, and one teenager was filming her over the back of the couch on which she was seated, doing a very bad job of trying to hide it.

"You're Farr and Away Events, right?" the girl said when she saw Catherine looking. "Can I get a selfie?"

Catherine pasted on a grin. "Sure, hon."

She walked over to the couch and leaned toward the girl. "You can tag me, but only if you promise not to mention the police."

"Bet," the girl said.

They smiled, took the pic, and the girl started jabbing away at the phone with her thumbs. "Thank you! My friends are gonna *die.*"

"What the hell was that?" Virgil asked when Catherine returned.

"Don't worry about it," Catherine said. From the look of this guy, he'd never even heard of social media. "Can we go somewhere more private?" she asked.

"Your room?" Magrin asked.

"Actually, it's kind of a mess," Catherine said truthfully. When she went on vacation, she allowed herself to be a slob, which was something she never did in her day-to-day life.

"You can use the manager's office," said the woman behind the desk, gesturing over her shoulder at an open doorway. "There's no one back there."

The office was small and bright and held only one chair, so Catherine stood against the wall on one side of the room, while the two officers hovered near the center. It made her feel claustrophobic.

"So what's all this about, Officer Virgil?" she asked, hoping to get it over with quickly. She put the bag containing her melting acai bowl atop some papers on the manager's desk.

"It's Detective Virgil."

"Sorry, I thought detectives wore plain clothes."

"Not in this town," he said, displeased.

"He's the only detective we've got," said Magrin, munching on another peanut. "But he also writes parking tickets."

"Oh, got it," she said. Though she really didn't. This town was rolling in money. They couldn't afford a full police force?

"Miss Farr, we received an anonymous tip," Virgil began, opening his notebook. "About a . . . conversation you had with Tilly Dansforth before her wedding?"

"A conversation *I* had?" Catherine said.

Magrin consulted her notes. "You, Mrs. Leanne Gladstone, and Miss Maya Romero."

*Oh fantastic*, Catherine thought. *So much for the pact.* She bet squeaky-clean Maya was the anonymous tipster. The woman didn't seem like the type who could handle anything morally gray, even though the pact had been her idea.

"Okay," she said, her fingers twitching for her phone. It was really well past time to call a lawyer.

"And she threatened to have Peter rescind his investment in your company, Farr and Away Events?"

"I know what my company is called," Catherine said stiffly. "And it wouldn't have mattered if he did take his money back. We've been profitable for three years. He's been seeing a return on his investment. Either she never asked him or she didn't believe him, but it was basically an empty threat."

"Was it, now?" Virgil seemed skeptical.

"Google me," Catherine snapped, resenting this line of questioning. "I mean, I'm no Jillian Fabre or Casey Crowley, but I'm very successful."

"We know you are," Magrin said with a placating tone.

Virgil shot her an admonishing look.

"What? It's true." *Crunch.* "She's doing the Beantonio wedding."

"The what? What is that, some kind of canned goods company?" asked Virgil.

Catherine and Magrin both laughed. "Oh my God, no. Bea Lively and Antonio Morrow? The ViaFit instructors? Catherine . . . I mean, Miss Farr here is planning their wedding."

*So Magrin's a fan. Nice.* Maybe she could use that to her advantage.

"I have no idea who those people are," said Virgil.

"They're two very famous fitness celebrities who aren't going to have a cocktail hour *or* a parting gift if I don't get up to my room and make some phone calls in the next five minutes," Catherine said. "So. Are there any other pointless questions you'd like to ask?"

Virgil glowered and Catherine's chest constricted. Clearly, that was a comment too far. She bit her tongue to keep from apologizing. If there was one way for a woman to instantly lose the upper hand in any conversation, it was by apologizing.

"What happened to your hand?" Virgil asked. "We didn't get to that earlier."

Catherine looked down at the large Band-Aid across her palm, held in place by an ace bandage the local pharmacist was nice enough to wrap for her.

"I cut it."

"How?"

"We've already gone over how drunk I was. I fell and cut it on a sharp rock."

It wasn't necessarily a lie. She just didn't remember.

"You did that on a rock," repeated Virgil, staring her in the eye. "Where? Was anyone with you?"

"I honestly don't know."

He dragged his gaze away absurdly slowly and wrote it in his notebook.

"Can I go now?" Catherine asked.

"Sure," Virgil said.

She snatched up her breakfast and made for the exit. "But don't leave town. And we're going to requisition your bank records to confirm your statement about your business."

"Feel free," she said breezily.

Catherine left them without a look back and didn't stop until she was safely inside her room with the door closed behind her. She texted Maya and Leanne.

> Someone tipped off the police about Tilly's little meeting. They already cornered me, so keep an eye out.

Leanne wrote back immediately.

> That was quick.

Three scrolling dots from Maya, then nothing. Then three scrolling dots, then nothing. Finally, a text.

> Any news on Hudson?

Catherine cursed under her breath. She'd completely spaced on Hudson. She typed quickly.

> I was just going to ask! Have you found him?

From Leanne:

> Nothing yet. Calling all his friends again.

Then, from Maya:

> Keep us posted. And please let me know if there's anything I can do.

*Like what?* Catherine wondered. *Put Serena Williams on the case?*

Outside the sliding glass doors to the veranda, the ocean churned and crashed, the sky overcast. The cops were not going to find anything suspicious in her bank records. But if they ever found out why Peter had invested in her company in the first place, they were both going to go to jail.

It was definitely time to call a lawyer.

She was about to ring Cash to ask if he had anyone to recommend, but the phone vibrated in her hand. It was Peter.

"Hello?" she said, sounding breathless.

"Cat?" His voice was strained.

"Peter? Are you okay?"

"Not really," he said. "This is all just . . . a lot."

"I know. I'm so sorry."

"I'm sure you're busy, and I know you and Cash probably have plans—"

"Cash went back to the city," Catherine said automatically.

"Oh." He paused. "Then, is there any chance you can come over? Just for a bit. I could really use someone to talk to who isn't on my staff."

Catherine looked around at her messy room. Thought of the call she still needed to make to Cash. But he could wait. He was the one who'd ditched her last night, after all. Peter's son was missing, and his wife was dead. She could spare him an hour or two.

"Sure," she told him. "I'll be there soon."

# CATHERINE

"I just don't know what I'm supposed to do here. I mean, I can handle a lot. You know I can. But this . . . ?"

Peter looked up from the settee where he was perched, his hair slicked back post-shower. His eyes were so desperate and sad. Catherine hated when he got like this. When he doubted himself. All his life he'd carried himself with confidence, putting forth the master-of-the-universe persona that was expected of him as the son of one of America's oldest and wealthiest families. But she knew that, deep down, all that privilege and expectation had done nothing but crush his self-esteem. Unlike so many of his peers, Peter worked hard at school and in life, trying to prove that he was worthy and that he hadn't had every little thing handed to him. But even so, he always felt less than. Like he would never be good enough to deserve everything he had. Even the things he'd worked for. Like his magna cum laude from Pepperdine. His Harvard MBA. His Philanthropist of the Year award from the city of New York.

Catherine blamed his father. When they were younger, Peter's dad was always telling him that, no matter what he did, some people would think he'd had everything handed to him because of his name. Peter had internalized this and made himself believe that it was the truth. That his hard work meant nothing.

"Peter, no one would know how to deal with this." She sat next to him and rubbed his back, feeling the warmth of his skin through his smooth, chambray shirt. "This is an extraordinary situation. Have they had any luck with Hudson?"

"No. Not yet." Peter picked up his phone from the seat next to him and glanced at it. "I keep waiting for him to call. And I keep waiting for Tilly to walk through the door. This is all so—"

A tear spilled over and he wiped it away quickly, sniffling. He straightened his posture and looked up at the ceiling, blinking rapidly.

"Shit, sorry."

"It's okay! You can cry. I'd be worried about you if you *didn't* cry."

Catherine got up and moved over to the dresser, which was covered in cosmetics bags, perfume bottles, and discarded jewelry, detritus left behind by a bride getting ready for her big day. She grabbed the gold tissue box and handed it to Peter, then stepped back while he blew his nose and wiped his face, pushing her hands into the pockets of her jacket. Her eyes trailed over a crystal tray. In it were a pearl necklace and earrings, a gold-and-diamond band, and a ring featuring a huge pink stone surrounded by diamonds.

Were these Tilly's wedding and engagement rings? Had they removed them from her body? Catherine reached out to touch the pink stone, compelled by some maudlin impulse. She could try it on. Just for a second. See how it felt on her hand. She picked it up between her thumb and her forefinger, the diamonds sparkling under the lights.

"I didn't want to marry her." Peter's voice was rough.

"What?" Catherine dropped the ring with a clatter. Drew her hand back. Suddenly sweating, she pulled her jacket off and hung it on the back of the chair.

"I haven't said this to anyone." Peter looked like a man on death row, making a final confession. "I didn't want to marry her."

"Then why—"

He stood up swiftly and crossed the room, placing his hands on her shoulders, squaring off so they were eye to eye.

"You know me better than anyone, Cat. You've always been there for me. You know. You know I'd never do anything like this. You know me."

Catherine's heart pounded. This was it. This was where he told her it was her. That it had always been her. This was where he apologized for wasting so much time, so much of their lives, apart. *I should have asked you to marry me years ago*, he'd say. *Let's make up for lost time.*

"You have to tell them I'd never do anything like this."

Catherine blinked. "Wait. Anything like what?"

"Murder someone. You know that's what everyone thinks." He released her arms and turned away toward the window. "Groom murders bride on her wedding night. Like I lured her down there in the middle of the night and . . . what, shot down the chandelier so it would fall on her head?"

"What?"

Catherine staggered back until her ass hit the bed. She braced her hands on her knees and breathed in a few times, trying to clear the dizziness that had randomly overcome her.

"That's how she died? The chandelier?"

"Yes! They didn't tell you when they were interviewing you? They found her this morning, crushed under the thing. The thing *she* had to have or it wouldn't be the wedding she wanted. Ironic, no?"

That chandelier must have weighed hundreds and hundreds of pounds. Tilly would have been flattened. Bones shattered, skull collapsed, all that blood. Catherine felt her acai bowl, which she'd eaten in fits and starts on her way over here, launching up her throat, and hurled herself across the room and into the adjoining bathroom. She almost made it to her knees before the entire breakfast came back up, spraying a colorful array across the white tile floor. She retched the last bits of it into the toilet before sitting shakily back on her knees.

Crushed to death? By two tons of carefully crafted metal and glass? Tilly was a lot of things, but she didn't deserve that.

"Are you okay in there?"

"Don't come in!" Catherine shouted.

She looked around at the disgusting mess and almost heaved again. Grabbing a few towels from the closet, she cleaned it up as best she could and shoved the bunched-up towels into the hamper. The cleaning staff was really earning their salary this weekend, thanks to her.

"Do you have an extra toothbrush?" she called.

"Bottom drawer on the right."

Sure enough, there was a box full of bamboo toothbrushes along with unused tubes of organic toothpaste. Catherine quickly cleaned her mouth, rinsed a few times, then dabbed some cold water on her face. Back in the bedroom she found Peter staring out the window at the ocean.

"I'm sorry," he said, turning to her. "I assumed you'd heard. Are you all right?"

"I'll live," she said, then immediately regretted her choice of words. Peter didn't seem to notice.

"I didn't kill her," he said, and trained his eyes on the horizon once more. "I mean, honestly, if I wanted her dead to get out of the marriage, why not do it before the wedding? There are a dozen decks and balconies on this house. I could have very easily just shoved her off here at any point over the past week and claimed it was an accident."

He gestured vehemently toward the French doors leading outside. The cliff beyond and the ocean stretching for miles.

Catherine stared. "Um. Okay."

"I mean, not that I would ever do that. I'm just saying."

He looked at her, and she laughed out her nerves. "No, I mean. Obviously."

Catherine took a step toward him and reached for his arm, running her fingers down his sleeve until she found his hand. "Peter, we both know you didn't do anything wrong," she said. "The truth will come out. You just have to be patient, be honest with the police, and have a little faith. It will all work out."

Peter turned toward her and squeezed her hand. Suddenly they were mere inches apart, his warm breath on her face. She tried not to think about the fact that she'd just barfed.

"You know, when you say it, I can almost believe it." His voice, gentle and full, rumbled inside her chest.

Catherine tipped her face up, praying she'd done a thorough job with the toothbrush. Peter's lips were right there, his eyes searching hers. She inched even closer, her leg between his.

And then, the door flung open and there stood Camilla Talbot-Frank, in full black, hair perfectly styled, makeup perfectly applied. She gave the two of them a look that could have withered the most hopeful of hearts as they sprung apart.

"Hello Catherine," she said, then turned her gaze on Peter. "Is it true my grandson is *missing*?"

# CATHERINE

Catherine left Peter to deal with his mother and went outside. The fresh air filled her lungs, dispelling what was left of her nausea and clearing her head. She had to get out of here and get back to her real life. Being around Peter was bad for her psyche. She knew this. And as much as she wanted to be there for him right now, she also knew how susceptible she was to him when he needed her. It had taken her three therapists and a very expensive desert retreat to accept the fact that she had not been put on this earth to rescue Peter Frank.

But even though she'd accepted it, she still had a hard time living it.

She rounded the corner of the house to the parking area, the broken-shell pathway crunching beneath her shoes, and came to an abrupt stop. Three men stood next to her Lexus SUV, embroiled in a heated, whispered discussion. One of them was Tilly's brother. Last night he'd had his blond hair slicked back, white teeth stark against his perfect tan, looking something like a character out of Gatsby. Now he was in a wrinkled Ralph Lauren linen shirt and a pair of madras shorts, and the longer she watched, the larger his angry gestures grew. The other two men wore the standard grounds uniform of the Frank estate—tan pants and dark blue polo shirts.

There was no way to get to her car door without interrupting them, so she finally strode forward, shaking her hair back behind her shoulders. The two workers noticed and straightened, one slipping something into the other's hand. Cash? He quickly shoved it in his pocket.

"Hello," Catherine said. "Is everything okay?"

Brandt turned. "Catherine? What are you doing here?"

"This is my car," Catherine gestured. The two workers nodded at Brandt, then turned and walked swiftly away. "What's going on?" Catherine asked, watching them go.

"Oh, nothing. Those two guys were just checking out my car and I got a little paranoid." Parked next to her Lexus was a sleek red Ferrari, and Brandt actually blushed a little as she ran her eyes over it. "I think that scene from *Ferris Bueller's Day Off* is permanently imbedded in my brain."

Brandt Dansforth was the CEO of the Dansforth Group, a private equity firm started by his great-grandfather, who never had to work a day in his life either, but who—as rumor had it—was bored after college and started the firm with his inheritance money after his own father died young of a heart attack. Since making those billions, the CEO-ship had traditionally been handed to the eldest Dansforth son when he turned thirty, and so far none of them had turned it down. Why would they? From what Catherine could gather, the board ran the place and the eldest Dansforth son simply lived the life.

Catherine and Brandt first met on a trip to Miami during spring break sophomore year. The Dansforths owned a two-story penthouse on the ocean and Brandt hosted an open house for Tilly and all of her friends, which had included Peter and, by extension, Catherine. Brandt had kept a low profile and a watchful eye as his sister's friends tore up the place, filled the rooftop pool with foam, and broke more than one priceless vase during an ill-advised bowling challenge. Catherine was never a huge partier herself, and some of the drugs being passed around that week—not to mention some of the orgiastic moments in the bedrooms—had made her wonder what she'd gotten herself into. She had appreciated the fact that Brandt stayed sober and had stepped in when the festivities started to get a little . . . much. She'd always wondered if he'd gotten in trouble with his parents for hosting it, but then, there never seemed to be any actual consequences for people like the Dansforths.

Then it hit Catherine that Brandt had come here for his sister's wedding and was likely only still here to help plan her funeral, and to top it all off, he'd lost his parents only six months ago.

"Brandt, I'm so sorry for your loss. I don't even really know what to say. It's such a shock."

"Thank you. I know. I just . . . it's almost like I keep forgetting it happened and expecting her to walk out the door and then it hits me all over again," he said. "I don't really believe it yet, I guess. The lawyers keep calling me, but I've been avoiding them all morning."

"Do they know what happened?" she asked, hoping to get some sort of inside info that might make Peter feel better—and look more innocent.

"At first everyone thought it was a freak accident," Brandt said. "But I don't know. Someone found something that made them think maybe not. Which I can't even believe. I mean . . . murder?" He scoffed. "Seriously?"

"What did they find?" Catherine asked.

He studied her for a second. Long enough for her to start to feel a bit under-the-microscope. "I don't know, actually. There's a briefing in a few minutes."

Catherine nodded, wishing like hell she could be a fly on the wall for that. "Well, I should go. It was good seeing you. I wish it were under other circumstances."

"Same here," Brandt said.

He waited and watched as she pulled her car out of her spot and maneuvered her way down to the driveway.

———

"I'm sorry, but your suite has already been booked for the week," the manager, a corpulent man by the name of Jean-Paul told Catherine, not looking the least bit sorry. "We're going to have to ask you to check out at your scheduled time." He checked his gaudy gold watch. "In twenty-two minutes."

Catherine groaned, slapping her purse down on the front desk. She had been told by the police to stay in town, but she didn't exactly want to share that information with this man. "Well, what about another room?"

"I'm sorry, but we're completely booked." The man sniffed.

"Look, I'm in the hospitality industry myself, and I know that there's no way you don't have a couple of rooms set aside for an emergency situation," she said.

The man looked her up and down, his light blue eyes fairly swimming in their sockets. "I don't see this as an emergency situation."

"Well, I do. I'll pay double." She took out her Amex Black and pushed it across the counter toward him. The man took a dainty step backward, gazing down at it as if it were made of worms.

"Miss, I'm afraid I can't help you."

"Why not?"

He leaned forward slightly and lowered his voice. "I cannot have guests at this hotel who are in the habit of receiving regular visits from the police and using my offices for interrogations."

Catherine's stomach dropped. So Jean-Paul wasn't just being difficult. He was rejecting her because she was considered bad for business. A PR risk. Nothing like this had ever happened to her before.

"Do you know how many followers I have on Instagram?" she snapped, desperate.

"I don't care." He glanced at his watch. "And now you have nineteen minutes."

Her jaw dropped. He stared her down. Catherine could feel the line forming behind her. She knew people were listening in. What else could she say without utterly humiliating herself? With all the dignity she could muster, she shoved her credit card back into her bag, lifted her chin, and strode toward the elevators. Halfway across the lobby, her phone rang.

Cash.

"Oh my God, hi," she said into the phone.

"Tilly's *dead*?" he said. "What the fuck?"

"I know!" she whispered, ducking behind a huge fern and pressing her back against the wall. "Cash, it's so horrible. I wish you were here."

"Holy shit, Catherine, what happened? Are you all right? All the news is saying is that police are investigating."

"I'm fine. I mean, I'm in shock, but I'm fine."

She was so glad he'd called her. After he left last night, she was worried she'd never hear from him again. Or that he was expecting her to grovel. It was kind of nice to know that wasn't the case.

"I'm so sorry I left," he said. "I mean, obviously I had no idea."

"Obviously," she replied.

"When are you coming home? Are you okay to drive?" He took a breath. "I'm supposed to fill in for a live this afternoon, but I can cancel if you need me to come get you."

Shit, he was so sweet. He would actually do it. Get in his car and drive all the way back out here to pick her up. What the hell had she been thinking, getting all emotional with Peter Frank? Imagining him *proposing*? She seriously had to get the hell away from here.

But then she remembered that she couldn't.

"I can't come home just yet," she said.

"What? Why not?"

"You heard it on the news, there's a police investigation. They're treating the death as suspicious."

"What does that have to do with you?" he asked.

Catherine swallowed hard, trying to come up with an answer that made sense. But none of this made sense.

"Wait, are you a suspect?" He laughed.

"No! I mean, not really. But—"

"Not *really*?"

"Someone claims Tilly and I got into a fight last night after you left," she said. "I barely remember it." She reached up absently to rub her jaw and wondered . . . had Tilly *hit* her? "But I guess somebody saw it and now they want to interview me."

She decided it was best not to mention she'd already been interviewed—twice—and they still wanted her to stay in town.

"You fought with the bride? About what?"

"Cash, I honestly don't know. I was pretty drunk, remember?"

"Yeah. I remember," he said ruefully. In the space of ten seconds his tone had shifted entirely from loving concern to bitter irritation.

"Look, I'm sure it'll be quick. I'll just tell them everything I do remember and then they'll let me go." She stepped over to the elevators and hit the up button. Before long, Jean-Paul was going to send some bellboys to throw her out on her ass. "It's not like I have a motive."

There was a long moment of silence on the other end of the phone. The elevator *ding*ed and the doors slid open. Catherine saw her reflection in the shimmering gold wall of the lift. She was clutching her phone like a lifeline and she looked haggard.

"You sure about that?" Cash said.

# MAYA

Maya Romero hated to lose. She hated it even more than she loved to win. Not that she would ever tell the press that. The trophies were nice. The accolades. The headlines. The sponsors. The prize money. But what really motivated her was the pit she felt in her belly when she was on the wrong side of the score line. It was facing someone who'd bested her four times and her absolute belief that it would not happen again. Not if there was anything she could do about it. Her favorite feeling in the world was burning that pit into cinder with the fire of her conviction, of her effort, of her mental toughness and focus, and making sure she just. Didn't. Lose.

That was part of the reason this felt so utterly devastating. Peter had chosen someone else. He'd *married* someone else. Someone she hadn't even known existed. She had lost a battle she hadn't even known she was fighting. If she'd known, she would have found a way to win.

But she hadn't had a clue. And she'd lost in the most public, spectacularly humiliating way possible. She could kill Peter for doing this to her. But unfortunately, she still loved him. Which made the whole thing even worse. She wished she had pressed him more when he was acting strangely during Wimbledon. If she could have forced him to tell her what was going on, maybe she could have prevented all of this from happening.

At least Tilly was no longer here to rub her nose in it. Was that awful to think? Maybe, but as long as she didn't say it out loud, no one could judge her for it.

"I just spoke to the police."

Maya stopped in the middle of what felt like her one-millionth Russian twist—she'd lost count—and dropped the medicine ball she was holding between her feet. Exercise had always made her feel better, no matter what was bothering her—embarrassment, anger, self-pity—but nothing seemed to be helping this time.

"And?"

Shawn stood over her, his light brown hair falling forward over his wide forehead. He had his hands in the pockets of his joggers and his right hand jingled his keys inside said pocket. His nervous tic.

Maya hated the term "life coach," and had floated other titles to him—personal assistant, personal wellness trainer—but he'd trained to be a life coach and that was what he wanted to call himself. In practice, he was Maya's sounding board, her calming presence, and her occasional juice-runner when Bekka wasn't around. If she was being honest, he was really her best friend. But the very idea that she paid someone six figures to be her best friend made her feel like the biggest loser on the planet, so she tried not to think about him that way.

"I told them we were on the phone for hours last night—for obvious reasons."

Maya bit her tongue, the pain washing over her anew. *Maya, sweetie. Your relationship with Peter is now over.*

"So, you obviously couldn't have had anything to do with what happened to that poor woman."

He held her gaze and she nodded. Maya reached for her water bottle, ignoring the fact that her cell phone was vibrating next to it. Peter's face, smoldering out at her. She'd taken the photo on a gondola in Luxembourg last Christmas. The single most romantic holiday of her life.

"You going to get that?" Shawn asked.

"You know me better than anyone. What do you think?"

Maya had waited upstairs at the Frank compound to talk to Peter for the better part of an hour. When he hadn't returned, it had become clear that he'd completely forgotten she was even there. That the fact that she'd made herself vulnerable by even coming back here in the first place didn't even register with him. So she'd left. And gone straight to the gym.

She drained the water bottle and shoved herself up off the floor, handing it to her trainer and hitting partner, Christopher McCoy, who ambled off to refill it. There was a shout and a slam and then someone in the distance reeled off a few eff-bombs. Every time someone left the room, the members of the press—who were lined up against the windows in the hall—seemed to lose their shit. Maya reached for the lat pulldown handles and glanced at Shawn.

"How many are there?" she asked.

"At least two dozen. Mostly photogs. But there's one news van."

Maya's shoulder muscles tensed, and not from the workout. "Good news travels fast. I knew we should've never gone public."

It was all Peter's fault. They'd been together for six months with nary a whiff of press, thanks to the incredible publicity team provided by her agency. Liz Phillipe headed up her crew, with her decades of experience with high-profile clients. She had known all the tricks for flying under the radar—showing up at events half an hour apart, separate cars, separate entrances, separate airports. The only people who had ever seen them together were people in their inner circles—people they trusted.

Then Peter had invited her to a "small family New Year's Eve gathering" at his house in Sag Harbor, and it had coincided perfectly with a little downtime she had before the Australian Open. What he'd failed to mention was that his cousin Max had just started dating the biggest pop star on the planet—one who leaked her whereabouts to the press as a matter of course. By the time they had arrived, the place had been overrun with photographers, TikTok influencers, and viral YouTubers, and within an hour her and Peter's relationship was trending. At least no one had given them one of those stupid name mashups—Petaya or Frankmero.

Peter had been apologetic, but he hadn't really understood her need for privacy. Why couldn't they be seen in public together? They loved each other. What did it matter who knew?

She wondered if he understood it now.

No longer was she America's Sweetheart—a powerful, poised, pristine star on the rise. Now she was the naïve idiot who'd been cheated on by her playboy boyfriend. Who'd been blindsided by his surprise wedding to another woman. She was tainted and tarnished. Maya had spent half her morning on a Zoom call with Liz, deciding on a game plan. For now, Liz recommended laying low, and she'd find Maya a good, philanthropic gala to attend where she could step out looking gorgeous and powerful and write a massive check so that all anyone would be talking about was how she hadn't broken stride.

"Oh shit."

"What?" Maya didn't like that tone coming from Shawn. He was staring down at his phone with his free hand over his mouth.

"What?" she repeated. The man was frozen. The last time she'd seen him like this was when the news broke that the Queen had died. "Shawn, you're scaring me. Let me see."

"Okay, but don't shoot the messenger."

Her pulse pounded as he handed her the phone. She saw a photo of herself from one of her recent matches, fists clenched, face contorted in a shout, hair plastered to her face with sweat, the headline **GAME, SET, MURDERER?** Stamped in red above her head.

At least they'd added a question mark.

Her phone vibrated. A text from Liz. A screenshot of the same headline.

> Plan B. We're going to need to make a statement. Crafting now and will send for approval.

It vibrated again. Incapable of any rational thought, she shoved Shawn's phone back at him, hit accept, putting it on speaker.

*Breathe*, Shawn mouthed to her. So she did. And while she did, Peter began talking.

"Maya? Are you there? Thank God you picked up. I need to talk to you."

God. Where the hell was Bekka with her new phone and number? She said she'd get a Zipcar and come right down.

"Are you sure you should be talking to a murderer?" she spat back, handing the phone to Shawn. He held it out so she could talk and hear and work out at the same time. This was not their first rodeo.

"So you saw it."

"The whole world saw it, Peter!" She yanked down on the lat cords, and the weights slammed up into the mechanism, making an awful clatter. "I am *not* a murderer."

"No one is going to believe that you are," he said calmly. "My lawyers are already on it. That reporter will be fired before lunch. Are you at the gym?"

"Yes."

She slammed the weights up again.

"Did you go back to Florida?"

"No, actually." *Slam.* "The police." *Slam.* "Wouldn't let me leave the state. Which I assume the press has also heard about." *Slam*. "So I'm at a lovely facility in Princeton."

"Good. Drop a pin. I can be there in an hour."

Maya let the weights clatter down and Shawn winced. "Peter, no."

"Look, I understand that you're pissed, but if you would just let me explain what happened—"

"I was going to let you explain. I sat in that stupid study at your house for over an hour, but you couldn't even be bothered to come back. Besides, I know what happened," Maya said. She took the phone from Shawn, took Peter off speaker, and brought the phone to her ear. "I stepped off the path."

"What path?"

"My *career* path," she said pacing the rubber floor. Sweat dropped onto her shoulders from her hair and she suddenly had perfect clarity. This was what she needed. This was what she *was*. Sweat. Hard work. Focus. "You are a distraction. That's it and that's all. You did me a favor by marrying someone else and waking me up to the truth. I have to work harder now, do you understand that? And I can't be distracted by some asshole who doesn't even respect me enough to break up with me before walking down the aisle with another woman!"

"Maya—"

"This conversation is over, Peter. We're over. Don't call me again."

She ended the call and dropped the phone on the nearest weight bench.

"Wow. Well done. How do you feel?" Shawn asked.

Maya sat down hard on the floor and burst into tears.

"Oh no! Maya, listen! It's going to be okay." Shawn crouched next to her and rubbed her soaking wet back. "No one's actually going to believe you're a murderer."

"I know! It's just. It's just—" Maya hated crying. It made her feel out of control. She tried to suck in breaths past her sobs, but she couldn't do it. It was all too much. To think that just forty-eight hours ago she'd been getting ready for a clambake and hoping for a reunion with her boyfriend, and now he'd been married and widowed, and a woman who'd had her whole life in front of her was dead and the press was calling Maya a murderer. How was this happening?

"I feel so stupid, Shawn. How? How could I have let all of this happen?"

He gripped her shoulders and made her look at him. "What happened to Tilly is not your fault."

There was just the slightest hint of doubt in his words as he said it. As if he wanted to add. *Is it?* Maya bit down on her tongue. She knew the press was only trying to sell papers and clicks with their headlines, but if *Shawn* was doubting her . . . she may as well quit right now.

"Of course it's not my fault. It's not like *I* brought that chandelier down on her head. I'm not talking about Tilly. How could I have fallen for someone who would do this to me?" She started crying all over again. "Ugh! I don't want to feel this way."

This was worse than all the times her father had let her down. Almost worse than when her mother had died.

"Listen, it's okay. This is perfectly natural. You have to grieve before you can heal. Just breathe with me, okay? In, one, two, three, four. Hold, one, two, three, four. Out, one, two, three, four."

She breathed in a square until her heart rate calmed. Until the tears slowed down.

Her phone vibrated again, and she groaned. "He can't be serious. I *need* to get a new number."

"It's not Peter. It's a random nine one seven," Shawn said. "Do you want me to get it?"

"It's probably a reporter," Maya said.

They let it go to voice mail. She sniffled and wiped her nose on the hem of her shirt.

"Can you get us some tissues, please?" Shawn asked Christopher, who had returned with the water in the middle of Maya's breakdown.

"Yeah, cause that's my job," he said. Maya glared at him, and he lifted his palms. "Sorry, I'll go."

She and Shawn looked at each other. "Attitude," they said under their breath in unison. Then they both chuckled. It felt good to chuckle.

A text came through. Shawn picked up her phone. "Same number." He read the text: "'Maya, it's Camilla.'"

Her stomach thunked. "Peter's mother," she explained.

"Oh." His eyes widened and he kept reading. "'I think we should meet. Tea tomorrow? Please confirm and I'll have my assistant send you the details.'"

Shawn looked at her quizzically. He almost looked as if he thought she should accept.

"Give me the phone."

He did and she texted back, her fingers shaking so much she had to restart five times.

> No thank you and I'd appreciate it if you and the rest of your family would kindly leave me alone.

She hit send, then pressed her thumb down on the power button until the screen went mercifully blank.

Christopher came back and handed her a tissue. "We going to keep crying or are we going to work?"

"Load another twenty on there," she told him, taking a swig of water and then blowing her nose. "I think I underestimated my strength."

# CATHERINE

Cash broke up with her. So. There was that.

He said he thought their relationship had "run its course." That he'd never left a woman he cared about alone and drunk somewhere before (ouch), so maybe they should take that as a sign. At least he did it over the phone instead of sending a text after they hung up.

Catherine woke up on Monday morning in her new, very pink, very rose-scented bedroom and grabbed her phone to check whether he'd said anything yet on social media. Nothing on TikTok, nothing on Insta, nothing on X. She wondered if he'd be willing to talk about it and make a plan. Obviously she'd prefer it go down as a mutual breakup, a conscious uncoupling. She decided to call him after she showered.

One thing she did notice on all platforms were the hundreds of notifications from reporters, bloggers, and randos asking what she'd seen at the wedding. If she'd been there when it happened. Whether she was okay. Like CycleBearMama44 really gave a crap if she was okay. But it wasn't as if she could blame them. What else was social media for aside from stalking semi-famous people and forming parasocial relationships? She got up and padded into the teeny tiny bathroom attached to her teeny tiny room.

The Nosy Elephant Bed-and-Breakfast was the only place in town Catherine could find with a vacancy. She could have looked farther afield—maybe gone inland a bit to a Best Western or a Courtyard Marriott—but something told her she should keep close. And besides, she'd sworn off mid-level chain hotels once her business had become profitable three years ago.

Not that the Nosy Elephant had all that much going for it. Her room was on the third floor at the top of some seriously skinny, winding stairs, and it was roughly the size of the walk-in closet off the bedroom in her Chelsea apartment. It was also—like the exterior of the house—very pink. And flowery. And full of elephants. There were elephant figurines on every surface, elephant bedding on the full-sized bed, and dancing elephant wallpaper not just on the walls but, questionably, on the ceiling. When she opened the closet last night, she'd half expected an inflatable elephant to pop out at her, but had been happy to find plenty of empty hangers and shelves of extra bedding. In the small bathroom she discovered elephant-shaped soap and a pink, plastic elephant mat in the stall shower.

"Well, at least it's not cats," Catherine muttered, stepping right on said elephant's smirky little face.

After a long, hot shower, Catherine put on a flimsy pink robe she found hanging on a hook in the bathroom. She pulled her wet hair back into a tight bun and did her face at her makeup mirror, which took up almost the entire top of the dresser. She opened the voice memo app on her phone and started a to-do list.

"Call the florist to confirm the flowers for the ceremony . . . Finalize the guest list . . . Check on VIP flights . . . Oh! Make sure Murphy booked that extra room for the groom's parents." (It seemed that when they went away on vacation, Antonio's parents needed two rooms so that if his father got too drunk, his mother could throw him out.)

She turned off the recording, then blew her hair out, repeatedly slamming her elbow into the furniture in the small space.

She needed to find a good coffee shop where she could set up a temporary office for the next few days. This was not going to cut it.

The second she put her hair dryer down, her cell phone rang. Bea Lively. Her heart sank. Had Cash called her to talk shit? Was she about to be fired? Catherine paced the infinitesimal space in front of the bed, then steeled herself, and picked up.

"There's my favorite bride!" she said with forced brightness.

"Catherine, oh my God I heard. Are you all right?" Bea asked.

She lowered herself onto the bed, realizing there were several things Bea could be referencing here.

"Sorry, heard what?"

"About you and Cash! And the dead bride. And that you were there when it happened! What a douchebag, dumping you when you've just been through so much."

Hope bloomed in Catherine's chest. "Yeah, it was not a cool move."

"The boy has got to get over himself," Bea said. "He wasn't even on anyone's radar until you came along."

"I don't know about that," Catherine said, blushing.

"Puh-lease, it's true. He had followers, but they were, like, his mom's friends. Now all the young hot women love him and it's all because of your Insta feed. Don't get it twisted."

"Wow, thanks, Bea. That means a lot, especially coming from you."

"Hey, I found you first, remember?" Bea said. "I got your back. Do you want me to disinvite him?"

Oh, God. She hadn't even thought of that. He'd be at the wedding, which was a little more than a month away. Would he bring a date? The very idea made her eyes sting. Maybe she'd been more into Cash than she'd thought. But she couldn't impose her own feelings on a client's wedding.

"No, no. That's fine. I'll be fine, really."

"Well, you just let me know if you need anything."

"I will. Thanks."

"So what the hell happened to Tilly Dansforth? They're saying it was murder? Did I ever tell you about the time that bitch cut in front of me on the bathroom line at the Met Gala? Girl had an ego the size of my daddy's truck."

Catherine smiled and scooted back on the bed to dish about Tilly. Fifteen minutes later, when she and Bea had hung up, she felt about a hundred times better. And Bea had also asked her to switch out the pink anthurium in her bouquet for red hibiscus because red was her new signature color. It was time to get back to work. Maybe Mrs. Booker, the Nosy Elephant's proprietor, would have some recommendations for quiet coffee shops.

On her way out the door, her phone vibrated again. It was a local, unknown number. Worried it might be the police, she answered.

"This is Catherine Farr."

"Catherine, it's Farrah." The person on the other end of the line was crying, her voice broken. Catherine racked her brain for the name.

"From the wedding? I showed you the . . . the . . ."

"Chandelier, yes! Of course. Farrah, what's wrong? Are you okay?" Catherine had given the girl her number for networking purposes. She'd seemed smart and organized and like someone who might not want to work for her mom forever.

"No! It's my mother. They just brought her in for questioning."

"Okay. But they're interviewing everyone, aren't they? I'm sure they're just gathering information."

Farrah sucked in a broken breath. Catherine heard her blow her nose. "Maybe, but, like, we *were* in charge of the murder weapon. And they found out that Tilly stiffed my mom for half the price of the party."

"Why did she stiff her?" Catherine asked.

"Something about not honoring the NDA," Farrah said, starting to sound calmer. "But she didn't tell a soul about the wedding. I didn't even know until after the announcement. I just thought we were handling the annual clambake. If she didn't tell me, she didn't tell the press."

"Okay, how much money are we talking here?" Catherine asked.

"Low six figures. And before you ask, yes, that's a lot for us."

"I know, I know." Catherine took a deep breath. "I'm sorry for asking this, Farrah, but why call me?"

"They asked her to bring receipts and any information on the setup of the chandelier. I'm just worried. What if they think she rigged it so that it would fall or something? I just thought maybe you could sort of back her up. Tell them it was all done the way it should be? Can you be, like, my wedding-planning expert witness?"

Catherine had met Farrah's mother, Felicia, briefly when Farrah had shown her the chandelier. She didn't seem like the type of woman who couldn't handle herself, but Catherine was moved by Farrah's pleas.

"I don't know how much it will mean to them, but of course I'm happy to help in any way I can."

"Oh my God, thank you!" said Farrah. "Can you meet me down at the police station? It's on Main Street across from the mochi donut place. They've got my mom down there right now."

Catherine stood up and grabbed her bag. "I'll be there in ten minutes."

———

Catherine felt a bit like a star on *Law & Order* as she and Farrah rushed up the steps into the small brick police station. She would never have said as much to Farrah, but this was sort of exciting.

She was about to offer her own expertise in a murder investigation. Who knew a party planner could even do such a thing?

She flung open the door and nearly collided with Felicia, who was being escorted out by none other than Detective Virgil. Her very favorite person.

"Miss Farr," he said. "We're seeing a lot of each other lately."

"Mom? Is everything all right?" Farrah asked.

Felicia was in her late fifties, with short dark hair cut in a stylish pixie, and a timeless look about her. She wore a pressed white button-down, jeans rolled halfway up her calves and a pair of red Rothy's. Her makeup was flawless and, though Farrah was still beside herself, she looked preternaturally calm.

"Everything's fine," she said, squeezing her daughter's arm. "The police just wanted to know the party particulars."

"We'd like to talk to you next, Miss Cox," Virgil said. "If you wouldn't mind following me . . ."

Farrah's face lost its color so fast, Catherine was sure she was about to faint. "Me? Why me?"

"I already told you, you won't be speaking to my daughter without a lawyer present." Felicia tightened her grip on Farrah and steered her right around and out the door.

"We'll be in touch," said the detective, his voice like a warning.

"Let's get out of here," Felicia said, slipping a pair of Chloe sunglasses on over her eyes. Outside again, the wind went out of Catherine's sails a bit. She'd been ready for some drama and now she didn't know what to do with all that adrenaline.

"Mom, why do they want to talk to me? I don't know anything more than you do."

"I know you don't, hon," Felicia said quietly. "They're just trying to be thorough. And who's this?" she asked, turning to Catherine.

"Catherine Farr, Farr and Away Events." Catherine offered her hand.

"Oh, yes! Farrah mentioned you were at the wedding! We love your Instagram." They shook hands. "What are you doing here?"

"I called her," Farrah offered. "In case you needed someone to explain why you could have never set up the chandelier to fall when it did."

"Oh, Farrah. You're so dramatic." Felicia laughed. "Well, thank you for coming down here. Of course, I already explained the mechanics of what happened to the police. They think they can charge me with negligence, but there's obviously no way that rope wasn't going to hold."

"Wait a minute . . . you used a rope to hoist the chandelier?" That was unheard of. Especially for a piece of that size and weight. There were mechanical hoists for such things. Chains and safety latches and counterweights. Perhaps these people *had* been negligent. At the very least, they were amateurs.

Felicia and Farrah exchanged a look, and Felicia began walking toward the parking lot. "Obviously we rented a hydraulic system to lift the chandelier and had everything in place to secure it according to regulation," she said crisply. "But the system failed that morning."

"It wouldn't even turn on," Farrah put in.

"So, of course, I went to the bride to let her know the chandelier wasn't going to happen, and that I had some lovely backup options in our warehouse."

"I can imagine how that went over," Catherine said.

"The bride was . . . displeased," Felicia said, pursing her lips. She pulled a set of keys out of her bag and used a fob to unlock a BMW sedan. "So, I had her sign a liability waiver and called in a favor." She looked at Farrah over the top of the car. "That's why they want to talk to you. They know you, Tilly, and I were the only ones who knew about that waiver. And since you found the body . . ."

Catherine's jaw dropped. "Wait. *You* found the body?"

Farrah nodded meekly, looking nauseated. "I was the first on-site for cleanup yesterday morning."

It was on the tip of Catherine's tongue to ask Farrah for details. Was there a lot of blood? Had she been crushed entirely? Was it like when the house fell on the Wicked Witch of the East and only her legs were sticking out?

*What the fuck is wrong with me?*

"Oh my God, Farrah. I'm so sorry. That must have been—"

"I don't want to talk about it," Farrah said. "I don't even want to think about it."

"I don't blame you." Catherine blushed over her gruesome thoughts. "I'm impressed you're even functioning right now. I'd be in bed under the covers if I were you."

"Well, some things are more important." She gave a wan smile in her mother's direction.

"So . . . wait," Catherine said, refocusing on Felicia. "You couldn't get a replacement machine?"

"Not that quickly," said Felicia. "But I know a guy who's good with ropes. And hoists. And heavy loads."

"Who?" Catherine asked, face screwed up in confusion.

Felicia popped open the door of her car. "Tony Gladstone."

Catherine's heart gave a small lurch.

"Leanne's husband?" Catherine asked.

"You know Leanne?" Felicia asked.

"Yes, I . . . we go way back."

"Well, wish her luck for me." Felicia slipped into the driver's seat as Farrah got in on the other side. "He's next on the cops' shit list."

# LEANNE

"What's the problem here?"

Leanne joined Barbara behind the counter, hoping to break up the argument she was having with one of the summer people. The woman in question was tall, tan, and wearing her tennis whites. She lifted her chin to look down her nose more effectively at Leanne. This woman had no idea what she was dealing with. If there was one thing Leanne wanted right now it was a fight.

She shouldn't even be here. She should be out scouring the streets for Hudson. But the police had assured her they were on it and that there was nothing more she could do, and then Tony had convinced her that she was going to lose her mind if she didn't find something to distract her. Well, what better way to distract her than by slinging Linzer tarts to rich bitches with tennis rackets up their butts?

"She won't sell me that chocolate tart." The woman gestured at the box Barbara was holding, half-open, with the last chocolate tart inside.

"As I've told the *nice lady*, someone just called to reserve it," Barbara said in her gravelly voice. "Priya Singh," she added pointedly to Leanne.

Priya only ordered the chocolate tart when she was going to visit her father at the old folks' home where he currently lived in the memory ward. Mr. Singh had taught history at the regional high school and had been one of Leanne's favorite teachers. He'd forgotten most things, but still remembered how much he loved her chocolate tart.

"Oh, well then, it's already been sold. My apologies," Leanne told the woman. "We have plenty of other chocolate desserts—"

"But I want *that* one," the woman said haughtily.

Leanne took a breath for patience. "I understand that, but as I mentioned, it's already been sold."

"Has it been paid for?" the woman said, presenting a hundred-dollar bill as if she'd conjured it from thin air. The tart was fifteen dollars.

"Yes. It has been paid for," Leanne lied, not that it mattered.

The woman stared at her with her ice-blue eyes, like she could not believe that someone in Leanne's position was saying no to her, let alone turning down an extra eighty-five dollars.

"How about a chocolate cream pie?" Leanne said, forcing a smile through her barely contained rage.

"You really have no idea how to run a business, do you?"

Just then, Priya came barreling in, harried, and rushed to the end of the counter where Barbara quickly tied twine around the box.

"Oh my gosh, thank you. I'm double-parked. Some idiot in a Tesla is taking up about three spaces."

Leanne saw the blonde flinch, and the two of them locked eyes. Clearly her Tesla.

Priya scrounged through her massive bag and produced a twenty-dollar bill, holding it out to Barbara as Barbara handed over the box.

"It's on the house," Leanne told her, and the tan woman made an incredulous noise. "Tell Mr. Singh I say hello."

"Leanne Gladstone, you're a goddess," Priya said. Then she ran out with her tart.

The woman across the counter narrowed her eyes at Leanne and Barbara who now stood side by side facing off with her. Leanne could see the war going on in her mind. Did she storm out, offended, or did she capitulate and buy something else?

"I'll take the cream pie," she said finally. "And in my defense, your parking spaces are insanely tight."

"Thank you for your business," Leanne said as Barbara pulled out one of the pies. Then she walked back to the front of the line, still shaking.

Where was Tony? He had called her to tell her he was going down to the police station to answer some questions, but he hadn't told her what those questions were about—only that they were *not* about Hudson. He had sworn on his beloved mother's grave. But Hudson was still missing. And it couldn't be a coincidence that the cops wanted to talk to her husband.

Did they think Tony knew something about Hudson's disappearance? It was the most ridiculous notion she could possibly imagine. Tony loved Hudson more than he could have loved his own child, had they been able to have any. And yes, he was a giant of a man—six foot five with broad shoulders, huge hands, and muscles chiseled from thirty years of working on fishing rigs. But he was a gentle soul. A teddy bear.

Well, unless someone he loved was threatened. Then the grizzly came out.

The doorbell chimed and Leanne looked up, not sure whether she was hoping for Tony or Hudson to walk through, but it was Tony, and he gave her a look that said she wasn't going to like whatever he had to say.

"Barbara, I'm going on break."

She turned and walked into the kitchen, past her crew cleaning up from the morning's bakes and out the back door, knowing Tony would follow. In the small alleyway out back, she had set up two café tables with bright yellow umbrellas, and several lattice boxes full of begonias, which bloomed all season. She and her girls used it as a de facto breakroom, and she immediately bent to pick up a couple of cigarette butts that had been crushed into the asphalt.

Barbara just couldn't get it through her head that she should dispose of her butts properly.

The door opened as she tossed the detritus into the small trash can. She swiped her hands against the ass of her jeans.

"What? What happened?" she asked Tony.

"Let's sit down," he said, his low voice smooth and calm. He hadn't shaved in two days and reddish-gray stubble covered his chin and cheeks.

"Tony, just tell me." She held herself around her waist as if prepping for a body blow.

"Fine," his large shoulders slumped slightly. "The police called me in for questioning. About Tilly Dansforth."

All the air went out of Leanne and she did sit, almost knocking over the nearest chair as she fell into it.

"*What?* You weren't even *at* the wedding!"

"But I was there earlier," he said. "At the Franks' place. Me and the boys . . . we helped put up the chandelier."

Leanne's mind went blank. It was a sensation she'd never had before. Like everything had stopped making sense so the constant whir of thoughts and worries and stresses in her mind just came to a halt and faded into nothing.

"Explain, please."

Tony sat across from her, the tiny chair screeching under his weight. He leaned forward, elbows and forearms on the tabletop, almost covering the whole thing.

"We'd just gotten the boats settled when Felicia called me. She said the hoist they rented for the chandelier had malfunctioned and the bride was freaking out. She asked if I could come take a look, figuring lifting a two-ton chandelier couldn't be much different than lifting two tons of bluefish."

"It weighed two tons?"

"No." Tony ran his hand up and down his face, his gold wedding band glinting in the sun. "Just, you know. An expression. Anyway, me and Bobby and Caleb went over there and we figured it out, got the thing up there, secured it, and said we'd come back to help take it down the next day."

"So what happened?" Leanne asked.

"Fuck if I know."

"Tony!"

"I'll tell you the same thing I told the police. We used a double-braided HMPE rope to hoist that thing in place. That product has the highest tenacity on the market. It's like steel, Leanne. Someone would have had to climb up there with a twelve-foot ladder and use a chain saw to bring it down. That or harpoon the thing. There's zero chance anything we did could have caused that chandelier to fall."

Leanne's pounding heart quieted somewhat. "And what did the cops say to that?"

"They said *we'll see*."

"What the hell does that mean?"

"I don't have a clue. I told them I'd never met the woman. They said something about how she was going to be Hudson's new mom, but I shrugged that off. It wasn't as if Peter marrying some socialite was going to change anything. Hudson's ours and everyone but the courts knows it."

Leanne's insides rearranged themselves. She hadn't told Tony about Tilly's pre-wedding threat. And now did not seem like the time. According to Catherine, though, the police knew. Was that why they'd said *we'll see*? But that conversation had come well after Tony and his men had done their work on the chandelier. There was no way he could have known that Tilly was planning to take Hudson away from them at that time, because *she* hadn't even known.

Just thinking about it made her feel shaky all over again. Tilly had threatened to take away the one thing that meant more than anything else in the world to her, and then, just a few hours later, had ended up dead. Why weren't the police swarming her house, her business—grilling her under a single lightbulb like they did in all the cop dramas? Forget Tony. She could have done it. She half wished she *had* done it.

"Speaking of which, we should get back out there and keep looking for him. Screw what the cops said. Do Barbara and the girls have things covered here?"

"Yeah," Leanne said, feeling a bit dizzy, a bit fuzzy, a bit not-herself. "Yes." She shoved herself up and removed her waist apron, dumping it on the table. She had already spent one sleepless night in her house without Hudson. She wasn't sure she could survive another. "Let's go find our boy."

# CATHERINE

Tuesday morning, Catherine was sitting in the window of Café Quatre, a cute little beignet place that made an excellent caramel latte, trying to reconfigure the seating arrangements for Beantonio's wedding, per a new email from the groom's mother outlining a recent feud between uncles. But her thoughts kept floating off. To Peter, to Brandt, to Maya, to Leanne and Tony and Felicia and Farrah.

Could one of these people really have committed murder?

If Catherine didn't know her better, she'd have put her money on Leanne. The look of rage on her face when Tilly had said she was going to take Hudson out of her life was epic. Leanne most definitely could have snapped. And it was interesting that Tony had been involved in the chandelier's setup. Plus, the two of them were locals. They probably had a couple dozen neighbors willing to help them cover up a crime out of solidarity against the rich summer people. Absently, Catherine wondered why Leanne and Tony had never had their own children. They seemed like the types to be swimming in diapers and onesies and minivans and soccer games. But she knew these things could often be complicated, even if it was something she'd never contemplated seriously for herself.

The TV behind the bar showed a clip of Maya Romero holding

up that dish-trophy thing from Wimbledon, and Catherine's lips pursed. Could *she* have somehow figured out a way to bring down the chandelier? The *New York Post* seemed to think so. But come on. Just look at the girl. Fresh-faced, wide-eyed, innocent, she was like one of those Disney Channel stars from Catherine's youth, minus the eventual drug problem.

She leaned back in her chair and sipped her latte. Across the street, she saw Farrah, carrying a plain brown paper bag and walking swiftly, weaving around families and window-shoppers. Catherine's eyes narrowed. Farrah looked stressed. She wondered if she'd talked to the police yet. What possible motive could sweet little Farrah have for squashing Tilly like a bug?

Ugh. She really had to stop allowing her brain to think disgusting, disrespectful things like that before one of them came blurting out of her mouth.

Suddenly, Farrah stopped, looked over her shoulder, and shoved the whole paper bag and its contents into a public garbage receptacle. Then she walked off quickly, hands in her pockets, nose thrust to the sky, playing at being someone who hadn't a care in the world.

The base of Catherine's skull tingled. Something was up.

She slapped her unused laptop closed and shoved it in her bag, grabbed her coffee and hustled out, crossing against the light and eliciting a honk and a stream of curses from a bunch of shirtless dudes in a top-down convertible. Catherine ignored them and paused next to the garbage can.

Was she really going to do this? Well, obviously she was. She shoved her hand into the hole and, mercifully, it hit the paper bag immediately. She grabbed it and shimmied it back out. With a quick, silent prayer that the bag would not contain a dead animal or severed head, Catherine opened the bag.

It took a moment for her to process what she was looking at, but when she did, her shoulders slumped.

Three cans of red spray paint, no lids, obviously used.

The exact shade of red that had been used to paint the word *LIAR* across the hood of a very expensive automobile.

# MAYA

Maya wore a new Adidas tracksuit to the interview, white with green piping. It was meant to evoke Wimbledon. To remind the reporter of her recent, stunning achievement, to keep herself focused.

Focus was the key going forward. Tennis. Avoiding injury. Staying healthy. Winning. Winning. Winning. There would be no more relationships. No new people. She was circling the wagons, raising the drawbridge—whatever old-timey metaphor one wanted to drag out. As she sat down at the café table in the juice bar at the Princeton Tennis and Pickleball Club, she swung her blond ponytail behind her, knowing she looked fresh-faced and dewy, with just the perfect spot of pink gloss. She uncapped her water—VOSS, of course, because sponsorship—and nodded at her publicist, Liz, who stood near the door. Liz nodded back and let the reporter in.

The reporter was Nadine Force, a well-respected journalist on the tennis press circuit, who had given up a career as a hard-nosed investigative exposé writer to follow the pros. Maya had known her since she was about fifteen years old, when Nadine had interviewed her for a roundup of future stars. (Today, Maya was the only one of the eight girls featured who had even cracked the top fifty, so that just went to show how much Nadine knew.) But to her credit, in the interview, Nadine had never once brought up Maya's background, her notorious father, her tragically deceased former-tennis-star mother, the fact that she lived with her aunt, Elina, who had been her mother's doubles partner. And of all the reporters on tour, Nadine was the one who could have done so with some credibility. Early in her career, she had run a series of stories about the Romero crime family, back when Maya was just a toddler. Maya knew this because she'd googled Nadine once and learned that it was soon after that series was published that Nadine had turned to sports. She claimed it was because she'd always loved tennis—had played as a girl and worshipped Monica Seles and Amélie Mauresmo—but Maya had always wondered. Was that really why she'd quit? Or had Maya's father somehow gotten to her?

Whatever the case may be, Maya trusted Nadine, which was why she was the perfect person for this particular interview. She'd sworn to Liz that she was only interested in a post-Wimbledon status report and in hearing what Maya was looking forward to as a next step in her career. There would be no questions about Peter or . . . anything else. Maya was in control.

She rolled her shoulders back, closed her eyes, and took three square breaths. When she opened her eyes again, she plastered a huge, welcoming smile on her face. One that became instantly rigid. Nadine was not alone.

"Maya! It's so good to see you!" Nadine slid into the chair across from her. Her plain brown hair was back in a low braid, and she wore a gray suit that did nothing for her coloring, along with sensible shoes. "I hope you don't mind, I brought our summer intern along as a learning experience. Rafael, this is Maya Romero. Maya, meet Rafael Carrero. He's at University of Chicago's J school."

Maya gave a quick glance over her shoulder at Liz. *Do you want me to call it off?* Liz asked with the raise of a brow. Maya shook her head almost imperceptibly.

"That's great!" Maya said, regaining her composure. "It's so nice to meet you."

"The pleasure's mine," Rafael said smoothly. He perched on the edge of his chair, knees spread wide, feet planted, like he was the one about to be interviewed. He wore pressed khakis and a pink polo, his impressive biceps muscles challenging the sleeves. His black hair was slicked back from his face with some sort of product, and he had oddly deep dimples. He placed a tiny digital recorder on the table and hit a button, then caught her staring. "Oh, sorry. First day on the job. Is it okay if I record our interview?"

"Of course," Maya said.

Nadine pulled out a notebook and pen. "I'm a bit more old-school, as you know."

Maya turned more fully toward Nadine.

"So. Shall we jump right in?" Nadine asked.

"Yes, please."

"First of all, congratulations on your incredible run at Wimbledon. Winning your first major and dropping only one set to boot? That must feel . . ."

"Incredible?" Maya supplied. "Life-changing?"

"Which?" Nadine asked, eyes sparkling.

"Let's say both," Maya replied. "I still feel like I'm walking on air. Sometimes I don't fully believe it happened. And my life has definitely changed. My coach is—"

"Well, yeah, your boyfriend married someone else and is now under investigation for murder," said Rafael. "Care to comment on that?"

Maya's entire body seized. She may have blinked, but it seemed impossible considering how coiled she suddenly felt.

"Raf, we talked about this," said Nadine through her teeth.

"I'm sorry, but are we really going to come in here in the middle of one of the biggest stories of the year and ask her nothing?"

"That's what we agreed to, yes," said Nadine. She looked apologetically at Maya. "I'm sorry. He's very ambitious."

"It's fine. I—"

"I'd prefer you not speak about me as if I'm not even here," said Rafael. "Now Maya, when did you actually find out that Peter Frank was set to marry someone else? Because he was still posting romantic pictures of the two of you a little over a week ago."

"I have no comment," Maya said, her skin beginning to pulse with heat.

"Well, do you think Tilly Dansforth was really murdered? Were you there when it happened? Have the police interviewed you yet?"

"Rafael!"

"I have no comment," Maya took a sip of her water and shot Liz a look of pure venom.

"Are you going to get back together with him?" asked Rafael. "You two were America's Sweethearts, after all."

"This is really none of your business," Maya heard herself say.

"Do you think he did it?"

"That's enough!" Nadine said, just as a large hand came down on Rafael's shoulder. Her agency had sent over a temporary bodyguard after the mayhem at the gym yesterday. Tito Alonzo was big as a bulldozer and had the squarest jaw Maya had ever seen outside of Buzz Lightyear.

"I think it's time for you two to go," Tito said.

"The both of us?" Nadine asked shakily, looking at Maya. "I'd prefer to stay and finish the interview we agreed upon. I'm very sorry about this, Maya."

Tito and Liz both looked at her. She shook her head once, hardly able to imagine speaking.

"Maya, please. I apologize for the rudeness of my . . . colleague," Nadine said the word as if it left a sour taste on her tongue. "I hope this won't affect our working relationship going forward."

She leaned toward Maya slightly. "They made me bring him. He's the boss's nephew and I—"

Maya looked Nadine in the eye. "Please go."

Nadine stood up straight, hesitated. "Fine. I understand. I'll call Liz to reschedule."

"No. You won't," said Maya. "We're done here."

Nadine's face fell. She looked over at Raphael, who seemed incredulous. "Not *done* done, Maya. We've known each other for—"

"See them out," Maya said to the bodyguard. "Please," she added, remembering her manners.

Then she got up and walked out the far door toward the courts, ignoring Nadine calling after her. She was, in some ways, her father's daughter. But her legs shook as she left. Because she was, after all, still her.

———

Freshly showered after a long practice with Christopher, Maya stood naked in front of the mirror in the locker room. She knew no one would walk in because she'd paid through the nose for a few private hours. But she wouldn't have much cared if someone had. Maya had spent the last ten years turning her body into a high-performance machine, low on body fat, high on lean muscle mass, and the only scar she carried was the tiny incision from her appendectomy at age sixteen. The only visible one, anyway.

Carlito Corsica, the two-time Wimbledon champ and Olympic gold medalist, had been her coach when her appendix burst. She had been living at his tennis academy in Boca, and her roommate, Benita Shu, had alerted their floor monitor once Maya had started screaming from the pain. Carlito had driven her to the hospital in his Porsche, frantically trying to get hold of her aunt Elina, who was her legal guardian at the time, but Elina had been on vacation in Tulum and couldn't be reached.

It was Carlito who had sat in the waiting room while she was operated on. Carlito who had masqueraded as her guardian to sign off on the surgery. Carlito who had made sure she got the proper rest and recovery time afterward. When her aunt had finally returned from Tulum, her first act had been to withdraw Maya from the academy, claiming fraud and negligence and threatening to sue.

Two months later, Maya filed for emancipation, won it, and moved back into the academy, where she waited tables for extra cash, aced all her sophomore-year academics, and went pro.

Now, Maya stared herself down in the mirror. She saw a young woman who had been hardened by the people in her life, but clearly not hardened enough. She had to protect herself better. Peter had been the first person she'd ever allowed herself to trust outside of her tennis family, and look where it had gotten her. She wouldn't even have Nadine Force to fawn all over her anymore, thanks to him.

Her phone rang. She threw on a T-shirt and stepped into a pair of underwear before answering, then laughed at herself, wondering why she had to be clothed to answer the phone. Five seconds later she felt so exposed, she was shivering.

"Holy fuck. You actually picked up the phone."

It was her father.

"How did you get this number?"

"Maya," he sounded exasperated. "This morning I woke up to a coupla green ass cops knocking down my door asking if I know anything about the murder of some dumb blond socialite back east. You wanna tell me why that happened?"

"Oh, I dunno, Dad, maybe they know you're a cold-blooded murderer so they just drew the obvious conclusion?"

She realized she wasn't breathing and sat down hard on the metal bench next to her.

"Allegedly," he said.

"Dad, don't talk to me like I don't know who you are and what you've done." Her fingers curled around the edge of the bench seat.

"What about what you've done, Daughter dear?"

Maya froze. She had no idea what he thought he knew, but she didn't like his tone. He chuckled.

"Not so high-and-mighty now, huh? How about you don't talk to me with such disrespect?" he shot back. "I'm sick and tired of all the disrespect, Maya."

"What disrespect?" she shot back, heart hammering. "I haven't even spoken to you in three years!"

"Exactly! That right there is disrespect. Who the hell raised you after your mother died?"

Nannies. Aunt Elina. A parade of coaches and trainers and mentors and psychologists and hitting partners.

"Who the hell paid for all your court time and your fancy rackets and those little skirts you were always running around in?"

"Back off, Dad. I haven't asked you for a penny in over ten years."

"That doesn't mean I deserve to get sucked into your little socialite drama!"

"You don't deserve? I'm sorry, *you* don't deserve?" she shouted. "When I was five years old *I* was woken up by a fucking SWAT team and dragged out of my bed so that a DEA squad could search my room for cocaine and firearms with a pack of dogs!"

She could still remember the woman who had held her in her arms and carried her to the van in the driveway of their lavish Las Vegas villa. She'd had curly red hair and smelled of cigarette smoke and lavender.

"Oh, boo-hoo! Your life has been *so* hard! I didn't see you crying when you were curtsying to the goddamned king of England!"

Maya ended the call and threw her cell phone across the room. It smashed satisfyingly against the wall and exploded into half a dozen pieces. It felt good, but it wasn't enough. She turned around and ripped her bag out of the locker. Grasping it in both hands, she slammed it repeatedly into the bench, whipping it over each shoulder in turn like she was chopping wood. Her things flew out the open zippered pockets. Lip balm and earbuds, racket tape and sunscreen, hair ties and eyedrops and the rosewater dish keychain Peter had bought her in the Wimbledon gift shop. Tears squeezed from her eyes, and she let out guttural wails and screeches and screams until her throat hurt. Until her chest ached. Until her head throbbed.

"Maya! MayaMayaMaya!"

Shawn burst into the room, locking the door behind him, and raced over to her, he batted a flying hairbrush out of the way and grabbed her in a bear hug, pinning her arms to her sides.

"Maya, stop!"

"Let me go!" she cried.

"Nope. Not gonna happen. You have to breathe."

"Shawn, I swear to God—"

"You don't want to do this, Maya, remember? Breathe with me, okay? Breathe."

She didn't want to breathe. She wanted to tear this whole fucking room down. She wanted to rip his arms off her and kick him as hard as she could. She wanted to hurt somebody. Badly.

And the second she realized that, the shame slammed into her like a bus. Shame, embarrassment, fear. She bent at the waist over Shawn's arm, and wept, her mouth open as she gasped for air.

Slowly Shawn turned her around so that she could sit, sweeping her crap out of the way, and sat down next to her. He kept one arm around her as she bent forward, head between her knees and cried.

*I'm such a piece of shit. I'm such a piece of shit. I'm such a piece of shit.*

*I hate him. I'm just like him. I hate him. I hate me.*

"It's okay," Shawn said, reaching up now to run his hand over her wet hair, over and over again. "It's going to be okay. It's all going to be okay."

Slowly, Maya's heartbeat returned to normal and she was able to breathe again. Shaky breaths in through the nose, even shakier as she blew them out audibly through her lips. She sat up, her head light.

"You all right?" Shawn asked.

She nodded, a lie, but at least she was no longer murderous.

"Okay." Shawn got up and started to clean her mess, picking up her clothes and makeup and accessories and putting them carefully, methodically back into her bag. He knew where everything went, folded her dirty clothes neatly. Finally, he retrieved the pieces of her phone and put them all into the pocket of his windbreaker.

"Bekka was supposed to get me a new number," Maya said, her throat raw.

Understanding dawned on Shawn's face. He knew her history. He knew how many times she'd had to change her cell phone number and that there had only ever been one reason why.

"She's out running errands right now. I'm sure that's on her list."

Maya nodded slowly, absently. She felt like she always felt after one of her fits—like she'd just been drugged.

"I was so close, Shawn. I was so close to having everything. Now I've lost it all."

"Hey. You just won fucking Wimbledon."

"But I lost Peter. And now my dad's back? What's the universe trying to tell me? I can only have one good thing at a time?"

Shawn rubbed her back gently. "We'll get you a new number. And if you want Peter back, just go get him. What's standing in your way?"

Maya gave a short, wry laugh. Her pride. Her ego. Her secrets. The trust that no longer existed between them.

"So I should just forgive him? He chose someone else."

"Yeah, but have you asked him why?"

Maya stared at Shawn. She had not asked him that. After everything that had happened . . . would it make a difference?

"Come on," Shawn said. "Let's get you some rest."

# CATHERINE

"**T**his is where you're staying?"

Peter stood at the foot of the steps outside the Nosy Elephant, batting away the bees that populated the forest of hydrangeas on either side of the short walk. He looked handsome in a pair of aviator sunglasses and a black polo shirt, like a proper prepster in mourning on a sunny summer day.

"It's not bad, actually. They had scones this morning." Catherine joined him, slipping her own sunglasses on.

"Were they elephant scones?" he asked, glancing at the stones beneath his Tevas. They were pink and gray and every other one had an elephant carved into it. One was sunbathing, another frolicking in the ocean, a third snoozing in a hammock.

Catherine laughed a bit too hard for the joke.

"I'd invite you to stay at mine, but—"

"Oh, no, Peter. That's okay."

"No, seriously. You're my oldest friend at this point. We *should* give you a place to stay. But there's so much going on with Hudson missing. And I'm not sure how it would look, my ex moving in right after my . . . wife . . ."

Catherine blushed. "They still haven't found him?" she said, trying to ignore the mention of Tilly.

Peter swallowed. "No. Last night I went into the city, to our apartment, and there was no sign of him there . . . I don't know, I keep wanting to *do* something, but the police keep telling me there's nothing I *can* do."

"I'm so sorry. I'm sure he's okay. Kids today are resourceful."

"I hope you're right," Peter said.

"Come on. Let's go for a walk."

He tilted his head quizzically. "You're being weirdly mysterious." They headed back out to the sidewalk, and Catherine turned her steps in the direction of the ocean. "Not that I'm not happy to get the hell out of my house, but what's going on?"

"I saw something today that I think you should know about," Catherine said.

"What?" Peter said, looking genuinely confused.

Catherine paused at the corner of Ocean Avenue and Tenth Street, giving herself half a second to rethink what she was about to do. Even though she knew she was going to do it. Peter deserved to know who had vandalized his car. And she wanted to confirm, for her own selfish reasons, that she was right about him and Farrah.

They waited for a couple of cars to drive slowly by, then crossed.

"The police have a new suspect."

"They do?"

She gave a quick nod. "Farrah Cox."

Guilt passed so quickly over Peter's face that she would have missed it had she not been looking for it. He gazed ahead, chin up, shoulders back.

"You mean that wedding planner? Why? She and Tilly didn't even know each other. What motive would she have?"

Catherine stopped walking and gave Peter her best *Don't lie to me, Peter* look. He paused, the sand on the sidewalk crunching beneath his feet as he turned.

"What?"

"Peter."

He removed his sunglasses and squeezed his eyes shut, pinching the bridge of his nose between thumb and forefinger. "You know?"

Catherine wanted to crow and cry at the same time. "Well, I do now!" She threw her palms up and let them slap down at her sides. "What the hell, Peter? Is it really that hard for you to keep it in your pants?"

"How did you find out?"

"I saw her throwing out a bag full of empty spray paint cans this morning. Red."

Peter gawked, then turned away from her, walking off a few paces before coming back. "She's the one who fucked up my car?"

"Yep. What were you thinking?" Catherine wanted to shake him. Peter, as far as she knew, had never been faithful to anyone in his entire life. She had thought, when they were together, that he had been faithful to her and that this had proven that they were meant to be together, but then Monica had happened. Monica, who had been Catherine's friend. Monica, who had claimed that Peter was so not her type and had encouraged Catherine to break it off because she was sure Peter was cheating on her.

As it had turned out, Monica had been trying to warn her that Peter was cheating on Catherine with *her*. And then Monica had gotten pregnant. Monica had been the reason she and Peter had broken up.

It pissed her off to no end that she had been made a fool of, but somehow, it didn't make her love him less. She had even tried, against her friends' advice, to get back together with him after Hudson was born and it was clear he and Monica would not be making it official. They had met up in the Bahamas, where she'd been assisting on a wedding, and he'd flown in from Boca, where he was visiting his grandparents. They'd had a night of incredible, mind-blowing sex—doing things Catherine had never done before, nor since—and when they'd woken up curled against each other the next morning, she'd laid her heart on the line.

"You're it for me, Peter," she'd said. "I want you back."

His eyes had filled with emotion, and he'd had to look away. "I can't. I'm so fucked-up, Cat. You can do so much better than me." He shoved himself up from the bed and pulled his underwear and jeans on.

"That's crap," Catherine had said, sitting up and clutching the bed sheets around her. "We're perfect together. You know we are."

"No," he said. "*You're* perfect. I'd just fuck it up again."

He was yanking on his shoes now, looking around for his shirt.

"Why are you getting dressed so quickly? Are you really that afraid to have this conversation?" she asked.

"We're not having this conversation." He yanked his T-shirt over his head, then came over to sit next to her. He took her hand in his. "I can't be with you, Catherine. I care too much about you."

She laughed a bitter laugh. "That makes sense."

"Actually, it does." He turned slightly on the bed to better face her. "I wouldn't trust myself not to hurt you again, and I don't think I'd survive it if I did."

So she'd let him go. But she knew, deep down, that all he needed was to grow up. To understand what he had in someone. And then he would settle down. And she'd always believed that that someone would be her. She and Peter had something. Something that transcended all those other random flings. He always came back to her. Always.

And this latest development proved it. Peter had even cheated on Maya Romero. A perfect, gorgeous, famous, world-class athlete. With not just Tilly, but also this Farrah girl. Clearly, Maya was not the woman he was going to drop his playboy ways over.

"I don't get it," Catherine said now. "You've been with Maya for like a year, and you were obviously recently fooling around with this . . . child."

"Have you been social media stalking me?" Peter said with a coy smile.

"Peter!"

"Oh my God, Cat, she's legal, okay?"

"So what? She looks like she's twelve!"

Peter groaned. "Fine. So she's immature. And she proved it by fucking up my car. But she's not a murderer, Catherine. Farrah doesn't have it in her. She still sleeps with a Pooh Bear, for God's sake."

Catherine didn't want to think about how he knew this. She took a breath.

"Fine. If she didn't do it, I'm sure the cops will figure it out. But I'm still confused. Why Tilly? What happened? Why did you marry her if you had two other women already?"

A young mother pushing a stroller shot them an alarmed look, overhearing this last question. Peter blew out a sigh and walked away, toward the beach, which was less than half a block off now. He sat on the bench at the foot of the ramp to the sand, took off his sunglasses and squinted up at Catherine.

"Tilly was pregnant."

Catherine stepped back, feeling as if the wind had been knocked out of her. Pregnant. Again. What the hell was wrong with his sperm? Why were they always impregnating the wrong people?

"Peter, oh my God," she said, as she realized what this meant. Tilly wasn't the only person who had been crushed under that chandelier. Peter had lost a son or daughter as well. "Oh my God. I'm so sorry."

She sat down next to him and put her hand on his leg. He put his own warm hand over hers.

"Does Maya know?" she asked.

Peter swallowed and shook his head. "No one knows." He looked her in the eyes. "You're the first person I've told."

A pleasant warmth sprouted inside Catherine's chest and radiated throughout her body.

She knew what the look in his eyes meant. She was the only person he'd told, because she was the only person he could trust.

# CATHERINE

Sweat dripped down Catherine's back as she broke down one of the round tables under the tent at the Frank estate on Wednesday morning. It was hot and humid and her tank top was soaked through, but she felt good. It was nice to do something useful, to get out of her stuffy little room and away from her computer for a while. That morning she had found a daily yoga class on the beach and signed up for the next day's flow. If she was going to be here for a few more days, she needed to start getting back to her normal routine. She'd automatically thought about texting Cash to tell him about this act of self-care before remembering, with a heart squeeze, that she couldn't do that anymore.

Farrah approached with an armful of linen tablecloths, all bunched up and tangled. "Thank you again for doing this," she said.

"Of course. Happy to help."

Catherine had always sort of enjoyed the manual labor that came with being one of the crew, and it had been a while since she'd broken down anything herself.

"Any idea what's going on with those two?" Farrah said, casting a glance past Catherine's shoulder. Catherine didn't have to turn to know who she was talking about. The Franks' butler, Liam, and another fairly buff guy in a black suit—clearly security—were keeping an eye on the proceedings. "Are they afraid we're going to steal something?"

"I know, right?" Catherine replied. "But stranger things have happened. I did a celebrity wedding in Cabo once, and two weeks later found out a member of the crew was selling some of the unused bottled water on eBay for two hundred bucks a pop."

Farrah's eyes widened, half-disgusted, half-impressed before she went back to what she'd been doing.

A member of the crew rolled away the table Catherine had been working on, and she looked around. The chandelier had been removed from the center of the dance floor, along with the section of the temporary floor where Tilly had fallen, but shards of glass and metal were being swept up by a pair of teenaged employees of Felicia's. The police had supposedly taken the end of the rope off and bagged it for evidence, and the rest of it had been shoved over to the side of the tent and forgotten about. As Farrah moved off to dump the tablecloths in one of the laundry bins, Catherine glanced over her shoulder. Liam was talking to one of the crew members, and the security dude was staring at his phone.

Slowly, nonchalantly, Catherine walked over to the corner to check out the rope. It ran along the edge of the tent and disappeared outside, where it was likely attached to some sort of winch or pulley system. But as she looked down at the brown coils of fibers, her heart rate ticked up a beat.

This couldn't have been the rope that had held the chandelier. It was about half as thick as she would have expected to raise and hold in place something that large. She crouched down, wondering it if was maybe heavier than it looked, but she could lift it easily with one hand.

"Everything okay?"

Catherine nearly jumped out of her skin. She stood up so fast she got a head rush. As she turned, she fully expected to see the security guy standing there, but it wasn't. It was a young man she'd been working alongside, whom she'd also noticed clearing tables at the wedding. He was hard to forget with his light blue eyes and brown skin, a tattoo of a snake running up his neck and around one ear.

"Oh yeah, fine. Can I ask you a question . . . ?"

"Marcos," he said.

"Marcos. I'm Catherine."

"I know. Everyone's talking about how we have a famous influencer among us," he said with a grin that had likely stopped a thousand hearts.

"Oh! Well, thanks. I think."

"So what's up?" he clapped his hands together.

"Was this the rope that was attached to the chandelier for the wedding? Or is this here for some other purpose?"

"No, that's the rope," he said. "Still can't believe what happened. We're lucky it was only one person who was under it when it fell, to be honest." Then he blanched. "I mean, it wasn't lucky for her obviously. The bride. I just meant—"

"It's okay. I know what you meant. Thanks."

"Anytime. Can I get a selfie?"

"Oh . . . sure. Hang on."

Catherine pulled her lip oil out of her pocket, reapplied, quickly retied and smoothed her ponytail, then leaned in for the photo. "Thanks!" he said. "Hoping to get some new followers for my band."

"Can I just check it really quickly?"

He gave her the phone, she applied a few filters to make herself look less sweaty and more tan, then handed it back.

"Cool." He winked at her, then walked away. Catherine looked up to see that the security detail was now watching her, standing across the tent. She looked back down at the rope and a shiver went through her. Marcos was right. If that thing had been used to hoist a three-hundred-pound chandelier, it was a miracle more people hadn't been hurt.

# MAYA

Peter was passed out on a chaise longue under a huge umbrella on the main deck when Maya arrived that afternoon. She whispered to Liam that he could leave them, but he hesitated, almost as if he wanted to ask her something. The man's light blue eyes were so intense, she felt like they were boring into her soul.

"Is there something else?" she asked quietly.

*Please not an autograph. Not now.*

"Pardon me if this crosses a line, but I just wanted to say . . . he really cares about you," Liam said.

Maya blinked, at a loss for how to respond. "What makes you say that?"

"You see things, in this job. You overhear things. I know you don't know me, but trust me. I know."

He nodded deferentially, then walked quickly away.

Feeling oddly exposed, Maya sat down quietly on the chair next to Peter's. Sleeping in the middle of the day was not like him. She didn't smell any alcohol and there were no glasses or cans or bottles around. Did this mean he hadn't been sleeping well? She felt a pang before she remembered that he had every reason not to be sleeping well and that all of them went back to his betrayal.

"Peter," she snapped loudly.

He startled awake, sitting up as if he'd been given an electric shock. It took him a second to focus on her, but when he did, the excitement on his face nearly broke her heart all over again.

"Maya! Oh my God! You're here!"

He threw his legs over the side of the chair and leaned toward her, but she put up a hand to stop him. "I only came to tell your mother to stop texting and calling me. And because I thought maybe you and I should get some closure."

"Closure? No. Closure is the last thing I want." He paused and leaned back. "Wait. My mother has been calling you?"

Maya took a breath for patience. "I figured you asked her to."

"No. I didn't. I'll talk to her. I'll take care of it. She won't bother you again."

"Thank you, but I can do it myself." She said this pointedly, reminding him that she was going to be doing everything herself again. As she always had before him. As she always would do from now on.

"Maya, please. We need to talk. You have to hear me out."

"I don't have to do anything," Maya said flatly, though inside she felt a small, hopeful, traitorous window open. What did he mean, hear him out? Had he been brainwashed? Drugged? Under some kind of spell? Why *had* he chosen Tilly? Why hadn't he given Maya any warning?

He reached for her hand, and she let him take it, but deadened her arm, refusing to curl her fingers around his or respond in any way. "I didn't mean for any of this to happen," he said. "You have to believe me."

"Excuse me, Mr. Frank?"

They startled apart and Peter stood. Standing in the sliding doors to the deck, flanked almost comically by two, wrought-iron statues of cats sitting up on their back paws like dogs, were Liam and two police officers. Maya's pulse thrummed in her ears.

"Is it Hudson?" Peter said.

The tall male detective skated his gaze over Maya. "Can we speak privately somewhere?"

"Whatever you have to say to me you can say in front of Maya," Peter said firmly.

Maya stood as well. She wasn't sure she wanted to hear whatever they had to say. Being raised by a mobster in the Vegas hills, Maya had learned an avid distrust of the police. Even if she did believe her father to be a very bad guy, she'd had it ingrained in her from a young age that all cops cared about was furthering their careers and they would do anything—lie, plant evidence, falsify documents—to look like they'd been right all along.

"Fine then." The man cleared his throat. "Ms. Dansforth-Frank's autopsy has come back. It turns out she wasn't pregnant as you'd stated."

"What!?" Peter blurted.

"Pregnant?" Maya demanded.

"No, that's not possible. She showed me the test. She showed me an ultrasound."

"According to her hormone levels, doctors suspect she had recently been pregnant and had likely miscarried." The man paused to take a breath. "There were no signs that an abortion had been performed."

Maya sat down again, suddenly light-headed. What the hell did this mean?

"Are you all right, Miss Romero?" asked the other officer, a young woman, as if the two of them had ever been introduced. Maya was accustomed to people knowing her name, acting like they knew her, but at this moment it felt like a personal attack.

"I'm fine," she spat. "Now that the two of you have seen Peter's reaction to this news with your own eyes, which I'm sure was your intention in coming over here to tell him in person, we'd appreciate it if you'd leave us the hell alone."

The woman stepped back, raising her hands as if in surrender, and she and her partner exchanged a look.

"We'll be in touch," the man said.

Then the two of them, along with the butler, disappeared inside.

"Holy shit," Peter said, pushing his hands into his hair and pacing the wide deck. "Holy *shit*. I can't believe this. I can't believe she didn't tell me."

"Peter, what is going on?"

"She was a sociopath," Peter said to himself, staring out at the ocean. "She was a bona fide sociopath."

"Peter!" He turned to look at her, eyes wide. She stood up again and joined him at the railing, the afternoon sun bright on their faces, the waves crashing down below. "Take a breath," she said. "And tell me what happened."

"She tricked me. She tricked me into the whole thing. The day I got to the UK, she sent me a photo of this pregnancy test she'd taken a month ago, and then an ultrasound from the week before. It was nothing but a blob, but it had her name on it."

"Okay . . ."

"And I was trying to figure out what to do, how to handle it, how to tell you, but then she went and told my parents. She told them we were getting married without even consulting me."

Maya was still. Her brain was slowly processing what she was hearing. Tilly had said there was a baby. Peter had believed it was his. Which obviously meant that Peter and Tilly had had sex. While *she* and Peter were together.

"This is why you were acting so strangely at Wimbledon. Because you knew you were about to marry someone else."

Peter turned to her. "I tried to get out of it. I did everything I could. But it wasn't as if Tilly was going to be bought off. She had more money than God. And I wanted to tell you, but you were winning."

And winning is everything.

He took both her hands before she could make a move to step away. "All I wanted to do when I saw you in my room that day was kiss you," he said. "I just wanted to grab you and run. This proves it, Maya. I'm the victim here. She wasn't even pregnant anymore when we walked down the aisle."

Maya's body was at war with itself. Part of her wanted to just surrender. To step into his arms and let him hold her and let all of this melt away. He was right. He'd been played. He'd never wanted to hurt her. Another part of her, the harder, more practical part, was stiff as a board, poking holes in everything he said.

"If you were marrying Tilly because you thought she was pregnant then you had to have a good reason to think *you'd* impregnated her."

Peter fell silent. He stood up straight.

"Which means that you cheated on me. Sometime in the last few months, you had sex—*unprotected* sex—with another woman."

Peter sucked in an audible breath, his broad chest—the chest she had rested her cheek on so many times, had taken comfort in so many times—expanding. Then he blew it all out.

"Maya, let me explain."

"I have to go train," she said. She paused at the door and looked back. "Please tell your mother to back off."

# LEANNE

Leanne had no idea how long she'd been staring at the tray of croissants she'd just pulled from the oven when Barbara poked her head into the kitchen. She'd been imagining Hudson tied up in the back of a van, scared out of his mind, tears staining his face, wondering where she was and why she hadn't come for him. Yes, the cops had ruled out kidnapping due to the amount of wedding security at the Franks' place and the lack of a ransom note, but that didn't mean someone hadn't taken him. A staff member or a stalker who had cleverly talked themselves onto the grounds. It could have happened.

Everyone seemed to be hoping that he'd just run away, but in some ways, that was worse. Because that meant he was so miserable he preferred to go live on the streets. An eleven-year-old boy. It meant he was doing this on purpose. It meant she'd failed him. And her sister. And herself.

"There are some people here to see you," Barbara said. "Not the police."

"Okay." Leanne's face was so dry it felt brittle when she spoke. She went over to the sink, pulled off her plastic gloves, and splashed cold water on her face. Barbara still stood there, looking confused. "What?"

"Aren't you going to ask me who it is?"

Why bother? If it wasn't the police and it wasn't Hudson, then what did she care? She shooed Barbara off in front of her and walked into the café. The line was out the door. It was their morning rush hour. The world hadn't stopped because Hudson was missing. The tourists still needed their elephant ears and crumb cakes and assorted jelly donuts.

Catherine sat at the corner table, wearing a stylish black jumpsuit, red lipstick, and tons of eyeliner, flagging Leanne down. Sitting across from her was Maya, in a dark baseball cap, mirrored sunglasses, and a full Adidas tracksuit in black. They looked like two thirds of the new Charlie's Angels. The glamorous one. The sporty one.

"What're you two doing here?" Leanne yanked out a chair and sat. "Do you want anything? Coffee? Pastry?" she asked—good hostessing was in her blood. She couldn't help it. Even though she would have preferred both of these women stay as far away from her as possible.

"Oh, thanks. Thank you. I'm sure everything is amazing, but I just ate," Catherine said.

"I try to limit sugar," said Maya.

"Well then, what?"

"Any news on Hudson?" Catherine asked.

Maya sat forward.

"No, nothing," said Leanne curtly. "But that's not why you're here."

"I'm sorry. I'm sure he's okay. He'll turn up soon," Catherine said.

Leanne's last nerve was quickly fraying. She pressed her eyes closed. "Can we talk about whatever you came here to talk about, please?"

"Sorry. Yes. Of course." Catherine cleared her throat. "I asked

Maya to meet me here so I could tell you both about something odd I found at the crime scene."

"The crime scene? How very Wednesday Addams," said Maya, leaning back in her chair, slim arms crossed over her tiny waist.

"Well, it *is* a crime scene," Catherine said snippily.

"What was it?" Leanne asked.

Catherine leaned in and lowered her voice. "The rope that was holding the chandelier . . . it was too lightweight to hold the chandelier. There's no way it was safe. All of us would have been crushed."

"No way. Tony and his crew hung that thing themselves. He told me it was indestructible."

"Who's Tony?" Maya asked.

"My husband. It's a long story. But he knows what he's doing, trust me."

"I believe you. Because if that rope had been used to hoist that chandelier, I don't think it would have even made it all the way up," Catherine said. "The rope would have snapped before they could have secured it in place."

"So then, what?" Leanne said. "It's not like someone could have replaced the rope after the chandelier was hung. There was no time and there were too many people around."

"And it wouldn't have held anyway, apparently," Maya put in.

"Exactly, so all I can think is that someone replaced the rope *after* the chandelier fell," Catherine said, looking quite pleased with herself.

Leanne and Maya exchanged a dubious look.

"Why would anyone do that?" Leanne asked.

"I don't know for sure, but I've been thinking about this a lot and what if . . . what if they got rid of the rope they cut to bring down the chandelier? So the cops wouldn't see how it was cut. And then they replaced it with this other rope."

"Holy shit," said Leanne.

Maya shimmied forward in her seat slightly. "That seems kind of . . . elaborate. Are you sure? That the rope couldn't have held?"

"I know it sounds stupid, but I—" Catherine said.

"Why do you do that?" Maya asked.

"Do what?"

"Put yourself down all the time. Start every other sentence with *I'm sorry*, or say that you *sound stupid*," Maya said. "You're clearly a successful woman. You should own that."

Catherine stared at her. Leanne stared at her.

"What?" Maya said and looked at Leanne. "I've never heard *you* apologize for anything."

"Fair," Leanne said.

"So . . . where's the original rope?" Maya asked.

Catherine, blushing over being admonished by a twenty-five-year-old, cleared her throat. "That's what we need to find out."

"Not us," Leanne said. "The cops."

"She can't tell the cops this," Maya said.

"Why not?" Leanne asked. At the very least it would take their attention off Tony, which would be a massive relief right now.

"Think about it. For someone to have done this, they had to have known how the chandelier was hung. They'd have to have access to the grounds and the tent. Which means unless it was the wedding planners for some reason—"

Catherine hiccupped. "Sorry."

"It wasn't," Leanne said. "I talked to a friend of mine at the station and Felicia and Farrah were both interviewed and released."

"Then it was someone in the family," Maya finished.

Catherine looked suddenly green. She hiccupped again.

"Like who? Camilla? Tate? That guy can barely lift a golf club anymore," Leanne scoffed.

"She's talking about Peter," Catherine said.

Maya looked away, her arms crossed over her stomach.

"Wait. You don't think—"

"He didn't want to marry her," Maya said to the wall. "She faked a pregnancy to entrap him."

"The pregnancy was fake?" Catherine blurted.

"He told you about it?" Maya asked.

"Um . . . not to split hairs, but since when does a pregnancy inspire Peter Frank to get married?" Leanne snapped.

"Maybe he's matured," Catherine posited.

Leanne snorted.

Maya took a breath. "Look, all I'm saying is, Peter had a motive." She squirmed a little in her seat. "But he didn't do it. We need to prove that before we go to the police with this."

"So you want to protect him. Even after what he did to you," Leanne said.

"Well, I don't want him to go to jail for murder!" Maya whispered. "Do you? He's Hudson's father."

They all fell silent. Customers came and went, the doorbell ringing each time it opened to let someone in or out. Outside a man laughed a throaty, happy laugh.

"Okay. Okay. Who else could it be?" Catherine said. "We need a list of people who (A) were aware of the 'surprise' wedding, (B) knew the chandelier was hung by a rope, and (C) could be on the grounds without suspicion."

Leanne's mind spun. Clearly, a long list of people knew about the chandelier. Peter, Tilly, Fiona, Farrah, Tony and his crew, Camilla—because nothing around that place happened without her knowing—and anyone else who had helped set up the tent. It was possible Sam knew because she was working that day, but it wasn't like she'd done anything to Tilly. What about Brandt? He'd just doubled his already ridiculous inheritance. Was that worth killing your only remaining family over?

She wondered what Tilly might have done to make someone hate her that much. To come up with a plan like this? There were so many opportunities for this person to rethink it, to back out. Whoever it was must have really hated Tilly.

"How did she fake a pregnancy? Didn't he ask for proof?" Catherine asked.

"They think she *was* pregnant, but miscarried and didn't tell him," Maya said flatly. Then she leaned forward, took off her sunglasses, and put her head in her hands. "I don't know why I'm telling you both this. I'm so tired."

"Hey, it's okay. Everyone needs people to talk to, and you've been through a lot," Leanne said.

"Not as much as you," Maya replied with a wan, apologetic smile. "I really am sorry about Hudson. My mom went missing for a few days when I was a kid. I remember how awful it was, the not knowing. If there's anything I can do . . ."

Shit. Leanne was starting to like this girl.

"What happened with your mom?" Leanne asked.

"She died. My dad had her murdered. He put out a hit because she left him."

Catherine hiccupped again.

"Shiiiiit," Leanne said, leaning back hard in her seat. She knew about Maya's family history. It was one of those stories the press loved to trot out every time there was another tennis tournament. But her dad had murdered her mom? How the fuck was she even functional?

"Yeah. My family makes Peter's family look like the Binghams."

"Who are the Binghams?" Leanne asked, screwing up her face.

"Influencers," Maya and Catherine said at the same time, then looked at each other and chuckled.

"Anyway, the more I hear about Tilly, the more I think she might have actually been insane," Maya said. "I don't think Peter should go down for her death. Especially if he didn't do it."

"We'll figure it out," Catherine said. "And you know what, fuck it." She turned to Leanne. "Do you have any cheese Danish?"

"Only the best in the state," Leanne said.

"I'll have one too," Maya said, smiling over at Catherine. "Fuck it."

Leanne got up from the table. Annoyingly, both these women were starting to grow on her. "Coming right up."

# MAYA

Maya was running on the beach as the sun rose the next morning, longing for her treadmill, her home gym, the predictable humidity of the Florida summer. So many people hated to train in humidity, but Maya found it useful. Working against the environment, the very air, made her stronger and gave her more stamina in matches. The longer she was stuck in New Jersey, the more out of control she felt. She needed to get back to her regular training facility, her regular schedule. She'd already had to pull out of one tournament because of this mess and she didn't want to have to rearrange her entire summer schedule because of it.

*"Never let a man run your life, dearest."*

Her mother's voice was so clear in her head it was as if they had spoken yesterday. It wasn't long after Maria had said this to her eight-year-old daughter that she'd left with nothing but her passport, her jewelry, and a bag full of designer shoes. And it was less than a month after *that* she'd died in a mysterious one-car accident on the streets of Paris. Maya had spent most of her life telling herself there was no way her father had killed her mother. The two of them had been together on a rare family vacation—to Disneyland, no less—when they'd received the news. But she'd stopped telling herself that sometime in her mid-teens. When he and her uncle Cozzo had been arrested for a triple-murder-by-arson (her dad had gotten off, Cozzo was serving a triple life sentence), she started understanding how the world really worked. The three men who had died had been proven to have cheated her father out of some huge real estate deal. Cozzo had been their partner.

You didn't screw over Nico Romero. Her mother had left him, and then she'd ended up dead. Sometimes, Maya wondered why she, herself, was still alive.

Her phone rang, pausing the music that was pumping into her ears, and she slowed. The caller ID read Camilla.

How had Camilla gotten her new number? It really shouldn't be this easy to find people.

For a half a second Maya considered not answering, but curiosity got the better of her. Was it about Catherine and the bomb she'd dropped yesterday? Had her theory gotten back to the doyenne of the Frank clan? She answered.

"Hello?"

"Maya, good morning. I knew you'd be up early."

"What is it, Camilla?"

"I heard you've been talking to the press."

Maya pulled a face. "It's kind of my job."

"I understand that, but I hope you're being discreet. You know I don't like to see my family's name in the papers unless it's connected to one of our charitable foundations."

Maya did not, in fact, know that. She'd never spoken to Camilla this much in her life. She wouldn't have been able to tell the press when Camilla's birthday was or how she took her eggs.

"If I talk to the press, it will be about my tennis," Maya assured her. "I'd rather forget any of this ever happened."

"Ah. About that. I'd like to talk to you. In person. I've made us a reservation at the club for breakfast on Saturday morning, eight a.m."

"No thank you," said Maya, pulling her right foot to her glute to stretch out her quad. She really hoped to be back in Florida by Saturday, with Peter and all this drama squarely in her rearview mirror. She'd been telling the truth yesterday, at the bakery. She didn't want to see Peter go down for this murder. But she was really starting to regret ever coming back here after fleeing the first time. She should have collected her gift baskets and gone straight to Florida.

"Please. There's no reason for you to cut ties completely," Camilla said. "Peter loves you so much, Maya. All I'm asking for is a breakfast. I've already made arrangements for you to use the outdoor courts at the club. They're reserved for you and your team all morning. Completely private. All you need to do is message me a list of names."

Maya breathed deeply. She closed her eyes. She waited. She wondered if Peter knew his mother was doing this. If he was standing right next to her.

*She won't talk to me, Mom, but maybe she'll talk to you.*

"Goodness, Maya, don't make me beg."

"Fine," she said. "I'll meet you there."

# CATHERINE

Catherine couldn't find her favorite lipstick. She'd dumped out her purse and her makeup bag, checked under the bed at the Nosy Elephant, and ransacked the bathroom, but nothing. She was about to get on a Zoom call with Cash to talk about how to roll out the news of their breakup on social and she needed her power lipstick, no question.

When she'd seen his name pop up on her phone, she'd been surprised that her heart had caught in hope. Only to falter when he explained that he wanted a PR brainstorm.

Catherine turned out pockets and shook out a scarf, then grabbed her favorite jacket and shoved her hand deep into the right pocket. Her fingers closed around . . . a ring.

She pulled it out and froze. It was Tilly's engagement ring. The one she'd admired in Peter's room the other day.

Her breath went shallow. What the fuck? She turned around in her small room, as if someone was filming her. As if this was some sort of TikTok prank.

"How the hell?"

She sat down on the edge of the soft bed, holding the ring between thumb and forefinger. There was a severe tightness in her chest. She thought back. Had she been wearing this jacket when she went to Peter's? Yes. She remembered putting it on that morning because it was like her security blanket. But how had the ring gotten in her pocket? Had it fallen in? Or worse, had she pocketed it without thinking?

Closing her eyes, Catherine tried to remember. Had the ring still been in her hand when she'd gotten nauseous? Maybe she'd shoved it in her pocket as she ran for the bathroom. The whole episode was a blur, but did it really matter? Whatever had happened, she had the ring. The very large, very expensive, property of a murdered woman.

A door slammed on the floor beneath her. This was bad. This was very, very bad. If anyone found out she had this ring . . . She'd look like a klepto at the very least, a raging, jealous, psychotic, murderous ex-girlfriend at the very worst.

She had to get this back to Peter's house, back in his room, back on that dresser, before anyone realized it was missing.

But her call with Cash was in minutes. She didn't have time to invent an excuse to go over there now. She was going to have to take a breath and come up with a plan. She stashed the ring in the zippered coin purse of her wallet and went to the bathroom to apply her second-favorite lipstick.

# LEANNE

Leanne was sitting at the same corner table she'd shared with Catherine and Maya the day before, calling all the parents of Hudson's friends for the tenth time, when Jackson Larson walked in and joined the line. Jackson was a local kid who Hudson sometimes met up with at the skate park. He was two years older than Hudson and came from a semi-notorious Cape Crest family. His father, Mike, had been in Tony's high school class, and to Leanne's knowledge had never held down a job for more than six months at a time. His mother worked two jobs to keep things semi-stable, but that meant she was never around to look after her three boys. The eldest had joined the military a couple years back, and no one had seen him since. The middle child, Dante, was still in high school and charged with looking out for Jackson, as far as anyone could tell, because he was the only family member anyone ever saw with Jackson in public. And then there was Jackson, always polite, but always up to no good.

Today he seemed rather jittery. Leanne kept an eye on him as he edged forward in the line, checking his cell phone screen every half second. She wondered if he was going to try to steal one of the forty-dollar cookie trays on top of the bakery case. Instead, he ordered four banana chocolate chip muffins and paid with cash, which of course made Leanne feel guilty.

When he turned around with his wax bag, his eyes caught Leanne's and he completely froze. Leanne's heart did an odd stutter step.

"Oh. Uh . . . hi Hudson's mom."

Then he turned and tore out of there like his pants were on fire.

Leanne hesitated half a second, then tore after him, nearly knocking over the table and scaring the crap out of an elderly couple stepping through the door.

"Jackson!" she shouted. But he was already on his skateboard— no helmet—speeding around the corner. Leanne blinked against the sun, then went back inside and grabbed her keys.

Banana chocolate chip muffins were Hudson's favorite.

———

The Larson home was inland—a good twenty-minute walk from the beach—a tiny Cape Cod on a street jammed with tiny Cape Cods. Most of the homes here belonged to locals, but there were a few cheaper rentals as well, and one could always tell which they were by the number of cars jammed into the tiny driveways.

There were no cars in the Larson driveway. The flimsy curtains were closed over the front windows and there was a crack in the one window facing the road on the second floor. Leanne stared out at the house from a parking spot across the street. Was Hudson in there? If so, would he run if she rang the bell?

The very idea of him running from her cracked her chest wide open. She got out of the car and approached slowly. Her entire body shook, and she realized she couldn't remember the last time she'd eaten or even had a sip of water. Jackson's skateboard had been abandoned on the front walk, the wheels facing the sky, reminding her of a dead bug. The grass out front was overgrown in spots, brown and patchy in others. Leanne heard thumping bass coming from somewhere, but she couldn't tell if it was the Larson house or the house next door. Then she heard a shriek.

*Hudson.*

She ran around the back of the house, vaulting over a rusty Weedwacker and past dozens of crushed cigarette butts.

And there was Hudson, wearing a T-shirt that was three sizes too big over his formal pants, which were caked with mud and grass stains, swinging high on a rickety old swing set, half a muffin squeezed in one hand. Screaming in delight.

"Hudson!" she shouted. "Oh my God!"

He skidded to a stop with both feet and ran. But he didn't run away from her. He ran into her arms.

———

That night, after speaking to the police, giving Hudson the longest shower in history, and sitting next to his bed until he fell asleep, Leanne turned her attention to cleaning out his backpack. It was heavy, and she wondered what the heck he'd been lugging around. Hudson had promised he would never disappear again. He said he was upset about the wedding and the fight and he'd taken off. He said he'd been at Jackson's the whole time, and that Jackson's brother Dante had been making them dinner each night. He'd barely seen Jackson's mom, and when he had, she'd been in a rush to get out the door.

The police had interviewed the Larsons earlier this evening. None of them had known that Hudson had been reported missing.

"Do you believe them?" Leanne had asked Tony.

Tony shrugged. "They're so busy keeping their heads above water, it wouldn't surprise me if they didn't notice anything that was going on around here."

He'd decided to sleep in the second twin bed in Hudson's room. Just in case.

Leanne opened Hudson's backpack in the kitchen of their home and stopped breathing. She had been expecting to find candy wrappers and books and his Switch, in sore need of a charge. All of that was here, but shoved in at an angle and barely fitting inside were a pair of gardening shears. The blade was wrapped up in the shirt Hudson had worn to the party, much of the fabric bunched up at the point, ostensibly to keep them from ripping through the canvas fabric.

"What the—"

And then it hit Leanne all at once. Catherine's theory that the original rope had been cut, sending the chandelier down on Tilly's head. The coil of rope in Hudson's hideout on the Franks' property.

No one had seen Hudson after Leanne's fight with Tilly. No one knew the Franks' estate better than the little boy who had been forced to stay there every other weekend, and who was then left to his own devices by the adults who supposedly wanted a relationship with him.

No one had a better motive than the child who had just seen his life turned upside down.

# MAYA

At the country club on Saturday morning, Maya greeted her coach, Joanie Kurchov, and felt a renewed sense of excitement. Joanie had just arrived with her too-pink eyeshadow and her perpetual scowl. It made her feel like things were getting back to normal. It also meant she was going to work harder than she had in days. She couldn't wait.

She left her team at the juice bar near the tennis courts and headed off to the restaurant alone. Her plan was to stay long enough to consume a spinach-and-cheddar omelet to fuel her workout and then get the hell out of there. She'd let the woman state her case, and then hit the court.

Unless, of course, Peter was there with his mother. It had crossed her mind that this could be some kind of ambush. That he might think that meeting her in public would force her to hear him out. But she hoped that after their last conversation, he would at least respect her boundaries.

"Oh! You're Maya Romero!" said the middle-aged hostess behind the stand, then blushed, clearly embarrassed at speaking before thinking. It gave Maya a little thrill, though, in her current, upbeat mood. She liked being recognized, though she'd never admit that to anyone other than Shawn.

"Yes, hello. I'm here to meet Camilla Talbot-Frank?"

"Of course, yes. Right this way."

The woman led her through the well-appointed restaurant, where hushed conversation was underscored by violin music being played through speakers at an unobtrusive volume.

"Congratulations on Wimbledon," the woman said. "I don't know how you do it. Three match points saved! My daughter plays, and she was screaming at the TV the entire time. You've really inspired a lot of young girls in this country, you know."

"Oh, wow. Thank you," Maya said humbly.

The woman had no idea how much she needed to hear this. Especially after everything that had happened. There was a point to it all. She was a good person. An important person. A person who inspired other people.

They walked through a pair of open French doors and out onto a paver patio dotted with umbrella-topped tables. Maya could see the ocean glinting beyond a well-kept hedgerow. The air smelled of coffee and something sweeter and more natural, coming from the flowerbeds, she assumed. She turned right, away from the water, to follow her hostess, and stopped dead in her tracks.

She couldn't be seeing what she thought she was seeing. Her intestines tied in knots, and she felt the immediate need to use the bathroom. Chrissy Evert had once said, watching Maya in the middle of a championship match at a 1000-level event, that nothing seemed to rile her. She was emotionless on the court. She gave nothing away.

But Chrissy had never seen Maya in the presence of her father.

Her father, Nico "The Nut" Romero, the most notorious gangster in the history of the Las Vegas crime world, now sat at an intimate table with Camilla Talbot-Frank, his polo shirt open at the neck to expose graying chest hair and a gold chain that bore her mother's wedding ring—the sight of which made her want to retch. They were laughing together like old friends.

Maya started to turn, hand on her abdomen. Which way? Which way out? She was going to run. To a toilet, then to a car, then to an airport. She had to get away. Get out of here. As fast as humanly possible. But there was the hostess, blocking her path.

"I'm sorry to ask this, but before you sit, could I possibly get your autograph?" the woman asked nervously. "My daughter is such a big fan."

This is where her reputation for being America's Sweetheart got her in trouble. If she were Valentina Vielo, the woman would have been too terrified to ask.

"Maya!" trilled Camilla. "There you are! Your father and I were just having the most interesting chat about you."

People at some of the neighboring tables looked up. They recognized her. They started to whisper. They picked up their phones and aimed them at her. She could still run. Of course, she could. But then there would be tweets. And maybe a leaked video. And then headlines.

## AMERICA'S SWEETHEART TAKES OFF IN TEARS

### TENNIS ACE CAN'T HANDLE OWN FAMILY

#### WHY IS MAYA SO AFRAID OF DEAR OLD DAD?

So instead, Maya smiled at the hostess. She took the offered pen and pad and scribbled her name. Then she turned toward the oddest couple she'd ever seen and clenched every muscle in her body.

Her father smiled at her, his eyes hard as emeralds. She'd seen this look on his face before. It never boded well for the person on the receiving end. She heard the echoes of slammed doors. Of screaming. Of begging and a single gunshot.

"There's my angel," her father said.

And that's when she knew she was screwed.

# CATHERINE

Catherine stood in the parlor at the Frank house, tapping her hand against her thigh in an uneven rhythm, a fake cat staring out at her from a nearby planter. She had texted Peter twice this morning, but he hadn't responded. She had to assume he was either passed out—she knew he was having trouble getting to sleep at night because of Hudson and everything else that was going on—or in some important meeting with the police or his board of directors. Part of her wanted to just run up the stairs, break into his room and put the ring back where she'd last seen it, but there were too many people around. Every time she so much as flinched, another woman with a duster or a man with a vacuum strode by. Perhaps Camilla's way of coping with death was to have everything deep cleaned.

She respected that. Catherine herself was a stress cleaner. Earlier today she'd taken everything out of her closet and bags at the Nosy Elephant, refolded and rearranged it, and put it all back. All because seeing Cash had proven more difficult than she could have imagined. Yes, they had made a plan for their conscious uncoupling, but he'd also apologized—for leaving her at the wedding, for the callous and curt breakup. He'd seemed honestly regretful. Which had left her questioning everything.

"Catherine, hey!"

She turned to find, not Peter, nor the butler she'd sent to get Peter, but Brandt Dansforth. He looked like he'd just come from a board meeting himself, in a gray suit and a pristine white shirt, his blond hair flopping over his eyes in a mid-part.

"Liam told me you were in here," he said. "Waiting for Peter?"

"Yeah, have you seen him?"

"No." He smiled apologetically. "Sorry. But could I . . . talk to you for a sec? I mean, if you have a minute?"

He tilted his head toward the front door, and Catherine was intrigued. She glanced toward the interior of the house, checking one last time to see if Peter had miraculously appeared. He hadn't.

"Sure."

Outside, the sun was bright and yet more workers dotted the landscape: sweeping walks, clipping hedges, and washing windows. She expected Brandt to stop on the porch, but he led her down the steps and over to the parking area, where her SUV glinted in the sun.

"I don't know how to say this, so I'm going to just say it," he began. "The morning after the wedding, when you saw me out here with those guys? I'm ninety percent sure they were in your car."

"What?" Catherine blurted. "What do you mean they were in my car?"

"I saw one of them close your trunk when I came around the corner. And when they saw me coming, they started acting *way* too casual, you know? Like a couple of kids who'd just stubbed out their cigarettes when they saw a teacher coming."

"Oh my God!" Catherine fumbled her keys out of her bag before realizing she hadn't locked her car. What was the point? The Frank property was as secure as Fort Knox. Or so she thought. She walked over and popped the trunk. There were a couple of paper grocery bags shoved in one of the side compartments, but nothing else. She kept her trunk empty most of the time in case she randomly had to pick up a flower order or some linens or stemware. She popped up the latch and checked the spare tire—still there—and nothing seemed amiss.

"Was there anything in here that day? Your luggage or a change of clothes or jewelry? Anything they could have taken?" Brandt asked.

Catherine shrugged. "Not that I can think of." She hadn't planned on staying over that night, after all.

"My mom used to keep an emergency hundred tucked between the headrest and the seat."

*For what?* Catherine wondered. *Emergency drug deals?* Didn't everyone pretty much take cards or Venmo these days?

"Nope. I don't even keep a charger in my car," she said. "I park in too many public garages and lots and on side streets in the city."

It seemed like everything was fine, but still, her heart pounded out an alarm. If they hadn't been in here to steal something, what if they had somehow messed with her car? She wished she knew how to check the brake lines. That was what always happened in movies. Cut brake lines. Her high school had forced everyone to take one semester of basic car care—something her father had thought was genius. Of course, the only thing Catherine remembered from the entire class was when Manny Valestro had kicked over the car jack and almost taken off Nestor Shahanian's head.

But what if? What if whoever had killed Tilly was coming after her next? Could someone be taking out all the women in Peter's life?

She dropped the floorboard back down over the tire and something odd caught her eye. Little fibers were sticking up off the tan car carpet. She ran her hand over the surface, and they pricked at her palm. She plucked one out and studied it.

"What's that?" Brandt asked, leaning in.

It was a rope fiber. Long and wiry and pale, almost the same color as her car's interior carpet. If she hadn't been looking for it, she would have missed it. She ran her hand over the carpet a bit more deliberately and came up with dozens of them.

A cold coil of fear ran right down her spine.

"Oh, nothing. I did some rattan accents at a wedding last weekend and haven't had my car cleaned yet." She dusted her hands together and slammed the trunk closed.

"Huh. So you're sure nothing's missing?"

Catherine looked him in the eye. She had perfected her lying-through-a-smile abilities over many years of telling bridezillas and their moms that everything was fine, even when the flowers had been set up at the wrong church or the groom was so hungover that he was upchucking in the bushes.

"I'm sure."

———

Someone was trying to set her up. Not kill her. Set her up. To take the fall for Tilly's murder. They'd planted rope fibers in her car, the same exact color as the rope she'd seen in the tent the other day. They'd planted Tilly's engagement ring in her pocket to make it look like she'd taken it off the body—or simply stolen it in a fit of jealousy from Peter's room. But who would do this? Why?

Why her?

Catherine didn't even realize she was walking around the house until she almost tripped over a cord on the pathway and had to grab on to one of the landscapers to keep from taking a header. The woman turned off her power tool and lifted her goggles.

"What the fuck? You scared the shit outta me. I coulda taken your head off!"

Catherine staggered back a step. It was the same woman she'd seen watching her the morning after the wedding, and she was holding a buzzing chain saw. "Sorry. I'm sorry. I'm not—"

"Hey." The woman suddenly looked concerned. "Are you okay?"

"Fine. I'm fine. Sorry."

Catherine kept walking but was now shaking from head to toe. The buzzing had felt familiar—a weird wisp of a memory she couldn't quite grasp. She had to find Peter. She had to figure out what the hell was going on. And she had to get rid of this goddamned ring. She was just pulling her phone out to call him when she heard him shout her name.

"Catherine! There you are!"

He jogged down the stairs from one of the patios toward her.

"I'm sorry I wasn't here when you got here. They found Hudson!"

"They did!?" Catherine's voice broke and she hoped he thought it was from happy emotion. "That's amazing! Is he okay? Where was he?"

"He's fine. He was at a friend's house. Punishing us, I guess. He's going to be grounded forever, but he's fine." The smile on Peter's face was almost enough to make her forget about the fact that someone was framing her for a capital crime. "I just got back from Leanne's."

"Is he here?"

A slight cloud crossed his features but was gone quickly. "No. He's exhausted, so he's conking out over there." He turned his steps down the pathway toward the beach. "Come on. Let's go for a walk."

"Actually . . ." She looked up at the house. "I need to talk to you."

"I know, so let's walk. I have all this pent-up energy. I want to be outside."

Catherine's fingers closed around the ring in her jacket pocket. "Okay. But just for a bit."

They walked down the paver pathway and then up and over the dunes via the wood plank walk to the beach. The beach grass clicked and clacked in the breeze and a pair of seagulls chased each other, flying low over the breakers. The sky was a bright, almost surreal blue, with wispy clouds far out on the horizon. Peter paused to take off his flip-flops when they reached the sand and inhaled deeply, filling his lungs and puffing out his chest.

"God, it really is a beautiful day, huh?"

"Definitely." Catherine wished she could enjoy it. Enjoy being alone with Peter. But she felt shaky, like someone was watching her. Maybe she should tell him about the ring and the fibers. He would protect her if he thought she was being threatened. But what if he didn't believe her? Or laughed off her suspicions? She didn't think she could take that right now.

"So, what did you want to talk about?" he asked.

Catherine had come up with a few different topics on her way over here, decoy conversations that would last long enough to get her upstairs so she could sneak the ring back where it belonged. Now she could remember none of it. Why the hell would she need to talk to him?

"Oh, I was just wondering if . . . I mean . . . I know it's an odd time, but Tilly actually got me thinking about your investment in my business."

"Yeah?" he said.

He was leading her up the beach now, toward his secret spot. Catherine's palms itched and her mouth felt dry. He looked confused and a bit concerned, which was understandable. Even she didn't know where she was going with this.

"Well, I mean, I just wanted to let you know that if you did want to pull your money out, it would be okay," she said. "I'm doing really well. I don't—"

She stopped talking. They both heard what she'd been about to say.

"Need me anymore?" he finished.

He looked away from her, up the beach. His expression was suddenly dead serious, his jaw tight.

"That's great, Cat. Really good to hear."

He glanced at her quickly, then started walking faster, up the hill toward his little hideaway. Catherine's chest cracked open. He was hurt. Seriously hurt. Why had she even started this conversation? She didn't want him to pull out of her business. She wanted to keep him as close as possible. She wasn't thinking straight, and now . . . Now she fucked everything all up.

"Peter, wait!"

She jogged after him, her knees wobbly and the sand working against her. She knew he could hear her, but he kept walking anyway. Hands in his pockets, head thrown slightly back, blowing her off. When she finally caught up to him, he was standing in the middle of the sandy area he loved so much, surrounded by the rock walls.

"Peter, come on. Look at me." She touched his taut shoulder. He turned around so swiftly she flinched. The emotion on his face was devastating. It was full of sadness and longing and regret and . . . fear?

"Peter?" she said quietly.

And then he yanked her into his arms and kissed her. Catherine was so surprised, she lost her balance and found all of her weight leaning into him. He kissed her roughly, shoving his hands into her hair and his tongue into her mouth like his life depended on it. When Catherine tried to shove him off her—more out of shock than anything else—he pulled her closer and his kiss grew gentler. Slower. More deliberate and less desperate. Catherine's heart gave a catch and she melted against him.

His fingertips trailed down her neck and over her shoulders, and she shivered all over when he tentatively brushed his knuckles down the side of one breast.

She pulled back, wanting to look into his eyes, to see what he was thinking. "Peter—"

But he stopped her with another kiss. He walked her backward until her back was against the rocks and his full weight was against her, and it was perfectly clear what he was thinking. A jagged rock jutted painfully into her right hip, but she ignored it as he broke away from her mouth and trailed kisses down the side of her neck and across her collarbone. She tipped her head back and let out a low moan when his fingers found the hem of her dress and pushed it higher up her thigh.

Then his mouth was back on hers and she pressed into him. She wanted him so badly, and they'd never had sex outdoors. Why not here? Why not now? They were both clearly in need of a release, and this spot was his favorite for a reason. For its privacy.

Her hands found the button on his shorts and she popped it open, reaching down inside to cup him with her fingers. It was his turn to moan.

"Mr. Frank?"

Peter backed up so fast, he wrenched Catherine's wrist. Every inch of her throbbed so distractingly it took her a moment to focus on the people standing just yards away, at the entrance to Peter's spot.

It was Officer Magrin and Detective Virgil. Magrin's eyes were trained on the ground. Virgil's eyes were fixed on Peter like live wires as he rebuttoned his shorts.

Catherine did not like the way Virgil was looking at Peter.

"Yes?" Peter said.

"We have some new evidence. We need to talk to you," the detective said. "Back at the house."

# MAYA

A waiter came to deliver a plate of melon, sliced thin and fanned out around a pot of cottage cheese, to Camilla. He refilled Nico's coffee—black—then turned to look at Maya with an accommodating expression. She waved him away before he could ask what she would like to order. She must have had fire in her eyes because he practically cowered as he rushed off.

"What are you doing here?" Maya asked, staring down her father. It took every ounce of her willpower to do so. Her heart jackrabbited around her chest, willing her to run—reminding her that flight was the only option when it came to Nico. But she needed to find out why these two were together. What, exactly, had they been talking about when I arrived?

"Camilla reached out to me. She's worried about you," said Nico. "And honestly, so'm I. I've been worried about you for a while, kid."

Maya barked a laugh. "I'd love to know why. There was more to be worried about when you were in my life than there is now."

Camilla sliced off a millimeter square of melon and placed it on her tongue with her fork.

"That's not what I hear." Nico watched her over the rim of his cup, eyes amused. Maya glanced at Camilla, but her expression betrayed nothing.

Fine. She'd call his bluff.

"Really? What have you heard that's so worrisome?"

Camilla ate another morsel of melon. Maya's father leaned forward, his elbows braced on the table, his beefy forearms up. He kneaded his hands together, making the tattoo of two dice on his wrist dance. She could hear how dry his skin was as he chafed one palm against the other.

"I know all about it," he said, lowering his voice in a way that hollowed out Maya's stomach. "The temper tantrums. The destroyed hotel rooms. The locker room you had to pay twenty grand to have repaired, and then another five grand of hush money to keep it quiet. I even know about the airport bathroom in Cali. Someday you gotta tell me how you managed to flood the place."

He chuckled.

"You must be stronger than you look."

Maya was having an out-of-body experience. With each word he spoke, her rising panic pushed her soul a little farther out, up through the top of her skull, until she felt so empty, so light-headed, she thought she might actually vomit on the pristine white tablecloth. Everything around her suddenly sounded very, very loud. The clanking of silverware. The thwack of a golf club against a ball on the driving range next door. A round of laughter at a nearby table.

"How?" she heard herself say, barely a breath. "How could you know?"

"That hardly matters," snipped Camilla. "What matters is that you're not denying it. Which obviously means it's all true."

Maya closed her eyes. She'd forgotten that Camilla was there. The woman had heard all of it. Probably been regaled with more stories before Maya had arrived. It was over. All over. All the work she'd done to make her outbursts stop. All the money she'd paid to cover up the times she lost control. It was all for nothing. She'd kept it out of the press, yes, but if her father knew, that was worse. Because that meant he knew she'd never really escaped him. That the worst part of him—the part she despised more than anything— lived within her. And had the power to destroy everything she had worked so hard for.

She had to get control of this situation. She had to try. One point at a time. Figure out what the opponent's strategy was, then counter it. Adjust accordingly.

"Why am I here?" she asked. "What do you two want from me?"

"I want you to get back together with Peter." Camilla reached for her water glass, then sat back, bringing it to her lips for a dainty sip. "My son loves you. He tells me he was going to propose to you when Tilly stepped in with her own demands."

"And if I don't want to get back together with him?" Maya asked.

Though, inside, her traitorous heart had skipped a few beats. She knew Peter was no good for her. She *knew* this. But if she was forced . . .

"Then I'll go to the press with the information your father has so helpfully supplied," Camilla said, placing the water glass down, precisely on top of the water ring it had made on the tablecloth. "He even has video."

"What?" Maya blurted. It had come out louder than she intended, and she lowered her voice. "*How?*"

Her father's smile was back. "Some of the people you think are your friends? They're more my friends."

Maya felt violated by those very words. She'd worked so hard for so long to cull the people around her down to a very sparse team of trusted friends and mentors and coaches. That her father had somehow infiltrated this group, that he would even take the time to try, and that someone would *let* him in . . . she couldn't process it. It didn't make sense.

"Money always talks," her father said. "I taught you that."

"Who?" she croaked out.

But even as she said it, she knew it had to be Shawn. He was the only person who had been anywhere near her when she'd somehow busted that pipe in the bathroom at the Burbank airport. It wasn't like her to crack that many hours after a match. But it had been the anniversary of her mother's death, and she was always emotional on that day. And Carolina Tabakova had bageled her in the third set, then celebrated as if she'd just won the US Open. At the net, she'd told Maya, with a smile, that she really had to work on her drop shot, which was *all* Maya had been working on for the three weeks prior.

Somehow, Maya had managed to smile back, congratulate her, get cooled down and showered and changed and over to the airport for her flight. Then some jackass in the terminal had yelled "Better luck next time!" in a thick Russian accent, and she had made a hard right into the bathroom, where she'd promptly gone berserk. Shawn had followed, making sure the one woman who'd been peeing in a stall while Maya lost it would say nothing, and barring the door from anyone else coming in.

He'd also paid the facility's bill and never told her how much it had cost.

Shawn was always there for her. But maybe she wasn't the only one paying him to be there.

"Is this how you keep getting my number?" she asked. "He's feeding it to you?"

"Every so often." Her father smiled. "I like to keep you on your toes."

She got up and walked away.

A chair scraped back behind her, but she did not turn to look. She was already in the indoor section of the restaurant when a cool, frail hand grabbed her elbow. Maya wrenched away, nearly knocking Camilla off-balance. Luckily, it being such a gorgeous day, there weren't as many diners inside as there were out. Maya blinked a few times, her eyes adjusting to the darkness after the bright sun of the outdoors. Camilla's face looked gray.

"I didn't want to resort to this," the woman said. "But you wouldn't reply to my texts or take my calls."

"So blackmail is the next obvious choice?" Maya asked. "Bringing evil incarnate here for a breakfast date is the next obvious choice?"

"If that's what will make you listen," Camilla said. "Tell me the truth, when you thought it was going to be me here, alone, did you have any intention of hearing me out?"

No. She'd been planning on getting a free breakfast and a day at the courts.

"I've spent my entire life working to get away from that man," Maya said. "My career is my life. I will not let him derail it."

"Your father or Peter?"

"Either," Maya said.

Camilla took a breath. "Peter won't derail it. Not again," she said. "Tilly's death, while unpleasant, has given you both a second chance. Don't you see that? I don't understand why you wouldn't want to grasp it. At least give him the opportunity to make it all up to you."

Maya's jaw clenched. The thing was, she had been softening toward Peter. She had started to think that maybe there was a chance. But she couldn't imagine ever trusting Camilla at this point. And there was no Peter without Camilla. At least until *she* kicked the bucket.

"He may have been able to before this," Maya said. "Before you bringing that man here. Before forcing me into his presence. But this . . . what you just did? He can never make up for."

With that, Maya turned and left Camilla behind.

———

"What's wrong?" Shawn asked, the second she walked into the clubhouse.

Of course he could tell something was wrong. He was her best friend. Her *paid* best friend. How pathetic was that? And worse, it hadn't even bought his loyalty.

Her team was listening to music through the small Bluetooth speaker she kept in her racket bag. She picked it up and almost—almost—hurled it at the nearest mirror, but instead, she simply hit the power button and turned to them, clutching it in both hands like the handle of a racket.

They all fell silent, watching her.

"Shawn," she said. "You're fired."

Shawn laughed. "Good one."

"Do I look like I'm *kidding*?" she shouted. "Get your traitorous face out of my sight before I fucking call security."

He went pale and glanced around at the others. Maya saw them all look away and wondered what the rest of them knew.

"Maya, what are you—"

"Don't insult me by acting like you don't know what I'm talking about, Shawn. I *know* you're on my father's payroll. He's *here*. He just told me *himself*." She got right up in Shawn's face, her entire body shaking with rage and despair. "Now grab your shit and get the hell out of here!"

"But, Maya, I—" Shawn's voice cracked. He took two steps back and covered his mouth with his hand. "Don't do this. Let me explain."

"There is not a single explanation on God's green earth that will be good enough," Maya said through clenched teeth, twisting the speaker between her hands. "You betrayed me. You sold me out to the *one person* you *know* I abhor. The one person who has the ability to use every single thing you say *against* me. How dare you?"

She finally flung the speaker, right at his feet. Her aim was so perfect he had to leap up to keep from being hit. The speaker cracked open, batteries spilling out and rolling across the floor.

"What the hell is the matter with you?" Shawn screeched. "You always resort to violence! Why? We've been working on this for three years!"

"Maybe you just suck at your job," Maya said.

Shaking, Shawn picked up his things from a nearby bench. "Fine. Screw you, Maya. Don't come running back to me when you get arrested for bashing someone's windshield in."

With that, he slammed through the double doors she'd walked through just moments ago, and was gone. Maya, strangely, thought of Peter. He had never liked Shawn. She'd always assumed he was jealous of their relationship, of how close they were. But it had all been a lie. Everything, it seemed, was a lie.

"Who else knew?" Maya whirled on the rest of the team.

"Maya," said Joanie, taking a step toward her. "Maybe we should take a walk outside."

"No." She batted the woman's hand away. "I wanna know who else Shawn has been talking to. Anyone?"

Christopher averted his eyes.

"You're fired too, Chris."

"Whatever. I'm sick of this shit anyway." He picked up his racket bag from the floor, shouldered it, and walked out the nearest door.

"Are you done now?" Joanie asked.

"Yes," Maya said, a single tear spilling over.

"Good. Then maybe we should take the day off."

"No." She shoved the back of her hand across her face and stood up straight. "Give me five minutes and meet me on the court. I need to work on my serve."

She grabbed a sweatshirt out of her open tennis bag and headed for the bathroom.

"Maya," Bekka said as she walked past. "Do you need me to—"

"Call Liz," Maya said, pausing, but not looking at Bekka. "Tell her I need to speak to her right away."

Bekka nodded. "On it."

Then Maya went to the bathroom where she locked the door and screamed into the balled-up fabric of her sweatshirt as loudly and for as long as she possibly could.

# CATHERINE

Catherine sat in the waiting area of Big Ron's Auto Detail later that afternoon, inhaling the scents of hot wax and motor oil, wondering how the hell she'd ended up here. In an alternate universe, she and Peter were locked in postcoital bliss in the sand right now. Instead, she was staring at an old issue of *Real Simple* magazine, Peter was meeting with the police *again*, and someone was trying to set her up for murder. But why? Who would do this to her?

There was Brandt Dansforth. It was a little odd that he was still hanging around so many days after his sister's death. Didn't he have his own home? A job to attend to? It was possible he'd found out about the wedding from Tilly before anyone else had and he'd had time to plan the whole thing. His motive was solid—Tilly's death had doubled his inheritance. As the sole living heir to the Dansforth fortune, he'd be one of the richest men in the country. But if he'd planted those fibers in her car, why would he have led her straight to them? And how would he have gotten Tilly's ring into her pocket?

Maya might have been able to get the ring. It was possible she'd been to see Peter and had snatched it while in his room. She had said she'd been talking to Peter—though why Peter hadn't told

Catherine about this, she had no idea. Catherine couldn't imagine when Maya would have had the opportunity to slip the ring into her jacket pocket, though. Besides. Maya was . . . Maya. She was America's Sweetheart. Catherine even sort of liked the girl. Plus, if she had known about the wedding before the announcement, she'd chosen the wrong career. She could have had three Oscars by now.

Although, she could be framing Catherine even if she hadn't cut the rope that had killed Tilly. It would be a convenient way to get Catherine out of the picture so that she could have Peter back. Catherine felt a zing of pleasure at the idea that Maya might see her as competition.

She checked her phone for texts from Peter. Nothing. Even though she'd sent him five separate texts asking what was going on and whether he was okay.

Surely the police couldn't think Peter was guilty. Though Catherine didn't know what he'd done in the hours between when she'd last seen him—around midnight—and when the chandelier had fallen—around three a.m. But no. She knew him. Peter was not capable of murder. So, who was?

Leanne? Leanne was a definite possibility for both the murder and Catherine's framing. Catherine's relationship with Leanne had been weird ever since Peter had gotten Monica pregnant with Hudson. Catherine could still remember the first time she'd met Leanne, the summer between freshman and sophomore year in college, when Catherine had come to visit Monica in her hometown of Cape Crest, New Jersey—conveniently, the same resort town where Catherine's new boyfriend, Peter, had a summer house. Monica and Leanne's close relationship had made only-child Catherine green with envy. Unlike older sisters in movies, Leanne and her cool, more mature friends included Monica and Catherine in everything—beach bonfires, Jet Skiing, cruising for summer boys on the boulevard. Catherine had returned the next summer, and the next, but then Monica had gotten pregnant with Peter's baby, and everything had changed.

Sometimes Leanne treated her as if she was the one who broke up Monica and Peter, rather than the other way around. Catherine supposed Leanne had just been looking out for her sister—making sure there was no chance that Catherine and Peter might get back together. But Monica had been dead for years now, and Leanne was still a bit odd around her.

Plus, Hudson was Leanne's life. She had a lot to gain from getting rid of Tilly, especially after her proclamation. And she'd said herself that her husband had been responsible for securing the chandelier. What if the two of them had planned it together, and now Leanne was trying to pin it all on Catherine? Leanne had to know that Catherine and Peter had never been out of touch. Did she suspect how close she and Peter still were? Did she think she could make it look like Catherine had murdered Tilly in a jealous rage?

Catherine's phone rang, startling her. It was flipped facedown on the magazine in front of her, and she almost dropped it when she saw the name on the screen.

*Leanne.*

Catherine looked around as if someone had been spying on her thoughts and told Leanne to call her.

She hit accept.

"Hey Leanne."

"Hey! Where are you?"

"Running errands. Why?"

"You aren't at the police station, are you?"

Catherine's pulse skipped ahead. "No. Why would I be there? Is Peter all right?"

"Peter? Why? Did they arrest him?"

Did she sound . . . hopeful?

"No! No. Never mind. What's up?"

"I was just thinking . . . it's probably better if you don't tell the cops about your rope theory."

Catherine stood up, dropping the magazine back into the basket next to the chair, and began to pace the small waiting area. She and the register lady were the only people in the room, and the register lady was focused on a puzzle she was working on the counter. Something with a lot of cats and yarn.

"Right. That was what we decided. I don't tell them until we come up with a suspect who isn't Peter."

"Yeah, but I mean . . . in general, I think it's a bad idea. I mean, what if it makes *you* look guilty? It does prove you know a lot about this stuff."

"I feel like my job title makes it clear I know a lot about this stuff. Besides, why would I tell them how I'd done it if I'd done it?"

"Reverse psychology?" Leanne gave a forced chuckle. "I don't know. Still. Better safe than sorry."

"I guess." Catherine still didn't really see how her telling the police she'd found a clue would make them think the clue led to her. Only an idiot would do that if they were truly guilty.

"Anyway, have you heard that Hudson is back?"

"Yes! Peter told me! I'm so happy for you!" Catherine forced excitement into her voice. "Is he okay?"

"He's doing great," Leanne said. "And I'm never taking my eyes off him again."

"He must *love* that," Catherine joked.

Big Ron poked his head into the room and gestured for her to come outside. Catherine nodded at him.

"I've gotta go. I'll see you later, okay?"

"Okay, but just . . . think about what I said. And don't go to the police without calling me first."

Catherine hung up the phone and picked up her bag. Leanne

was up to something, and Catherine was going to figure out what it was.

———

Catherine was waiting for a huge family of toddlers, parents, grandparents, aunts, uncles, and a couple of surly-looking teenagers to cross the road with their beach paraphernalia when it hit her. What if Peter *had* murdered Tilly? What if he'd murdered Tilly so he could be with Catherine?

Her body flushed hot from head to toe, and her palms were instantly slick. The family made it safely to the beach side of the street, and Catherine edged her gleamingly clean, new-smelling SUV into the first spot she saw.

Putting aside the fact that she didn't believe Peter could murder anyone . . . it was possible, right? Maybe when he'd seen Catherine in the hotel lobby that morning, he'd had an epiphany. How much he'd missed her. How much he loved her. How much time he'd wasted not being with her.

Perhaps seeing her on the morning of the wedding had sent him over the edge and he'd come up with a way out. Then he slipped the engagement ring into her pocket the next day as some sort of signal.

He wanted her to have it.

He wanted to marry *her*.

# LEANNE

Leanne tapped the steering wheel impatiently as Samantha chatted with her friends on the roller hockey rink, slapping hands and yukking it up under the lights. Her friend had called her for a ride home and Leanne had taken it as a sign. All day she'd been thinking about asking Samantha about the gardening shears she'd found in Hudson's bag—whether they were strong enough and sharp enough to cut through the rope Tony had used to hoist the chandelier. This gave her the perfect opportunity to do it outside the house, when Tony and Hudson weren't around. She hadn't told Tony about them yet. And Hudson must have known she'd found them, but he hadn't mentioned it.

"Hey! Thanks so much for the ride!" Samantha said, popping open the passenger door. Her blond hair was caked to her head with sweat, and she looked ruddy and happy. "Carter drove me here, but then his kid fell off a slide or something and now they're at the hospital."

"Oh, God. I hope he's okay!"

"Pop the trunk?" Sam asked, indicating her hockey bag.

"Actually, there's something I wanted to show you."

Leanne pulled the lever to open the trunk and got out of the car. Samantha shoved the trunk door up and paused. Her face lit up.

"Hey! Where'd you find these?" She dropped her bag on the

ground and picked up the shears before Leanne could stop her. Leanne had been handling them with gloves, just in case. "I've been looking all over for them."

"Wait. Those are yours?"

"Yeah, why?" Samantha tossed them back into the trunk, then threw her bag and hockey stick in as well.

Leanne narrowed her eyes at Samantha. "You didn't kill Tilly, did you?"

Samantha laughed. "Okay, non sequitur."

"Did you?" Leanne's voice went up an octave.

"Ummmm, no. Are you serious?" Samantha paused to wave to a group of her teammates who were walking past, lugging sticks and gear. "Why the hell would I murder Tilly?" she whispered.

Leanne felt stupid for asking, but her brain was grasping at any straw that might indicate Hudson had nothing to do with it. That he'd been hiding a pair of nasty, heavy-duty gardening sheers for some other reason.

"Well, I know you and Peter used to . . . have a thing."

Samantha snorted and slammed the trunk with an emphatic *bang*. "Yeah, the occasional afternoon hookup in the landscape shed. That doesn't mean I was in love with him or something. And, I mean, you can hardly blame him. I'm super hot when I'm sweaty and covered in grass clippings."

Leanne smiled. "Well, obviously."

"Come on. I'm dying for a shower and a bowl of pasta."

They got in the car and Leanne scrolled down the windows to let in the cool evening breeze off the ocean. "How did you know those were yours?"

"Not everybody splurges for Bilt tools. Those have been missing from the Franks' for a while now. Where'd you find them?"

Leanne's stomach twisted. "So you keep them on property? Where?"

"In the aforementioned tool shed." There was a pause, and Samantha's brain finally seemed to catch up. "Wait . . . you don't think someone used them to, like, fuck with the chandelier, do you?"

Leanne swallowed, staring through the windshield. "How long have they been missing?"

Samantha sat back hard in her seat. "I don't know for sure . . . a few days?"

"So, maybe since the day of the wedding?" Leanne asked.

"Shit," Samantha said. "Maybe I don't want to know where you found them."

"Yeah," Leanne said, flinging the car into reverse and pulling out of the parking spot. "You really don't."

# CATHERINE

"**H**ow do you lose four boxes full of custom-made gift bags? They were in the storage room when I left for the shore. How does this happen, Murphy?"

Catherine pressed her thumb and forefinger to her forehead, glaring out at the ocean. She was standing beneath the shade of the Eighth Street gazebo—a large structure where families picnicked all day and teenagers got stoned and made out all night—squeezing in some work calls before Leanne and Maya arrived. At this point she was really wishing she'd just ignored the cops and gone back to the city already. Because even if she didn't get arrested for murder, messing up this wedding would kill her career.

"I've talked to the housekeeping staff, the delivery guys, everyone who has access to the office. They have no idea," Murphy said.

"Well, you have to find them. There's no way we can get new ones made now. They'll never get here in time, let alone down to Turks."

"I know. But I have an idea. There are all these local artisans down there. Maybe I can hire someone to make something even better! Something authentic to the region!" He sounded so excited it almost hurt Catherine to let him down. Almost.

"Murphy, it took the bride six months and twelve meetings to decide on the design we had. Do you really think she's going to be okay with some random rattan bags with puka shells attached to them?"

There was a pause. "It was just an idea."

"Find. The damn. Boxes!" Catherine shouted. And she ended the call.

"Wow. Bad morning?"

Catherine turned to find Leanne standing behind her with a bakery bag and a tray of iced coffees.

"Whatever," she rolled her eyes. "It's not like I'm curing cancer."

Leanne tilted her head. "Huh. Maya's right. You really do crap on yourself a lot."

Catherine's face burned. "Oh my God, fine. I think my job is important. I do. Can I have whatever is in that bag?" She waved Leanne over and they both sat at the nearest picnic table. Catherine pulled out a chocolate croissant and tore into it, raining flaky pastry everywhere. "Thank you. I'm starving."

She took one of the coffees and dumped four sugar packets and three creamers into it just as Maya jogged up in yoga pants and a crop top.

"Hi," she said, and checked her heart rate on her watch. "Is one of those for me?"

Leanne handed over a coffee and Maya sat, perspiring prettily and barely out of breath.

"So. What's this emergency meeting all about?" She popped the top off her coffee and sipped it, black.

Catherine placed the croissant down on a napkin, got up, and walked over to the railing. She turned to lean back on it and looked down on them. She wanted to make sure she could see both their reactions clearly when she said what she was about to say. Her little moment of insanity, when she'd thought Peter had killed Tilly for her, had passed. Because while Peter *could* have slipped her the ring as a signal, it wouldn't explain the rope fibers in her car. Besides, she knew in her heart of hearts that Peter was not a murderer. Which brought her to this moment, trying to figure out if one of these women could be responsible.

"I think someone's trying to set me up," Catherine said. "To take the fall for Tilly's murder."

"What?" Leanne blurted.

Maya looked skeptical. "Why would you think that?"

Both responses seemed genuine in their surprise. Catherine took a breath, then a sip of her coffee. She told them about the ring she'd found in her pocket and the rope fibers in her car.

"Wait. Tilly had an engagement ring?" Maya asked. "But Peter never actually asked her to marry him."

"What do you mean?" Leanne asked.

"He told me that Tilly basically told him he was getting married," Maya explained. "It's not like he planned some big proposal." She looked green at the very idea.

"I don't know," Catherine said. "Maybe she picked it out herself. Or maybe it was a family ring?"

Maya faced forward on the picnic bench, her back to the ocean, as if processing this.

"You should go to the police," Leanne said. "If someone's trying to set you up, they need to know now."

"But what if they don't believe me?" Catherine said. "And yesterday you were both telling me not to go to the police."

"But that was before we saw all this. If someone's trying to set you up, then it seems like they're escalating," Leanne said. "You need to show them the evidence. The rope fibers, the ring. Someone's going to a lot of trouble if they're breaking into your car . . . and into Peter's room to steal jewelry. The police need to know what they're dealing with."

Leanne wasn't wrong. Catherine was kind of regretting having her car detailed at this point.

"Do you still have the ring?" Maya asked suddenly.

"Yeah . . . why?"

"Can I see it?"

Catherine and Leanne exchanged a look.

"Maya, I don't know if that's the best idea," Catherine said.

"Don't talk to me like I'm a child." Maya stood up, towering over Catherine. She could see how this woman could be intimidating on a tennis court. "I want to see it."

Catherine went to her bag and fished the ring out of the zippered coin pouch of her wallet. Reluctantly, she held it out to Maya.

The girl's face lost every ounce of its vibrancy. Her eyes went dull. She made no move to take the ring, and for half a second, Catherine was worried she was going to bat it out of her hand and into the sand dunes that surrounded the gazebo.

"That's my ring."

"What?" Leanne said. "What do you—"

"I . . . we picked out that ring. Together. Me and Peter."

Catherine pulled back her outstretched hand. "I don't understand."

"He was supposed to propose. After Wimbledon." She wrapped her arms around her abdomen. "I guess he gave it to her instead of me."

"Oh, Jesus, Maya. I'm so sorry," Leanne said. "He's such a little shit."

Catherine felt nauseous. Peter was going to *marry* Maya? What the fuck?

"I have to go," Maya said. She yanked her cell phone out of the back pocket of her yoga pants and turned toward the stairs to the beach.

"Maya, wait—!" Leanne said.

But Maya was already gone.

# MAYA

"Maya, hey! What're you doing here?"

Peter stepped through the sliding glass doors to the back deck and dropped his sunglasses and phone on a table. She barely had a moment to register how haggard he looked—how relieved to see her—before the rage exploded out of her. She flew out of the chair she'd been perched on and shoved him as hard as she could, two hands to the chest.

"You *proposed* to Tilly? You gave her my ring? You fucking liar!" she shouted, her voice raw and cracked. "You said you loved me! You said Tilly railroaded you into a wedding! But you gave her *my ring!*"

Tears burst out of her then, tears she'd been holding back all morning, maybe all week, definitely since seeing her father. She sobbed, her hands over her face, her neck bent.

"Maya. Maya, hey." Peter's voice was calm and soothing. He reached for her, fingers grazing her arm, but she flinched away.

"Don't touch me!" She scrubbed at her face with her hands, then glared at him. "You were my safe space," she said. "You said you'd never hurt me. And now I find out you've been lying to me over and over and over again."

"I know and I'm sorry. I'm really and truly sorry," Peter said. "I hate seeing you like this, Maya. If you'd just let me explain."

Maya turned and sat down on the end of a chaise lounge, knees together, feet apart, hunched forward. She looked down at her fingernails and picked at them. Her face felt hot and swollen and her eyes hurt. She was exhausted. She needed to find a new hitting partner. There were interviews and workout sessions scheduled. She shouldn't even be here. But she couldn't seem to pull herself away from Peter.

"Fine," she said weakly. "Explain. But I want the whole story. I need to know everything. No lying this time. You have to promise me."

"Fine. I promise." He yanked over another chaise and sat at the end, mirroring her. He reached over for her hand, but she pulled away again, and he sighed, running his fingers through his hair. There was no product in it, which was odd for him, and it flopped forward, feathering out on each side of his forehead. "Remember when I had to leave Paris suddenly right before the French?" he began.

"Yeah. Your mom got sick."

"Right, well. It was worse than I let on."

Maya squirmed back slightly and hugged herself. "How much worse?"

"They told us her cancer was back, and this time it was inoperable. She has a brain tumor."

"What? But she seems—"

"Fine, yeah, I know. They did radiation and we're waiting to see how it went, but they said all they can do is try to manage it. At some point it's going to become . . . unmanageable."

"God, Peter. I'm sorry." Even though she could have killed Camilla herself right now, Maya knew that his mother meant more to him than just about anyone, other than herself. And maybe Hudson. "Why didn't you tell me?"

"You were working. I know how hard clay season is for you.

And then with Wimbledon and everyone talking about how you had a shot . . . I don't know. I just thought I'd wait."

"Okay, so what does this have to do with Tilly?"

"Her mom and my mom were such old friends—my mother was like an aunt to Tilly. She was in the city when she heard my mom was in the hospital, and Tilly's parents had just died recently. I think she felt responsible to sort of represent her family, so she came to visit. She saw how upset I was and said she'd take me out for a drink."

Maya suddenly wondered whether she, in fact, did want to hear this.

"We got . . . very drunk," he said. "And there were a couple of celebrities at the bar so there were paparazzi outside. I sort of freaked out, knowing that if they got shots of me and Tilly it would . . . be bad."

He paused and looked out at the water.

"I was thinking about you," he said. "What the press would say."

"Okay, and?"

"So we went out the back and were hoping to sneak around them and call a cab, but there were these guys back there."

"Guys?"

"A waiter from the bar and one of his friends, I guess. I don't know. They were smoking pot and had a flask. Clearly we should have just avoided them, but they started up with me."

Maya's face burned. "Started up? What does that mean?"

"They were mocking me for being a drunk prissy boy or whatever. One of them took my scarf and started messing around. And the other one started fucking with Tilly."

"Oh, God."

"I just kind of lost it. I don't fully remember what happened, but I beat the shit out of one of the guys and the other one ran. By the time Tilly got me off him he was unconscious."

Maya leaned forward, staring down at the toes of her sneakers. Her brain was racing. Peter should have known better. He knew how he was when he got too drunk. Three drinks was his limit before all judgment completely disappeared. She should have been there with him. He should have told her what was going on with his mother. If she'd been there, she would have stopped him after that third drink. They would have gone home together. And whatever he was about to tell her happened next, never would have happened.

"Why didn't you call me? I could have come . . ."

"You were into the second round. I wasn't about to do that to you."

What he didn't say, but what they both knew, was that she wouldn't have dropped out of a major because his mother was sick. They both knew that her career had to come first right now. That it would only last so long and she had to take advantage of every opportunity. If his mother had *died*, that would have been a conversation. But in the hospital with no imminent threat? No.

She felt simultaneously guilty and justified.

"Anyway, the next thing I know, I'm waking up at Tilly's and she's on the phone with some reporter, paying him off to keep quiet. The guy I fought was in the hospital, but he'd recognized us and called the press. She paid him off, too. Him and his friend."

"Jesus, Peter."

"I know. I'm an idiot. I'm so sorry." He reached for her hand again and this time she let him take it. He held her fingers gently, as if he was afraid if he held on too hard she would pull away. "You can't leave me alone for five seconds."

Her heart squeezed. He needed her. Maybe even more than she needed him.

*No.*

She didn't need him. She didn't need anyone. She had to remember that. It was the only way to keep from feeling like this all the time. And she couldn't win when she was feeling like this. She could barely think when she was feeling like this. She pulled her hand away and braced her palms on the cushion by her sides.

"So you and Tilly had sex."

She needed to hear him say it.

"I don't know."

"Stop lying!" Maya stood up so quickly, Peter fell sideways off the end of the chaise. He jumped up, the tendons on his neck protruding.

"I'm not lying! At this point, I honestly have no idea what was true. She said we had sex. She *said* we made a baby. But the woman was obviously pathological, Maya. Who knows what the hell she was thinking?"

"How could you not know whether or not the two of you had sex?" Maya demanded with an incredulous laugh.

"I don't remember anything that happened after that guy shoved me. Nothing until I woke up on her bed, with my underwear on, by the way, and she was already in a robe on the phone in the next room." He took a couple of steps toward her, and Maya turned away, facing the ocean. "My clothes weren't thrown around as if they'd been taken off in a hurry or anything. There were no . . . condoms."

"Well, if you got her pregnant—"

"Who knows if she even was pregnant?" Peter blurted.

Maya blinked. She looked sideways at him. "Didn't the medical examiner say she had heightened hormone levels?"

"Yeah, but no baby. Heightened hormones could be caused by a lot of things," Peter said. "Maybe that ultrasound she showed me was fake. I wouldn't put it past her."

"Did you ask for a paternity test?"

Peter bowed his head. "No."

"Peter!" she threw her hands up.

"What? I don't know. The timing was right and I didn't want to insult her, Maya! Our families are very old friends."

"So, let me get this straight. You were willing to blow up our entire life together and marry someone else because your families are very old friends?"

Did she even know this person?

"That and . . ."

Her jaw tightened. "And what?"

"When she showed me the ultrasound, she said if I didn't marry her . . . if I didn't make us a legitimate family . . ."

Maya's entire body went cold. She felt she knew what was coming but couldn't wrap her mind around the diabolical nature of it.

"What, Peter?"

"She said she'd go to the police and the press about what happened in the alley. She still had those guys' phone numbers. They had the hospital records. With three eyewitnesses, including Tilly—"

"You would've gone to jail."

"Or at the very least been torn to shreds in the press." He looked at her, so hangdog she could hardly stand it. "And they would've dragged you into it. And your dad. Just imagine the headlines about you falling for someone just like your father."

"Don't try to make this about me. You weren't thinking about me," Maya spat. Though she could see the truth of what he was saying. This is absolutely where the press would have gone.

She wondered if Tilly had planned all of this out. If she'd hired those guys to be in that alleyway. If she also knew about his crap tolerance level. If she'd conned Peter from the very beginning. She didn't want to see him as a victim here, but what if?

"I'm sorry. I'm so sorry." He turned away from her, his body rigid. "God, I'm such a fuckup. I should have come to you. I would have, if it wasn't about . . . this. You always know what to do."

Funny, she'd just been thinking the same thing about him.

She'd been thinking it a lot lately. Wishing he was there when Adidas came calling. When Nadine brought her asswipe protégé to interview her. When her father showed up.

They'd made such a good team. It felt like a death to see it this broken.

"Did your mother know about all of this? The baby, the blackmail?"

"Why do you ask?" Peter looked wary.

"Because she keeps telling me she thinks we should be together, yet she planned this elaborate secret wedding for you and Tilly. It makes no sense."

"She knew," he said. "She wanted to pay her off, but Tilly already had more money than God. So instead, she decided to give her what she wanted."

"She decided. Like you had no say in the matter?" Maya asked.

Peter's Adam's apple bobbed. "Please, Maya, let me make it up to you," he said, his eyes desperate. "Let me at least try."

Maya just stared back at him. "Did you give Tilly the ring you bought for me?"

"I did, but only because she rejected my grandmother's ring and I had already picked up ours from Cartier so—"

"So lucky for you, you just happened to have a spare lying around." Her eyes filled with tears. "Good to know Tilly thought my ring was good enough."

"It wasn't like that. Maya, I was trapped."

"Yeah, you keep saying that."

"Maya—"

"Did she know?" Maya asked.

"Did she know what?"

"That the ring was meant for me. Did she know?"

"Well, yeah. Why else would I have had a five-carat diamond in my possession?"

She could tell that the moment he said it he knew it was a mistake. It was so blasé.

Maya wanted to scream. It didn't matter, in that moment, that the woman was dead. What mattered was that she had died wearing *Maya's* ring. She'd died thinking—knowing—that she had won. And wearing the spoils. She must have thought Maya was such a pathetic, naïve, childish *loser.*

"I'm sorry. I wasn't thinking. I—" Peter's eyebrows shot up. "You can have the ring. Do what you want with it. I have it upstairs." He went to move past her inside, but she grabbed his arm to stop him.

"If you think, for one second, that I want that ring anywhere near me, then you don't know me at all," she said. "I never want to see that piece of shit again."

# CATHERINE

The sun was setting in the distance as Catherine walked up the front steps at Peter's house. All day she had been obsessing about Peter. About their clinch on the beach. About the cops and whatever new evidence they'd found. She wondered if it would point her toward whoever was trying to set her up. She wasn't exactly sure what she'd do with the information if she had it, but it was killing her, not knowing. Every inch of her felt tense, and she kept checking over her shoulder as if someone was going to jump out and attack her. She had to talk to Peter about it. He'd help her figure out what to do.

She also wanted him to look her in the eye and tell her that, while he might not have intended to marry Tilly, he had intended to get married. To Maya. How many times was she going to allow this to happen to her? To let him humiliate her over another woman? She wasn't sure how much more of Peter's capriciousness her heart could take.

The guard at the gate had called ahead, announcing her arrival to the household, but she rang the bell anyway, and the door opened that same moment.

"Peter!"

He looked harried. And haggard. He had an uneven five-o'clock shadow and his eyes were rimmed in red. Catherine's indignation flew out the window.

"Are you all right?" she asked. "What did the police say?"

"Oh, Cat, hey," he said, looking around as if he'd forgotten where he was. "Not much. Just that they don't think Farrah is a viable suspect. And they also intimated I should probably stop sleeping around."

He gave a stiff smile, but the comment hit Catherine like a dart to the chest. She hated being reminded of his recent bad behavior. He *should* stop sleeping around. With everybody but her.

"What're you doing here?" he asked. He said it as if he hadn't expected to see her again anytime soon, burying the dart further.

"Oh, I . . ." *Thought we could finish where we left off back at the beach yesterday?* "Wanted to see if you were okay."

"I'm fine. I mean, aside from the fact that everything in my life is completely fucked-up." He gave a frown like a shrug. "I'm just heading out. Sorry you came all this way."

He descended two steps, then looked back up at her, squinting one eye against the very bright porch lights.

"Listen, I'm really sorry about what happened yesterday. That was totally inappropriate," he said. "It's just, being around you sometimes . . . it's so . . ."

*Maddening? Tempting? Provoking?*

"Comforting," he said. "You know?"

Comforting. Like a heated blanket. The back of Catherine's throat was so tight she didn't trust herself to speak.

"God, I'm such a mess." He ran his hand over his face and through his hair. "I'll call you soon. Thanks for coming by. Honestly. It means a lot. I'm glad you haven't written me off yet."

He jogged down the rest of the stairs and disappeared around the corner of the garage.

Catherine couldn't move. What the hell was he doing, apologizing to her? She had been a willing participant in yesterday's proceedings. He knew that. She was always a willing participant when he wanted her, as much as it pained her to think about that. Nothing had changed. She couldn't understand why he was acting so distant now. Now when they were so close.

Unless . . . something was wrong. Really wrong. This talk of writing him off . . . And how everything in his life was wrong. It made her suddenly nervous.

A few moments ticked by, and then Peter pulled out in a boxy, black Mercedes SUV, its exterior gleaming in the waning sun. Catherine decided to follow him. From behind the wheel of her car, she saw a light in the house flick on. It was the butler, looking down at her from a second-floor window. Glaring.

———

Peter parked his car at the docks. And not the hip, happening docks where the waterfront restaurants and bars were, where it was next to impossible to get a spot any time after three p.m. any day of the week, but the working docks. He pulled right up next to a couple of grizzled men fishing over the guard rail into the bay waters, smoking cigarettes and chugging beers with one hand, while they held their rods with the other.

He shoved something into his back pocket as he got out of the Mercedes, then pulled his shirt tail out to cover it. Catherine was too busy ducking down to avoid being seen, to get a good look at what it was.

Once Peter had walked down along one of the docks, she slipped out of the car and over to a warehouse, ducking behind a stack of wood pallets that reeked of fish guts and blood. There were a dozen boats already moored, and another half dozen chugging in after a day out on the open water. Peter paused in front of one of the docked boats and shouted something, but between the clanging of bells, the roaring of engines and the cawing of seagulls, his words were incomprehensible.

Then, Tony appeared. He stepped off one of the boats and onto the dock next to Peter. As they stood together, talking, Catherine was struck by how very different they were. Peter was tall and lean, and even with his afternoon scruff came off as clean-cut and wealthy. It was something about the way he stood, feet planted, arms crossed, chin slightly raised. Tony was taller still, and so much broader it was like the Hulk standing next to Ant Man. His T-shirt had holes near the hem and his cargo shorts were splotchy and wet. The back of his neck was brighter than the setting sun.

Catherine couldn't imagine being attracted to a man like Tony, even though she knew he was a good guy and everyone around here loved and respected him. There was just nothing . . . intriguing about him. She wondered how he and Leanne had ended up together. But then, there was nothing overly intriguing about Leanne, either. Maybe they just got each other.

Peter suddenly reached for his back pocket and Catherine held her breath. He whipped out a thick, white envelope, glancing around to make sure no one was watching. Which, of course, she was. Hello? She wanted to shout at him that he wasn't as great at subterfuge as he thought, but then Tony glanced inside the envelope and even from here, Catherine could see that it was stuffed to the gills with cash.

The two men shook hands, and then Peter rushed back to his car, while Tony shoved the money deep into one of his cargo pockets, and zipped it up tight. He glanced around quickly himself, before hopping back onto his boat. Then Peter pulled out of the spot and gunned the engine, spraying pebbles and shell shards all over the two fishermen. They cursed at his rearview lights as he disappeared around the corner of the warehouse, completely oblivious.

# LEANNE

Leanne hadn't taken a yoga class in about fifteen years, when she'd gotten so dizzy in one of the poses that she'd almost vomited and had to lay on her back in savasana for the rest of the class. But when Daisy Pangano offhandedly mentioned that Catherine had been taking her daily class on the beach, Leanne got up early, yanked on a pair of faded Old Navy leggings, and fished her old yoga mat out from the back of the junk closet.

She needed to talk to Catherine, but she needed the conversation to happen casually, and she refused to wait outside the woman's bed-and-breakfast and then just pretend to be walking by. She wasn't a total amateur.

As soon as she was over the dunes, she clocked Catherine in her full-black outfit, emblazoned with the logo of her boyfriend's fitness company. She pretended not to notice her, however, and walked right over to Daisy, greeting her with a quick hug. A large square of sand had been raked over to form a flattish surface for the class. There were half a dozen women and one very fit man already stretching out.

"Glad you could make it!" Daisy trilled. "Grab yourself a spot!"

Catherine waved at her as she turned around. Perfect. This would be easier than she thought.

"Hey! I didn't know you'd be here," Leanne said, striding over to

Catherine. The woman's eyelids sparkled with a light pink shimmer, and her eyeliner was, as always, perfectly applied.

"Hey Leanne," Catherine said. "Yeah, I love this class. You know the instructor?"

"Oh yeah." Leanne waved one arm in Daisy's direction, irritated at herself for noticing the flab of her bat wings. "We used to be in a book club together."

She rolled out her mat and sat down on it. Her knees cracked loudly, and Catherine winced.

"Sounds like you need this."

"Oh, totally." Leanne pulled a bottle full of iced coffee out of her bag and took a swig. "I don't know if you know this, but it's been a tad stressful lately." Leanne forced a laugh.

"You seem . . . different."

"Do I? How?"

"Like you're on something," Catherine said.

Leanne laughed loudly. "Just happy to have Hudson home," she said. "Not that the police helped in any way with that whole debacle."

Catherine pressed herself back into a child's pose, then up into a perfect downward facing dog.

"We'll get started in about five minutes everyone!" Daisy called out, as a couple more people joined the group.

"Speaking of which, I was thinking about what you said at my place the other day . . . about someone setting you up?" she whispered.

She went into child's pose herself, and her back cracked in three places. Shit. This actually felt kind of good. Catherine dropped back in a mirror of her pose.

"You have?" she whispered, glancing sideways at her.

"Yeah, and I was thinking . . . what if it's Maya?"

Catherine flung herself over onto her butt. "Maya?"

"Yeah, I mean . . . it kind of makes sense, doesn't it?"

Catherine crossed her legs in front of her, pressing her hands into the mat at her sides. "How do you figure?"

"Well, (A) she clearly had a reason to murder Tilly, and (B) she has a reason to want to get you out of the way."

This was sort of mean. Leanne knew it was. There was no way Peter was interested in Catherine, nor would he ever dump someone as glitzy and glamorous and famous and talented and young as Maya for someone he'd already been with. Even if she was glitzy and glamorous and *semi*-famous. Peter's ego ran Peter's life. Maya was good for his ego.

But she also knew that Catherine had never given up on Peter. She could tell by the way she looked at him, like a puppy watching its mother play with its other spawn. By the way she talked about him like she knew what he was thinking, like she knew him better than anyone. Plus, she had long suspected that Peter willingly led Catherine on, putting his . . . carrot out whenever it suited him. She was pretty sure he'd done it the night her sister died.

Leanne didn't *really* think Maya had done anything. But if Catherine went to the police with this, it would distract them. The more suspects, the better. If they kept looking into more people, they wouldn't ever think to look closely at her son.

"But she seemed so shocked when I showed her the ring."

Leanne lifted a shoulder. "So maybe she's a good actress. She definitely could have gotten it out of Peter's room. Then all she would have needed was an opportunity to slip it into your pocket. And the two of you have been together a few times. I'm sure she had a chance."

"What about the fibers?"

"Don't you think it's interesting that they appeared there *after* you told us your theory about the rope? She probably got the idea to plant them then."

"Huh. Interesting."

Leanne watched Catherine as she processed this. She wasn't reacting the way Leanne had hoped—horrified and certain, like everything was clicking into place. She was, instead, eyeing Leanne like she wasn't telling the whole story.

"Can I ask you a question?"

"Sure." Leanne sat and did a couple of head rolls. Yet more cracking.

"Do Peter and Tony ever hang out together?"

Leanne stopped rolling. "No, never. I mean, maybe at a family party here or there, but Tony avoids them like the plague. Why?"

Catherine looked away. "No reason."

Leanne's heart thumped with foreboding. She was about to ask a follow-up question, but then Daisy called for the class's attention, and every time Leanne tried to restart the conversation, Catherine shushed her.

So Leanne settled in for forty-five minutes of pain, nausea, and humiliation. She only hoped Catherine would take the bait and lead the cops toward Maya. Then it would all be worth it.

# CATHERINE

Catherine walked into Shore Bar, her pulse thrumming in every inch of her body. The music was loud and thumping, even though it was a Monday evening and the place was nearly dead. Maybe in a couple of hours the small, sandy dance floor would be teeming with twentysomethings who didn't give a crap what day it was, but for now, there were just a few single men and one woman at the bar, and one booth in the back occupied. By Peter.

She ordered herself a white wine at the bar, pointing to Peter's table. Peter was typing madly on his phone as she approached, and she kept waiting for him to look up. She knew for a fact she looked sexy in this particular little black dress, especially while walking slowly in low light, but he was too focused on whatever he was doing. She slid onto the vinyl-covered seat, feeling slightly irritated.

"Hey," he said, glancing sideways at her. "Sorry, just give me one . . . second."

Catherine said nothing. She gave the waitress a brief, close-lipped smile as she delivered her wine, then gulped down half the glass.

"So. What're we doing here?" she asked, reminding him that he was the one who had asked her to meet. And in this, the oddest of places.

He shoved his phone into his pocket and sighed. "Sorry. Just a lot going on." He finally, fully looked at her and the tension drained from his face. "Wow, Cat, you look amazing."

Catherine smiled, her annoyance forgotten. "Thank you."

"I'm not keeping you from something more important, am I?" He sipped his whiskey, keeping his eyes appraisingly on her.

"What could I possibly have to do on a Monday night down the shore?" she asked, and sipped her wine, holding his gaze.

"Well, I appreciate you coming. I wanted to get your opinion on something." He placed his glass down, centering it between the tips of his fingers, holding it lightly.

"I'm intrigued," she said, turning her knees toward his. They brushed, and that small touch sent fire up her legs.

"It's about Hudson. And Leanne. She's suing me for full custody."

Catherine blinked. She wasn't sure where she thought this conversation was going, but it wasn't there. There were so many things she *wanted* to talk about. Like had he really been planning to propose to Maya. Was he still? What was he doing with Tony down at the docks? She'd always thought he told her everything. Had she been an idiot for half her life?

"Okay," she said. "And you're fighting it?"

"Honestly? I wasn't really," he said with a grimace. "He basically lives with her and Tony, and she's way more involved in his life than I am. I love him, don't get me wrong, but when she tries to involve me in big decisions like should he get braces and should he switch therapists and is he ready for sleepaway camp . . . I'm like . . . what the hell do I know?"

He sat back, tipping his face toward the ceiling.

"God, I sound like a total prick."

"You sound like someone who was not ready to be a father," Catherine said. She stopped herself before adding *But Monica trapped you, hoping you'd marry her anyway.* At least he hadn't done that. At least he'd had enough sense to see through her manipulation. Catherine wondered if it was as bad to think ill of the dead as it was to speak ill of the dead, but she really didn't care. Monica had fucked up everything for everyone. It was a shame when anyone died young, especially a young mother, but it didn't negate all the crap she'd pulled when she was still alive.

"So what's the problem? It sounds like you're okay with her having full custody. Is she trying to completely cut you out of his life or something?"

"No. I'd still be in his life. That was nonnegotiable. It's just . . . I'm not sure that I can trust her." He sat up straight again. "I know this is going to sound crazy, but sometimes I think . . . now don't freak out."

Catherine's heart constricted. "What?"

"Sometimes I think that she *knows.*"

There was a moment, the briefest moment, when Catherine felt as if she had left her body. Was this what it felt like to have your greatest fear realized? But then she came slamming back and found herself pushing a few inches away from Peter on the bench.

"She can't know. No one knows." She suddenly felt hot all over, and not in a good way. "No one was there but us."

"I know. It doesn't make sense. But she's definitely been digging around, trying to find something to use against me in case I decide to fight her motion in court. She's obsessed with Hudson. Obsessed with getting custody. What if she found out somehow?"

There was a sudden commotion in the room. Ten women in short dresses and very high heels were screaming and screeching and cheering as they barreled their way into the bar. Catherine's jaw clenched.

"Honestly, it wouldn't surprise me if she killed Tilly just so she could frame me for it."

He gave a halfhearted smile, then tossed back the rest of his drink.

Catherine watched the women as they took their champagne glasses out onto the dance floor, twirling, gyrating against each other, having fun. She thought about her encounter with Leanne that morning at yoga. How she'd suggested that Maya might be setting her up. Had she come there just to tell her that? Maybe she wanted to make it seem like Maya and Peter were in on it together. She *had* seemed more and more miserable as the class had gone on. Her downward dog was for shit and she'd taken out two people next to her while trying to hold tree pose, the three of them toppling like dominoes. It was weird, wasn't it? How one minute she'd been telling Catherine to tell the cops about her rope theory and the next minute she was advising her not to. The woman was all over the place.

She took a breath. Part of her still wanted to tell Peter that she thought someone was trying to set *her* up, but now it felt as if she'd be trying to negate what he was feeling and make it about her. Of course, if Leanne did know what had happened on the night of the reunion, then this was about her. At least partially.

"I just wish I knew what she was thinking," Peter said finally.

"Let me see if I can find out what Leanne knows," Catherine suggested.

"Really?" his face lit up.

"I can't guarantee anything, but I'll try."

"Thanks, Cat. Really. I knew you'd know what to do." He reached over and put his hand on hers atop the bench. Catherine stared down at it, her heart suddenly pounding again. Peter shifted toward her and she stopped breathing. Then his face was next to hers, his breath on her ear, and he pressed his lips into her cheek. "Thank you," he whispered again huskily. "You're the only one I can trust."

Then he pulled away, his skin brushing hers . . . and slid out of the booth.

"I'll take care of this," he said, pulling out a credit card and motioning at the glasses. "Call me once you've talked to her?"

Catherine said nothing. She watched him cross the room, her body throbbing. He paid the bartender, winked at the women on the dance floor, and was gone.

———

Driving back to the B&B, Catherine felt like she was having a nervous breakdown. There were too many thoughts, conversations, suspicions, and memories sliding in and around and then out of her mind. It was barely nine o'clock and all she wanted to do was crawl into her comfiest pajamas and under the thick comforter in her room, but she knew she'd never fall asleep with her thoughts swirling like this.

Tilly's superior fucking smirk. Monica, all rosy and perky and pregnant. Peter crying. Begging forgiveness. Leanne's beady eyes behind her glasses. A rope on the ground. An envelope full of cash. Tony's shoulders. Broken glass. Smeared lipstick. A torn wedding dress. Her bloody hand. Beads everywhere. Blood everywhere. Mud and leaves and brick.

When her phone rang with an unknown number, she hit the answer button on her steering wheel right away, because why the hell not?

"Hello?" she sounded manic. The light up ahead turned yellow, and for half a second she thought about gunning it, and then a pair of tweens on bikes sped across the street and she slammed on her brakes. Shit. She had to get ahold of herself.

"Catherine, it's Maya. Maya Romero."

"Oh. Hi?"

"Listen, I'm sorry to bother you, but I've been thinking . . . what if it's Leanne who's trying to set you up?"

Catherine laughed. She couldn't help it. She brought her forehead down on her steering wheel.

"I know, but hear me out," Maya said. "We both know she had the most to gain from Tilly's death. The woman threatened to take Hudson from her."

The light turned green and someone honked. Catherine eased through the intersection. Everything outside seemed sharp. The colors, the angles, the contrast.

"And we know she knew about the wedding before everyone else because her husband helped with the chandelier. I mean . . . they very well could have been in on it together."

The cash. Peter had been so tense before that meeting with Tony. Was it all connected? No. It couldn't be. Peter would never.

"Her husband probably has a garage full of different ropes," Maya went on. "She easily could have replaced it."

Catherine suddenly realized she was holding her breath. She let it out as she pulled up in front of the Nosy Elephant, amazed that she'd made it back in one piece.

"Anyway, I just thought I'd let you know what I was thinking. In case you wanted to keep an eye out."

"Thank you," Catherine said. "I will."

# MAYA

Maya was in control. She could walk away at any moment. This evening was just an experiment. A chance for her to determine whether or not there was even the slightest possibility she could entertain getting back together with Peter. She could walk away at any time.

This was what she told herself as Peter ushered her upstairs to the private dining room at the club, his hand resting gently on the small of her back. She told herself this as they ordered, sea bass for her, lobster for him, white wine and potatoes and asparagus in garlic butter. She was in control as they watched the sun set outside the picture window. As he poured her another glass of wine. As he ordered dessert and inched his chair closer to hers.

The thing about Peter was, he knew exactly what she needed. The quiet, private room, away from prying eyes. The conversation focused on her career, her next move, the tournament she would hopefully be playing in next week. He didn't ask about Shawn. He didn't mention Tilly or Hudson or Catherine or Leanne. The ring or the wedding or the lies.

They were both playing pretend, but if she let herself, she could really start to believe it. That they could put this behind them. That everything could go back to the way it was.

She needed it to go back to the way it was as much as she

detested the idea of being the woman who needed it to go back to the way it was.

"How's the slice coming?" he asked as the waiter delivered two cappuccinos. "Have you been working on it?"

"I haven't had much time," Maya said, pleased that he remembered. It had taken him weeks—maybe months—to get down the names of all the different strokes and shots. "What with everything that's been going on."

"I'm sorry about that," he said, his eyes reflecting the dancing candlelight. He put his cup down and turned his chair so that he was fully facing her at the small, round table. She placed her hands in her lap. "This will all be over soon. The police are grasping at straws. They're going to rule it an accident, officially, any day."

"Did they tell you that?" she snapped, irritated that the bubble around them had been burst.

"No, but they will. Because it was. It had to be. No one we know could have committed murder."

He seemed so certain, she almost believed him.

There was a commotion just outside the door, raised voices. A hushed admonishment. Then someone called Maya's name.

Bekka? Maya stood up. Peter reached for her hand, but she batted him off. "Let her in!"

The maître d' stepped inside with Bekka, who looked pale and frazzled. Her eyes widened when she took in the romantic scene before her, but she gamely lifted her chin and crossed the room.

"I'm so sorry to interrupt, but you weren't answering your phone."

"What's wrong?"

Bekka glanced at Peter warily.

"It's fine. Don't keep me in suspense. What happened?"

"It's . . . Shawn. Liz's contact at the *New York Post* tipped her off. He's offered them an exclusive tell-all."

Maya's knees gave out. Peter shoved her chair behind her and she dropped into it, jarring her lower spine.

"No. No, no, no, no, no." She put her head in her hands, elbows braced on the white linen tablecloth. She felt suddenly dizzy, her life flashing before her eyes. All the glasses she'd smashed, the artwork she'd torn off walls, the broken furniture, the bloodstains. Shawn knew everything. Every move she'd made for the past five years. He could end her. "He can't do that, can he? He wouldn't!"

"Well, for the right price," Bekka said.

Peter got up and started to tap on his phone, pacing alongside the table. He came around behind Maya and placed one strong, steadying hand on her shoulder.

"Robert?" he said into the phone. "I need you to get Veronica Langford for me, okay? Have her call me right back."

"Holy shit. This is it. My career is over," Maya rambled. Worse, if there was video of something she'd gotten away with, something she hadn't apologized and paid for—like the locker room in Cleveland where she'd shattered that mirror when no one but Shawn was around—she could end up in jail. God, imagine how her father would revel in that plot twist. "How could I be so stupid?"

"Maya, listen to me," Peter said, "this is not the end of your career."

She shoved herself up and out of her chair, whirling on him, her breath short. Bekka took a few steps back, startled.

"How?" Maya demanded. "He's got *video*, Peter. He knows everything! You don't even know the half of it!"

"But I can fix this."

"How? How can you fix it? It's already done! I'm a monster. Me! America's Sweetheart! Can you even imagine the field day the press is going to have with this? The headlines alone!"

Maya saw herself making an apology video on TikTok. She imagined being interviewed by Robin Roberts and acting all contrite. She could *feel* what it would be like at press after every single match, being asked—not about the score line or her strategy—but about her temper. She couldn't take it. There was no way she would survive.

"Listen to me," Peter said firmly. He glanced at his phone as it buzzed, then put both hands on her shoulders, one still clasping the phone, and squared her to face him. "I can fix it. I *will* fix it. All you have to do is trust me."

Maya knew what he was doing. She knew he was trying to prove himself. To make it up to her. To find a way to erase what he had put her through. And even though nothing could ever erase it, she needed to believe in him. She needed to grab on to something before she went under, and he was here, in front of her, throwing her a lifeline. Right here. Right now.

"Fine," she said. "I trust you."

He gave her a firm kiss on the forehead and walked purposefully out of the room, his phone pressed to his ear.

# LEANNE

Leanne was surprised when, after the morning rush had dwindled, she looked up to find Catherine swanning into the bakery with a bag from Rosalita's. She was wearing a fit-and-flare sundress, her breasts practically spilling out the top, red lipstick, and dark sunglasses. She looked like a 1950s movie poster. Leanne was wearing denim shorts that showed off her cellulite and a V-neck T-shirt that had once been black but was now a shady gray. Her sweaty brown hair was back in a hairnet, and she couldn't remember whether she'd even washed her face this morning.

"What can I get you?" Leanne asked. Her stomach growled at the spicy scents emanating from the takeout bag.

"Nothing! I brought *you* lunch!"

Catherine placed the bag on one palm and gestured at it like a *Price Is Right* model. Leanne narrowed her eyes, suspicious. Catherine had been so cagey with her at yoga, and now this?

"Why?"

"Everything's been so crazy, I thought it might be nice to actually catch up," Catherine said. "I'd love to know how Hudson's doing. You know, in general. Before all this."

Leanne still sensed an ulterior motive, but she hadn't eaten anything all morning, and she never could resist Rosalita's food. She hoped there were some flautas in that bag.

"Mary! I'm taking my lunch!"

Mary, who was on the phone at the far end of the counter, taking an order, waved a hand in acknowledgment. Leanne cocked her head, then led Catherine through the kitchen and out the back door to her break area. Catherine set the bag down on the table and Leanne dove in, pulling in a deep breath of fried and cheesy air. Catherine produced two bottles of water from her oversize purse.

"So. How have you been?" Catherine asked, ripping open the wax bag of tortilla chips. "I mean, before the whole Tilly thing."

"Good. Fine." Leanne opened a container of Mexican rice and beans and dug in with a plastic fork. "It's hectic this time of year, but we enjoy it. And in a few weeks I'll be tearing my hair out wishing for September."

"It must be so weird, living year-round in a place that's so focused on summer."

Leanne lifted one shoulder and said through a mouth full of food. "It's the only life I know."

Catherine sipped her water, leaving a ring of garish red around the spout.

"And Hudson doesn't mind it? Spending most of his time here when his dad's in the city?"

A full-body flush hit Leanne so hard and fast she almost flinched. "Why would he mind living where he's always lived? It was good enough for me and my sisters. Why shouldn't it be good enough for him?"

"I didn't mean it that way," Catherine said quickly. "I'm sorry, I didn't mean to offend you. My parents got divorced when I was little, but they stayed in the same town. Which was, in and of itself, a nightmare. Whatever the arrangement, it's hard for a kid to have two homes and I'm just curious how Hudson handles it."

"Why?" Leanne snapped.

"Why?" Catherine replied.

"Yeah, why are you curious. Why are you interested in my kid?"

She saw Catherine bite her tongue. Could feel the woman wanting to correct her.

"I mean . . . Monica and I were friends. Of course, I'm interested in her son."

Leanne went still. Hearing Monica's name on Catherine's lips made her blood run cold.

"I still think about her, you know? About things we maybe both could have done differently. I miss her."

Leanne finished chewing the food in her mouth slowly and forced herself to swallow.

"Does Hudson remember her well?" Catherine asked.

Leanne wiped her lips with a paper napkin and balled it up in a clenched fist. "I don't want to talk about Monica. Not with you."

Catherine went still. "What does that mean?"

"It means what it means."

"I'm sorry, I just thought it might be nice to share some memories, you know? There aren't many people in my life still who knew her. I thought—"

"Well, you thought wrong." Leanne got up, scraping her chair back. "I think you should go."

"What? Leanne, sit. Eat. We don't have to talk about Monica. We could—"

"Please just go," Leanne was shaking. Everywhere. She couldn't control it. And that scared the living shit out of her.

"Leanne—"

"Please!" Leanne shouted.

Catherine flinched and stood, gathering up her purse and her bottle of water. "Fine. I'll go. I'm sorry, really. I didn't—"

Leanne closed her eyes, her arms clenched around herself. But still, she couldn't stop shaking.

"I'll just go."

Leanne counted to twenty and when she opened her eyes, Catherine was gone.

# CATHERINE

"Peter, I need to know something," Catherine said into the speakerphone in her car as she drove away from the bakery. "Why did you pay Tony Gladstone a wad of cash the other night?"

There was a long pause.

"Did he tell you I—"

"No. I saw you. But you're not . . . I mean . . . you wouldn't have—"

"I was paying him for a daytrip I took with my dad. We went out trawling for blues. Why? And how did you even see us?"

Jesus. How was Peter saying the phrase *trawling for blues* so damn sexy?

"It's not important." Catherine tried to focus her thoughts as she came to a red light. "No reason. I just . . . I think you were right. I think Leanne might have had something to do with Tilly's death."

"Shit, really?" Peter said. Did he sound a bit too excited?

"Yeah," Catherine said as the light turned green. "And I think she might also know what we did."

"What?" Peter snapped.

"We'll figure it out. I have to go," Catherine said, her heart pounding in her ears. "I'll call you later."

"Cat, wait—"

She hung up. Five minutes later, walking up the steps to the police station in her platform sandals, her entire being was on high alert. She no longer cared what Leanne thought she should do. The rope was important. She knew in her gut that it was. And now that she knew for certain that Peter hadn't been paying Tony off for rigging the chandelier to fall, it was time to tell the police what she had found.

She asked the receptionist if she could please speak to Detective Magrin, hoping she wouldn't have to lay eyes on Virgil, then perched on the hard bench in the waiting area. What the hell had happened back at Leanne's place? It was like she'd had a mini breakdown. And all Catherine had done was *mention* Monica's name.

The desk officer asked Catherine to follow her, so she did, around the desks at the center of the room to a tight hallway lined by small offices in the back. Detective Magrin was standing inside one of them, watching traffic footage on a crappy, flat-screen TV. Luckily, Virgil was nowhere in sight.

"Come in, Ms. Farr," she said, pausing the video as a Jeep with no doors clearly ran a red light. Bare legs and feet hung out back and over the sides, and someone had a Solo cup thrust into the air. "What can I do for you?"

"I have something to tell you." Catherine clasped her bag in front of her with both hands. "About your investigation at the Franks'."

Magrin's eyes widened slightly. "I should call in Virgil, then. He's at lunch, but—"

"No, I really would just like to get this out."

She sat down in one of two chairs facing the desk and Magrin sat in the other, rather than taking the desk chair on the opposite side. This close, Catherine could smell her—coconut sunscreen and coffee. "Okay, what is it?"

"I was helping with the cleanup at the Franks' the other day and we were in the main tent where Tilly . . . where, you know . . . it happened. And I saw the rope that supposedly held the chandelier that night."

"Okay," Magrin said, pulling out a tiny pad and pen from her breast pocket.

"And there's no way that rope could have hoisted that chandelier. It was too skinny. Too weak. It would have snapped before they got it four feet off the ground."

Magrin's brow furrowed. She jotted down a note. "And you know this how?"

"I've done a lot of weddings with a lot of chandeliers. Trust me, I know."

Catherine's palms were sweating. When she wiped them on the seat of the chair at either side of her hips, they left dark stains in the light gray fabric. Her face burned. If Magrin noticed, she was polite enough not to say anything.

The officer wrote something else down and then snapped her notebook closed. "Got it. Thanks. We'll look into it." She reached over to a bowl on the desk filled with M&M's, took a handful, and tossed one into her mouth.

"That's it? You're not going to ask me anything else?" Catherine asked.

"Like what?" Magrin asked.

"Like what I think happened."

"You've got a theory?"

"Yes! What if someone cut the original rope so that the chandelier would fall, then replaced it with the smaller rope so you wouldn't be able to tell how the rope was cut? What if someone got Tilly down there and sawed through the thing while she was standing under it? What if—"

"You do know you're making yourself look guilty as sin right now, right?" Magrin popped another M&M and crunched down on it.

"No. No! See, that's what Leanne said would happen, but why would I tell you how I did it if I did it?" She grabbed a tissue from the box on the desk and dabbed around her eyes and nose, sweating like mad. Her makeup was sluicing right off.

"Maybe you're trying to reverse psychology me," Magrin said. Another M&M, another crunch. "Or *maybe* you *want* to get caught."

"I don't! I mean, I didn't do anything." Catherine stood up and fanned her face with the stained tissue. "Is it really hot in here or is it just me?"

"Just you."

Magrin stood and walked around to the other side of the desk. "Lucky for you we have a statement from Felicia Cox saying that her and her daughter basically poured you into bed in an upstairs bedroom at two a.m. and that you were so inebriated you couldn't walk, so. That's a pretty good alibi." Shrug. Another M&M into the maw.

Catherine paused. Felicia and Farrah had been the ones to get her to bed? Why? How had they gotten her all the way upstairs if she was that drunk? She wondered why they hadn't mentioned it to her. She wondered if her hand had already been cut and bleeding when they left her there or if she'd somehow done that to herself later.

"Great. Okay. Well, I guess I'll go, then," Catherine said, turning toward the door. "But you'll look into it?"

"Look into what?" Virgil was in the doorway, glaring down at her like he was the stern principal and she'd shown up drunk to the dance. An expression made only slightly less sinister by the small smear of mustard to the right of his lips.

"Magrin will fill you in," Catherine said.

She stepped so aggressively toward the doorway that he had no choice but to move out of her way.

# LEANNE

When the doorbell rang, Leanne expected bad news. Why else would the doorbell ring with no warning at 9:17 on a Wednesday night? She was surprised to find Samantha standing on her doorstep. Even stranger was the fact that she couldn't tell if Sam was terrified or excited.

"What's wrong?" Leanne demanded.

"Where're Tony and Hudson?" Samantha slipped inside and looked around the foyer, tilting her head to see beyond into the living room, where the light was dim. Leanne had been going over invoices while watching old episodes of *Friends*.

"They went out to get ice cream. What's up?"

Samantha went into the living room, picked up the remote to mute the TV, then dropped it back on the coffee table with a clatter. There was something off about her. It was as if she was vibrating. And Sam never vibrated.

"Sam, Jesus. You're freaking me out!"

"The cops came by my place earlier, looking for those shears."

The room tilted. Leanne sat down on Tony's leather chair. On the screen, Chandler was having a heart-to-heart with the rooster and duck. She glanced at her cell phone. She wanted to call Tony and tell him not to come back. That he should take Hudson somewhere safe. But where? Peter was the one with the money, the extra houses, the hideaways. All she and Tony had, other than a massive second mortgage, were the boats. And the bakery.

Plus, Tony didn't know anything about the shears. She'd thought it was better if he didn't know his step-nephew was potentially a murderer. Not that Leanne thought Tony would ever suggest they give up their bid for full custody. But, well. Better safe than sorry.

"And? Did you give them to them?"

"Of course I did. What was I supposed to do?" Samantha hissed. "They said they were evidence in a *murder investigation*."

"Oh my God." Leanne put her head between her knees, clutching her arms around her middle. She'd fucking failed. She'd failed in so many ways. Peter *should* keep custody of Hudson. She couldn't protect him. She couldn't raise him. She was a failure.

"Are you okay? Do you need water or something? Vodka?"

Leanne just shook her head, still staring at the floor. Tears squeezed from her eyes. If they had the shears, it was only a matter of time before they found the rope. Why hadn't she done something about it? She could have gone in there and gotten rid of it . . . somehow. Talked her way past the guards, found some excuse to go to the shed. She should have burned the building down by now.

"Leanne, you didn't do something, did you? Because if you did, you could have told me. And I would have fucking thrown those things into the ocean, never to be seen again."

Leanne looked up, her head swimming. "No. I didn't do anything."

Samantha closed her eyes, crossed herself, then sat on the coffee table, facing Leanne. "Thank God."

Leanne's phone rang. Samantha full-body flinched, and Leanne lunged for it. Was it Tony? The police? Had they already found Hudson? Leanne turned it to face Samantha. The name on the screen was Catherine.

"Answer it!" Samantha hissed.

Leanne trembled as she brought the phone to her ear.

"Hello?"

"Leanne, oh my God, they've brought Maya down to the station for questioning. Like, officially."

Leanne stood up. "What? Why?" She paced into the center of the room, away from Samantha.

"I'm so sorry, Leanne. I told them about the rope."

*Shit.* "Okay . . ."

"I thought . . . honestly, after what happened at lunch, I thought that maybe you and Tony had . . . you know—"

Leanne closed her eyes and clenched her teeth to keep from spontaneously imploding.

"But then they found these massive gardening shears that weren't in the shed when they first searched it, and now they think Maya might have used them to cut down the chandelier."

"Wait, wait, wait." She looked at Samantha, who was now standing as well. Sam threw out her hands, palms up, like *Tell me!* "They think *Maya* cut the rope?"

Samantha's blue eyes widened.

"Yes!"

"Why?"

"Because they found her fingerprints! On the shears! Clear as day. Why the hell else would Maya Romero have ever even come into contact with a gardening tool?"

Leanne felt a crashing wave of elation engulf her, unlike anything she'd ever felt before. She didn't know how Catherine had found all of this out. She didn't care. All that mattered was that Hudson was in the clear. He was fine. Though now she really did have to ask him what the hell he was doing carrying those things around with him.

"What?" Samantha whispered.

"They found Maya's fingerprints on your shears," Leanne whispered back, pulling a WTF face.

"I've been thinking about what you said the other day, and maybe you're right," said Catherine. "Maybe it *is* Maya who's trying to set me up."

It took Leanne a moment to catch up to what Catherine was saying. She no longer cared one iota whether someone was trying to set up Catherine or who that person might be. Everything was going to be fine. Hudson's prints were not on the shears. That was all that mattered.

Then she noticed Samantha was at the liquor cabinet.

"Catherine, I gotta go. I'll talk to you later."

She hung up while Catherine was mid-reply. Sam had already taken a swig directly out of a bottle of Jack.

"Sam? What is it?"

Her best friend wiped her lips with the back of her wrist. "I know why Maya's prints are on those shears."

# MAYA

Maya was taking out her anger on the court, and poor Oona—
the woman interviewing to be her new hitting partner—could
barely keep up. She pounded the ball so hard, her shoulder was
screaming. Every time the strings made contact with the ball she
saw smug Virgil showing up at the door of the Airbnb. She saw
herself getting into the police SUV with him and his partner,
because they *had* to interview her *at the station*. The whole drive
there, not knowing what they were going to ask her, she'd wanted
to jump right out of the car.

But of course she couldn't. Because they'd locked her in there
like a criminal. What if there had been photographers at the police
station? What if someone had gotten a shot of them dragging her
in there? The headlines on this one wrote themselves.

### LIKE FATHER LIKE DAUGHTER

### THE APPLE DOESN'T FALL FAR

### IN THE FAMILY BIZ?

*Thwack.* The ball whizzed right by Oona's hip.

All because of those stupid shears. It was amazing, really, how one small, silly moment could have huge ripple effects. After her conversation with Peter about the ring, Maya had stormed down to the rose garden to walk off her anger until her Uber showed up, and she had stumbled upon one of the gardeners. Samantha—Sam, she had introduced herself. Needing an excuse for being there, Maya had said she'd come to admire the roses. She had a garden at home (true) and they never looked as good as these (false, as she also had gardeners). Sam had told her it wasn't as hard as people thought and offered to show her how to prune, and now . . . Maya's fingerprints were on the potential murder weapon.

*Thwack!* Oona raised her racket just in time to save herself from a black eye.

"Okay! Okay! I think we've seen enough!" Joanie called out, stepping over from the sidelines. "Let's take fifteen."

Looking relieved, Oona jogged to the bench, grabbed her Gatorade, and chugged.

"She can take fifteen!" Maya called back. "I'll be here."

Then she started serving aces. She didn't stop until Bekka came jogging onto the court in her pink Athleta leggings, excitement radiating from her pores. Oona had disappeared into the clubhouse, and Joanie was making notes on her clipboard in the shade of a sideline umbrella.

"Maya! Oh my God!"

"What?" Maya asked, walking over to join her at the bench.

"It's Shawn."

Even though this was clearly good news, the sound of his name brought bile up the back of Maya's throat. She grabbed her water bottle and drank, motioning with her free hand for Bekka to keep talking.

"He rescinded his story offer!"

"What!?"

"Yeah! He took some swank job at a super exclusive drug rehab facility out in Utah where all the celebrities go? And they make their employees all sign some ridiculous NDA. He can't talk to the press or he'll lose the job."

"Holy shit!" Maya felt as if someone had just lifted a brick off her chest. "Oh my God, how?"

Bekka tilted her head, the eye roll implied. "I think we both know how."

Maya slowly blushed as a pleasant, tingling realization moved through her.

Peter.

———

When he opened the door of his room on the second floor of the Franks' estate, his eyes nearly bulged out of his head. Maya gave him a smoldering, closed-lipped smile.

"It is your favorite, right?"

She was wearing a tennis dress—the one she'd worn to play the French last year. It had a white halter top that showed off her tan and a pink, pleated skirt, so short her boy shorts—pink and white striped—had flashed every time she moved on court. Maya had lost to a wild card in the second round and had wanted to burn the half dozen fits she still had left in the package. But the outfit was also Peter's favorite. So she'd kept one.

"It is," he said huskily. He was shirtless himself, wearing only a pair of soft-looking striped pajama pants. They were thin, summer-weight pants, and she could see how turned on he was at the sight of her. "What're you doing here?" he asked.

"I came to thank you," she said.

Then she shoved him backward into the room with two flat hands to his chest and kicked out a foot to slam the door.

# CATHERINE

The experts say that when you can't sleep you should get out of bed, go to another room, and read a book. Preferably one you've read before so that you already know what will happen. They say to sip chamomile tea or do deep breathing or watch TV to distract your mind. But none of that had ever worked for Catherine. Idle time did not suit her. If she was awake, she was getting something done. Down the shore, she had two choices—exercise or work. She chose exercise.

The town was relatively flat and relatively dead in the middle of the week in the middle of the night. Catherine put on a reflective headband and headed out, turning her steps in the direction of Peter's house, because of course. Who knew? Maybe she'd catch him coming back from grabbing a drink at one of the downtown bars—if they were even open this late midweek. Or maybe he'd be out for a walk or a run, like her, unable to sleep, and they'd bump into each other and he'd tell her all about how Maya was arrested and she's not who he thought she was, and does she want to come inside for a bit?

And then maybe . . . just maybe . . . she'd say no. See how he reacted. See how it felt.

Just past the gates, Catherine came to a long, partially hidden driveway—a service entrance to the estate. There was an SUV parked halfway down. Something about it felt familiar, and Catherine paused, her heart pounding from the run. She took measured breaths and looked around. There were no other houses on this stretch of road—she was pretty sure the Franks owned acres of property on either side, ensuring that no one could develop condos directly across from their estate. Slowly, Catherine crept over to the car. It had Jersey license plates. The back seat held a gym bag and there were a few chip bag wrappers—the snack size—and crushed tissues on the floor. She was just about to peer into the front seat when something moved in the corner of her vision.

Catherine ducked down behind the car. There was someone there. Creeping along the security wall toward the service gate. What the fuck?

She peeked out. The person was dressed all in black, including a black skull cap, even though it was still seventy degrees out. It was a woman. Shoulder-length dark hair. Catherine stood up all the way. Was that—

"Leanne!" she hissed.

Leanne whirled around so quickly, she lost her balance, slipped on the gravel drive, and fell on her ass. Catherine jogged over and offered her a hand.

"What the hell are you doing?"

"You scared the ever-living soul out of me!" Leanne said, struggling to her feet. "What are you doing here?"

"I was running!" Catherine whispered, glancing up and around in case there were security cameras. If there were, she couldn't see them. "I couldn't sleep."

"Same. Couldn't sleep," Leanne said, avoiding Catherine's gaze.

"So you drove over here in full black, like a ninja, to . . . what? Inspect the Franks' security system?"

"Oh my God, will you just go? I don't need you here right now."

Catherine threw up her hands. "Don't need me? For what? What does that even mean? I thought we were on the same side."

"Sides? There are no sides," Leanne whispered. "And if there were, I wouldn't be on yours."

"Why are you so pissed at me?" Catherine asked. "Why did you lose it on me when I brought up Monica?"

"Because I know, all right!?" Leanne shouted. "I know all about the night she died." She slapped her hand over her mouth as Catherine's entire life flashed before her eyes. Suddenly, Leanne was running back to her car and jumping in behind the wheel. Without thinking, Catherine followed her, terrified Leanne would get away before Catherine could get some answers. She dove for the passenger door, expecting Leanne to peel out any second, then realized the woman had not turned on the car or the headlights. She was just sitting there, slumped over the wheel, her arms crossed as a pillow for her forehead.

Catherine pressed her lips together. This was actually happening. Leanne knew about Monica. She should probably run away, get the hell out of town, figure out how people assumed new identities and disappeared. But first, she needed to know what Leanne knew.

She got in the car.

"Please just go away," Leanne said through tears.

"Leanne, I'm so sorry. I'm sorry about what happened to Monica," Catherine said, choosing her words carefully. "But what are you talking about?"

"I know you guys had a fight," Leanne said, turning her head to look at Catherine but not lifting it from the steering wheel. Tears sluiced down her face. "Right in front of everyone." She lifted her head and wiped her face with her sleeve. "I know Monica went to the reunion thinking that she and Peter had a chance to get back together. That *he* had basically told her this. So she went, all excited, all dressed up, thinking that the three of them were finally going to be a real family, and then, suddenly, the two of you are screaming at each other in the hallway and she's calling you a slut and a homewrecker and a backstabber."

Wow. Someone had really been taking notes that night.

"And then she was so upset she stormed out and took off," Leanne continued. "I know my sister. She never would have been driving that fast if she wasn't royally pissed. And probably hysterical."

Catherine stared at Leanne. Monica had definitely been both of those things.

"So what happened? What did you do? Did you and Peter hook up that night?"

Catherine sat back in the seat. Well, yes, she and Peter had hooked up that night. Being back on campus, in the student center where they'd first met, the warm night air, the scent of the primrose blooming against the backdrop of the ocean. It had been a heady night, to say the least. She and Peter had danced one slow dance, eyes locked, hands gripping, exploring, as much as was decent in public. But they couldn't help themselves. As soon as the song had ended, they'd run off to find someplace private and had ended up having sex up against the wall in a storage room they had found mercifully unlocked. It had been hot and forbidden and fucking amazing . . . until the door had opened. Monica, backlit by the hallway lights, her expression horrified as Peter came right in front of her.

So, yes, that had happened. And then the fight. Right there in the hallway, so loud it had attracted a crowd. One of whom had clearly been committing the whole thing to memory.

"We did fight. She was upset because Peter and I were spending a lot of time together that night," Catherine said carefully. "But we were back at school. That's what those things are about, right? Reliving old memories?"

"She was that pissed about you guys hanging out?" Leanne said.

Catherine cleared her throat. "Well, we did get a little . . . close on the dance floor. I always assumed that was what she was so mad about." She hated this. But she had no choice. Leanne clearly didn't know everything, and she had to protect the truth to the best of her ability.

"So. Are you going to tell me what you're doing here?" Catherine asked, hoping to change the subject.

"I think I know what happened to Tilly," Leanne said, looking out her window toward the house.

"Don't we all know what happened to Tilly?" Catherine asked.

"No. I mean I think I know how. I think I know . . . who."

Catherine stared. *Say Maya. Please say Maya.*

"I have to get on the property." Leanne paused. She turned to look Catherine dead in the eye. "Will you help me?"

There was a hard stone of unease in Catherine's gut. She was really regretting choosing a run over work. "Depends," she said. "Are we destroying evidence?"

Leanne sucked in a breath. "Kind of," she said. "But it's not to protect me." She paused and pressed her eyes closed. "It's to protect Hudson."

# LEANNE

"**T**his thing is so heavy!" Catherine grunted as she and Leanne carried the coiled length of rope between them down the service road to Leanne's car. "How the hell did Hudson move it?"

"I don't know. Adrenaline?" Leanne replied. She didn't want to picture it. Didn't even want to think about it. Her little boy, so distraught he was driven to murder. Him being up all night, covering his tracks, and then running to a friend's house to hide.

It was all too much.

They drove out of town and got on the parkway, driving north until they got to Tom's River, where they found a supermarket with a line of half-full dumpsters out back. Catherine had floated the idea of just throwing it in the ocean, but Leanne wasn't convinced the tide would take it out any time soon, and she wanted it as far away from the house as possible. They struggled the rope out and over the side of one of the fuller ones, hoping it would be the first to be emptied, and took off again.

It was only when they were back on the parkway that Leanne felt as if she could breathe. She'd done it. No one would ever find that thing. It was the last bit of evidence connecting Hudson to the crime.

She glanced over at Catherine. The woman was smirking.

"What's that face?"

Catherine immediately rearranged her features. "What face?"

"That! I saw you! You looked smug."

"I'm not smug!"

"Yes, you are! Why were you smirking?"

Catherine lifted her hands and slapped them into her lap. "Okay, fine, I'm a little proud that my theory about the rope was right, okay? I'm sorry."

Leanne rolled her eyes. "Great. I'm so happy you're happy. Congratulations, Sherlock."

"If it makes you feel any better, I don't see how Hudson could have done it."

Leanne gripped the wheel, kneading it with her sweaty hands. Everything about her was tight and tense and dry. It was after three a.m. She needed a shower. She needed to sleep. She needed all of this to be over.

"What makes you say that?"

"You saw how heavy that rope was. And could a kid really cut through that with a pair of shears?" Catherine lifted her shoulders. "I don't know. I think we might have just covered up someone else's crime."

"Well, I really hope you're right," Leanne said. "I don't want to believe that he could have actually killed someone. But you didn't see how upset he was, Catherine. That kid has been through so much . . ."

Catherine looked down at her lap. She pressed her palms into her thighs, wiping them on her Lululemons.

"I know," she said quietly. "For what it's worth? You're a good mom."

A lump instantly formed in Leanne's throat. "Thanks."

"I mean, my mom never would have done anything like this for me. Skulking around in the dead of night? Chipping her *fingernails*? Please."

Leanne snorted a laugh. "Mine either. She would have been like *Yo, officer! She's over here! Here's the one you're looking for!*"

Catherine laughed. "Oh my God. And then my mom *never* would have visited me in prison. She thinks wearing orange is a crime in and of itself."

Leanne was laughing hard now, the release sublime. "My mom would have let me go to prison just to see if she could get away with smuggling in a shiv for me."

"I'm sorry, darling, but that unflattering jumpsuit offends my eyes."

"I swear to God, officer, I just baked a sausage roll. I have no idea how that knife got in there!"

They laughed until they made it to the exit for Cape Crest and then they were silent for the rest of the drive. Leanne dropped Catherine off in front of the Nosy Elephant.

"This is between us, right?" Leanne said through the open window, as Catherine closed her door. "Swear on your life?"

Catherine leaned in, hands atop the window's lip. She looked Leanne dead in the eye. "I swear on my life. This goes to the grave."

Leanne nodded, Catherine took a step back, and Leanne drove off.

# CATHERINE

The sun was going down when Catherine found Peter on the beach, sitting in the sand with his knees bent, staring out at the ocean. She had slept half the day away after her adventure with Leanne, then spent the rest of it at her computer and on the phone with Bea, who was starting to get nervous that Catherine might not make it to Turks in time for the wedding.

Catherine had promised her bride that she'd be there—they were still a few weeks out—but she honestly was starting to wonder herself.

It felt good to be outside in the fresh air, away from her screen. Peter didn't notice her until her feet were right next to his. Then he squinted one eye as he looked up at her and smiled. "Hey there. This is a nice surprise."

She smiled back. "Wanna go for a walk?"

"Sure."

He pushed himself up, dusted sand off the seat of his athletic shorts, and turned south, as she knew he would, in the direction of his spot. She waited a few steps before she spoke.

"So, Leanne knows that Monica and I fought that night, but she doesn't know anything else."

Peter's head lifted. "You're sure?"

"Oh, I'm sure," she said. "She blames us for getting Monica so upset that she was driving like a maniac and crashed. That's it."

Peter pushed his hands through his hair, then laced his fingers behind his head, elbows jutting out on either side as he walked. "Wow. Okay. How do you feel?"

"Good. Fine. Okay," Catherine said. "I mean, it's a good thing."

Peter stopped walking. Catherine stopped too.

"What?" she said.

He reached out and took one of her hands, then the other. Catherine's breath caught. A warmth rose from between her legs and into her belly at just that touch. That was all it took.

"It's a very good thing," he said, his voice low. His thumb ran gently over the top of her right hand. Shivers went through her. "You have no idea what this means to me," he said. "What *you* mean to me. You're literally the only person on this planet who's truly always looking out for me, Cat. I can't thank you enough."

*Kiss me*, she thought, full-body flushed as she gazed into his eyes. *Kiss me kiss me kiss me.*

And then, she couldn't take it anymore. She kissed him.

And he kissed her back.

Everything after that was a blur. Somehow, they made it to his private spot. Jogging, giggling, laughing. They stood in the center of the rock circle, hands roaming. She ground her hips into him and felt how hard he was as he shoved his fingers though her hair, trailed his lips down her neck. She slid her hands into the elastic waistband of his shorts and shoved them down, then took him in both hands, stroking until he moaned. He did the same for her, pushing her skirt up, his fingers slowly, tantalizingly working their way inside her underwear.

Before she knew it, she was on her back and he was inside her. He pushed down the straps of her dress so that he could see more of her, and took her nipple into his mouth as he thrust deeper. Catherine tipped her head back in the sand. He always remembered. Everything. What she wanted, what she liked, what she needed. She opened her eyes and saw him smiling knowingly, lovingly. They came at the same time, and he leaned into her ear.

"I've never stopped loving you, Cat."

It was then that she realized she was crying.

Finally. Finally. Finally.

It was all happening. Peter Frank was finally hers.

———

Feeling blissful and light-headed and exhausted and satisfied, Catherine opened the door to her room at the Nosy Elephant, planning to pass out and not wake up until lunchtime the next day. She and Peter had spent the whole evening together, making love, going back to the house for a quick meal of sandwiches and fruit in the service kitchen, then heading back outside for more. At some point, she'd passed out under the stars, and when she'd woken up, it had been almost midnight. She'd left Peter sleeping and slipped away, knowing how mortified she'd be if they woke up in the bright sunlight and he had a chance to see what she looked like after a full night of sleeping outdoors. She needed to shower, wash her face, moisturize, and get some real sleep. That way she could go back there in the morning, fresh-faced and ready to talk about the future. But when she opened the door, something moved. The window was open, and someone dressed in black was flinging themselves through it and out into the night.

"Hey!" Catherine shouted.

She ran over to the window and peeked out. The person was running down the fire escape, then suddenly launched themselves over the side, landing on the ground like a cat.

Heart in her throat, Catherine turned around and barreled down the tight, creaky staircase. Late as it was, there was no one at the front desk or in the lobby. She ran outside and around the side of the house, but whoever had been there was long gone.

"Sonofabitch." There was a stitch in her side. Catherine held it as she hobbled back into the B&B. Mrs. Booker stood there in her robe, her hair back in a loose bun.

"What's going on?" she asked, breathless.

"Call the police. There was someone in my room."

Catherine was already halfway back up the stairs.

"What? How?"

"I don't know, but they went out the window!" Catherine called back.

Other residents of the B&B peeked out of their rooms as she passed, but she didn't stop to explain. Her laptop was in her room. All of her work. Her jewelry. Peter's ring!

She flew back into the room and started to check bags and drawers. Her computer was there. Her extra phone. She went to the closet. Her clothes were all there. The jewelry bag where she'd stashed the engagement ring was still zipped, safe and sound, in the inside pocket of her suitcase.

There were footsteps outside her open door. She shoved the ring back into her jacket and closed the closet. It was Mr. Booker, also in pajamas and a robe.

"Everything all right in here, Miss Farr? Did they get anything?"

Catherine sighed, her adrenaline seeping out of her, leaving her spent. "It doesn't seem like it. I'll double-check, but I don't think anything is missing."

"Mind if I come in?"

She shook her head. He shuffled inside and over to the window, peering out. He checked the latch and the lock and the up-and-down motion of the windowpane, then frowned.

"I don't understand it. No one came past the front desk, and it doesn't look as if this was messed with."

Catherine shook her head. "I don't know. Why would someone sneak in here and not take anything?"

# MAYA

When Maya opened the front door of her Airbnb at four a.m. to head to the courts and saw Peter about to ring the bell, she knew immediately what was going to happen, but she played dumb. He drove her in his freshly painted and detailed McLaren to the docks, where a rather large man, freshly showered and shaved, welcomed them onto his boat, introducing himself as Tony Gladstone.

"Oh, it's so nice to meet you!" Maya said. "I've heard a lot about you."

Both Tony and Peter looked surprised but said nothing. Maya wondered if Leanne hadn't told her husband that they had been . . . was *hanging out* the right term? Maybe she hadn't said anything because it was too bizarre of a relationship to explain.

Tony all but disappeared after the introduction, leaving Maya and Peter alone on the deck. The docks were hectic at that time of day, with men loading coolers and supplies onto boats, shouting to one another, but once they were out on the open water, it was so peaceful, Maya could hear herself breathe.

And her breath was very calm.

There was a breakfast of champagne and strawberries, croissants and fresh butter. When the first slivers of color began to appear over the horizon, she and Peter were kicked back on a cushion-strewn bench, sipping champagne, his arm around her shoulders.

"This is really beautiful. Thanks for thinking of it," Maya said, tilting her head back to look up at him.

He gave a small smile that seemed almost sad. No, tentative. It caused a frisson of doubt. She sat forward, putting her champagne flute down on the small surface they were using as a table—an excuse to pull away from him.

"I mean, I should be training right now, but—"

When she turned back to look at him, he was holding a ring.

"Don't say no," he said.

Maya's pulse raced. "Wow. That's some offer."

Peter shifted, pulling one leg up, crooked on the seat, to better face her. The ring, she saw, was pink, like the one she'd originally chosen, but much simpler. It was actually much more her. She was suddenly not sure why she'd chosen that large, garish rock in the first place.

"Hear me out," he said. "This whole investigation is going to be over soon. The second it is, I say we elope and then we take off for Australia, or maybe New Zealand, where you can train in peace while everything dies down. You can come back, play Cincinnati, and get some match play in before the Open, where you will undoubtedly kick ass."

Maya smiled, hiding it behind one hand. She loved that 99 percent of his proposal was about her tennis. She loved the ring. She loved him.

He'd made some mistakes. Some huge, honking, unforgettable mistakes. But maybe they were forgivable. No one was perfect. Marriage, she had heard, was all about compromise. She was no longer naïve. She knew that if Peter had cheated on her once, he would likely do it again. But as long as she knew that going in, she was willing to look the other way for what it got her. It got her him—the person who made her better, helped her focus, knew her better than anyone. It got her the man who accepted her—who loved her, flaws and all—firmly on her side, forever.

Besides, it wasn't as if she hadn't made her own mistakes the last few months. Done things that would be unforgivable if anyone knew about them. Well, a couple of people knew about them, but it wasn't as if they were going to talk. Not now.

He'd saved her from that. Saved her from Shawn. If ever anything like that were to happen again, she knew he'd have her back. She knew now, above all else, that she could trust him to take care of her. No matter what.

"Say yes, Maya. Be my wife." His eyes were pleading, raw, vulnerable. "You're it for me. Just . . . say yes."

# CATHERINE

"Is the flight all booked? I just don't want any surprises. I can't believe they're finally letting me go."

Catherine zipped up her bag and looked around her room, feeling that kinetic energy she always felt when leaving on a work trip. Did she have everything? Yes. Her passport, her sleep mask, her laptop easily accessible. She hadn't told Peter yet that she was going, but she'd call him from the car. She'd leave her SUV at the airport in Philly and just take the hit on the exorbitant long-term parking fees. The plan was to have the last meetings with all the vendors this week, then fly back for final prep with the bride in New York, before flying back down again the weekend before the wedding. Everything was coming together. Customs had even found the gift bags and they were en route to the hotel. It felt like a small miracle.

"Yes, you're all booked. Business class. I'll be at the airport with a car when you get here," Murphy said. He had flown down to Turks the night before. He sounded so relieved. She totally understood. She felt relieved, too.

"Fantastic," she told him. "See you soon."

By the time she'd struggled down to the first floor with her bags, she was sweating. The air in the small lobby was tight and warm and smelled of the bacon that had been served at breakfast.

Catherine was reaching for the doorknob when the front door flew open, slamming into her hand.

"Ow, mother—"

"Catherine! I'm so glad I caught you!" It was Maya, dressed in a white linen jumpsuit, no makeup, her hair up in a high ponytail. She saw Catherine's bags and frowned. "Are you checking out?"

"Yeah." Catherine shook out her injured fingers. "Got the all-clear to go to Turks. My flight's in a few hours."

"No! No, you can't go."

Catherine had never seen Maya this hyper. She was all nervous energy, so unlike the poised, still, controlled person she was used to.

"Why not? Did something happen?" Catherine asked, flashing on an image of Hudson.

"Yes! He proposed! We're getting married!" Maya flashed her left hand, then pulled Catherine into a strong, sinewy hug.

"Wait, what? Who?"

"Peter, duh. Who else?"

Catherine felt the walls closing in on her. Maya was talking, but she couldn't understand a word she was saying. Peter could not have proposed to Maya. Peter had told Catherine that he loved her. Yesterday. Yesterday, he had told Catherine that he had always loved her. He had come inside her, on a beach, with sand up her butt crack *yesterday.*

She reached out and grabbed Maya's left hand, staring down at the ring. A pink, square-cut diamond with a clear, triangular diamond on either side. Gold band. Pretty. Unpretentious. Something one could easily wear while playing tennis.

Catherine liked the other one better.

"Isn't it beautiful?" Maya said on a sigh.

"I don't understand. When did he . . . ?"

"This morning!" Maya stepped aside to let a family through the door. They bustled past with bags full of souvenirs, smelling of sweat. "He took me out on Tony Gladstone's boat to watch the sunrise. It was so romantic."

Catherine swallowed. Her throat was rapidly closing. He hadn't paid Tony for a fishing trip. He'd paid Tony to host his engagement. He'd lied to her face. About everything.

"We're going to get married here, ASAP, and then we're off to Australia. I was hoping . . . maybe you could help me plan it? It's not going to be big, obviously. Probably a luncheon on the beach? Leanne already said she'd do the cake."

She needed water. Or vodka. Maybe tequila. Frantically, Catherine looked around. Her eyes fell on the water jug on the counter, lemon slices floating at the top, and she grabbed one of the glasses nearby, filling it to the brim. She chugged it down, then filled it again.

*Peter will screw anything that moves.*

*I've never stopped loving you, Cat.*

*It was so romantic!*

She drank the second glass, then closed her eyes, one hand on the counter.

"Are you okay?" Maya asked.

"I'm fine," Catherine said.

*Except I'm an idiot. I'm a loser. I'm the biggest fucking dupe ever to walk the earth. He was never going to marry me. I hate myself. I hate Peter. I hate you. And I've wasted my entire life.*

She opened her eyes. "Of course I'll help plan your wedding," she said, and Maya squealed.

Catherine was going to plan for Maya the most fabulous ASAP wedding of all time. And then she was going to knee Peter Frank in the balls as hard as she could, and never look back.

# LEANNE

It was a humid, overcast day at the park, but Leanne couldn't have been in a better mood. Hudson was out on the field, playing soccer in the town's summer rec league, one of his very favorite things. He begged to join every year, even though Leanne and Tony were more than happy to sign him up. It gave him the opportunity to play with local kids—kids who hadn't been born with every privilege at the foot of their bed—and they thought it was good for him to see the way real people lived. Plus, Hudson loved his local friends. He never asked to hang outside of school with Connor Hilton or Trent Bartholomew—the two kids he had lunch with every day at the academy during the school year. All he ever wanted to do was ride bikes with the town kids or invite them over to play XBox. For the most part, he was growing up just like she and Monica had. But with a mansion and a helicopter to fall back on.

And good for him. Really. That was part of who he was. But she wanted him to know that wasn't all he came from. She wanted him to understand what real life was like when you had to work for your paycheck and could have pride in what you produced and felt good about providing for those you loved.

She was going to make sure that he understood all of that. And now that Maya and Peter were getting married, it was going to be so much easier. Leanne and Tony would have full custody before this summer was over. She knew this because when Maya had come to the bakery this morning to tell her the good news and order a cake and talk about her future, she hadn't once mentioned Hudson. Not once. A kid did not factor into her plans. Why should he? She was twenty-five years old. Just hitting the prime of a career that demanded every ounce of her attention, that kept her traveling eleven months of the year (Leanne had looked it up). She needed to eat right, stay in shape, *sleep* when she needed to sleep. Hudson still, periodically, wet the bed, and when he did, he never went back to sleep afterward. He also got fevers. And coughs. And had nightmares. Who was going to deal with all of that while she was in the middle of a grand slam in Paris? Peter?

Hardly.

Hudson stole the ball and took it upfield. He had a shot at the goal, but he passed it to Frankie Falestro, who scored. Leanne jumped to her feet.

"Nice pass, Hudson!"

He slapped hands with Frankie, and they jogged back upfield.

"He should have taken the shot."

Leanne turned to find Peter standing next to the bleachers in athletic shorts and T-shirt, mirrored sunglasses covering his eyes.

"What're you doing here?" she asked.

"I can't come to my own son's soccer game?"

Something about the way he said it twisted Leanne's insides. He took off his sunglasses and folded them into his pocket. "Can we talk?"

"Sure." She stepped down from the bleachers so she could face him. "I hear congratulations are in order. You're marrying the woman you actually want to marry this time, I presume?"

"Very funny," he said. "And yes. Thanks."

He was being weird. The charm wasn't there. This was all-business Peter. The tiny hairs on the back of her head stood on end.

"So, what's up?" she said, tense.

"I wanted to let you know that I'm not going to be signing the papers. I'm not giving you custody of Hudson."

"*What?*"

A couple of the parents on the bleachers turned.

"You okay, Leanne?" Frankie's mom, Dina, asked. In high school, Dina had once beaten up a girl from Belmar because she'd looked at Dina's boyfriend wrong. Leanne half wanted to tag her in, but instead she pulled Peter away from the bleachers.

"What are you talking about? Two weeks ago you were ready to sign."

"I've been thinking a lot about what happened the night of the wedding. Our argument, the fact that Hudson ran off." He paused and looked over at the field. "I don't think it's good for him, seeing his two primary caregivers at odds. I think he should be with his family."

Leanne had a sudden vision of her head exploding like a mushroom cloud. "Okay, (A) I am his primary caregiver. You see him ten times a year." It was an exaggeration, but whatever. "And (B) I *am* his family. I am his flesh and blood."

"But you're not his mother, Leanne."

She wanted to tackle him to the ground and pummel his pretty face into oblivion. She almost did. Would have if they weren't surrounded by kids and friends. Which, she realized now, was probably why he'd come here. He knew she couldn't freak out on him in a public place. Especially not in front of Hudson.

"You. Fucking. Prick," she said slowly. "If Monica were here she'd scratch your eyes out for saying that to me. After everything I've done?"

"But she's not here, Leanne. And we have to deal with that reality."

This condescending asshole. She dealt with that reality every goddamned day. It suddenly occurred to her why he had dragged out the custody process for so long. It was because he had never intended to give over custody of Hudson. He had just been waiting for a good reason. Something he could rub in her face. Something to push him over the edge from knowing what he should do in society's eyes, as the kid's father, and finding a reason to want to do it.

"What about Maya? What about her career? What're you going to do, stay in the city with Hudson while she globe-trots? Is that your plan? Because I don't really see that as a viable marriage."

"No, we're going to take him with us."

Leanne felt this like an elbow drop to the chest. "No."

Peter lifted his shoulders. "I think it'll be good for him to see the world. Learn about other cultures. I've already looked into tutors that can travel with us so he won't miss a beat in school. Hell, he'll probably do better with the personal attention he'll get."

She would never see him. At least if they were in the city, she had a shot. But this? This *plan*? He was taking her kid away from her in the most thorough possible way.

"Jesus, Peter, do you even hear yourself?"

"What?"

"What about friends? What about family? What about this?" She gestured at the field. "What about being a *kid*?"

"I didn't have any of this and I turned out fine."

Debatable.

"I know this is difficult for you to accept, but this isn't the only way to grow up, Leanne," Peter said. "God, you're such a snob."

"I'm sorry, *I'm* the snob?"

"Yes! You think you know everything and that your way is the only way," Peter said, the color rising in his face. "Well guess what, there are other ways to live that are just as valid as your homegrown, paycheck-to-paycheck struggle. And to be perfectly honest, I don't want my kid growing up to become some blue-collar bakery assistant in Bumblefuck, New Jersey."

It was at that moment that Leanne learned what it felt like to punch a man in the face.

# CATHERINE

It was the morning of the wedding. Catherine stared at herself in her makeup mirror, her face perfectly contoured, her eye makeup applied, everything done but her lips, which seemed almost gray. She stared at her reflection and willed herself to smile. The only way to get through this day was to fake it. But there was no light in her eyes. They looked dead. She felt dead.

She was about to watch the love of her life get married to someone else for the second time in two weeks.

Catherine turned away from the mirror and forced herself to go to the closet. To take out the black dress she'd purchased for the event. She pulled at the hanger, but it was stuck on something. So she pulled again harder. And harder. Tears filled her eyes. She yanked as hard as she could and the dress came free, but her jacket and another cardigan slid off their hangers to the floor.

She let out a wail of frustration, then started pulling out everything from the jammed closet. Her dresses, her jumpsuits, her shirts, flinging them to the ground. Teeth clenched, tears threatening, she gathered up the clothes in a ball and tossed them at the bed. When that didn't make her feel better, she turned back to the closet and yanked the bedding off the shelves. A blanket, a comforter. She grabbed one of the extra pillows and a plastic bag fell on her head.

Catherine stumbled backward, smoothing back the hair she'd so carefully styled, and paused. The bag at her feet was full of blood.

"Oh my God," Catherine said aloud.

Her own voice was startling to her after the very silent break-down she'd just had. Her pulse thrummed in her neck and wrists. She bent for a closer look, not wanting to touch it, and saw something familiar. White fabric with a thin, blue stripe.

Catherine stumbled backward and fell on her ass atop the pillows she'd thrown across the room.

It wasn't a bag full of blood. It was a bag full of bloody sheets. Her sheets from the morning after the wedding.

How the hell?

Moving to hands and knees, shaking like a leaf in the wind, Catherine peered up into the closet. There was nothing else there that she could see. How could these sheets have possibly ended up here? In this room? She hadn't even been staying here the night of the wedding.

None of it made any sense. And no one else had been in her room.

Except that someone had.

It hit her all at once, and the back of her skull throbbed. Someone had been in her room. The night she'd been with Peter. The night before he'd proposed to Maya. And they hadn't taken anything.

They'd *left* something.

Deep voices resonated up the stairs from the lobby. Catherine scrambled to her feet, kicking aside pillows, stepping over the offending bag. She crept outside and angled herself so she could see to the first floor.

Cops. Two of them. She couldn't see their faces, but she could see their blue slacks, their black shoes.

She heard one of them say her name.

*Shit!*

Catherine tiptoed back into her room, closed and locked the door behind her, and grabbed one of the pillows, yanking it out of its case. She picked up the plastic bag, holding her breath, and shoved it inside the pillowcase. It was slippery and protested the whole way, but she managed it.

Footsteps on the stairs, Catherine ran around the bed to the window—the very window whoever had done this to her had escaped from. Sweating now, she shoved it open, leaned out, and tossed the pillow to the left of the fire escape, into the bushes below.

They were at her door. She closed the window quietly and waited for the knock.

"Miss Farr? I'm sorry to bother you, but the police are here? They want to search your room. They have a warrant."

Catherine suddenly remembered the ring.

"One second! Just putting my robe on."

She fished her black jacket off the floor, pulled out the ring, put it on her own finger and then turned it so that it looked like a plain band.

Then, with the diamond that had been intended for someone else cutting into her palm, she opened the door.

# LEANNE

It wasn't Maya's fault. That was what Leanne kept telling herself as she helped Bekka lift the flowered headband and veil onto the crown of the woman's head. It wasn't Maya's fault that Peter was stealing Hudson away from her. In fact, if she could get Maya alone for five minutes, she had a feeling she could bring the girl over to her side. But not today. Not now. It wouldn't be appropriate. Maybe after the vows?

She had wanted to drop off the cake, collect her fee, and run, but Maya had been waiting for her when she got there, all aflutter, saying she couldn't get ahold of Catherine and the officiant wasn't there yet and she didn't know what to do. Farrah was there—Catherine had hired her to assist for the day—but she was troubleshooting the florist and the food.

So Leanne had stayed. She was, after all, a mom at heart. Maybe if she couldn't have her own children, and she couldn't have Hudson, she could just go around taking care of other motherless people.

At least Sam had been on the grounds today. She'd come the moment Leanne had called her. Leanne wondered if it bothered Maya that the people helping her get ready for the biggest moment of her life were basically strangers.

"Well, what do we think?" Maya asked, turning to face them.

She looked perfect. Her dress was a simple, strapless cotton gown that just scraped the top of her sandaled feet. The top was plain, but the skirt was an intricate eyelet pattern of swirling flowers and stood out from her hips in a stiff A-line. She wore a sapphire solitaire pendant—her something blue—and a pair of Camilla's diamond earrings—both borrowed and old. Everything else on her person was new.

"You look incredible," Camilla said from the doorway. She was wearing a cream-colored crepe suit, her hair back in a perfect bun. Leanne knew that people found Camilla Talbot-Frank formidable, but at that moment, she looked to Leanne like she could blow away in a stiff wind.

"You look lovely too, Mrs. Frank," Sam said with a smile.

"Thank you, Samantha. And thank you all for being here." She smiled around the room at the gathered women. "It's time for family photos on the deck."

"I thought we were doing wedding party first," said Bekka, picking up their colorful bouquets. She wore a dark pink sundress to perform her duties as maid of honor.

"Bekka always knows the schedule by heart," Maya joked. "I'd never get anywhere without her."

"No, no. We're doing that next. I just need Maya for now, dear," Camilla said, waving Bekka off and reaching for Maya's hand. "I'll have someone come get you in a few minutes."

Bekka handed Maya her bouquet and picked up her phone, perplexed, but Maya had already followed Camilla out of the room and down the hallway.

"This email from Catherine definitely says bride and maid of honor first," Bekka said. "But whatever. I have to pee anyway."

She walked out, leaving Leanne and Samantha alone with the champagne and strawberries, the makeup detritus, and the boxes full of various shoes Catherine had ordered so that Maya could try them on that morning. Where was that woman? Leanne checked her phone. Nothing.

Samantha handed her a flute full of champagne and Leanne moved over to the windows to look out at the patios and gardens. She could still see where the stakes for Tilly's wedding tent had been driven into the ground, though Samantha and her crew had smoothed it over and planted new grass seed. Her jaw clenched as she recalled every detail of that night. Tilly's cryptic text, the humiliation, the slap, being escorted off the grounds.

"It's hard to believe we were all here with Tilly just a couple of weeks ago," she said to Samantha, taking a sip of bubbly, "listening to her ridiculous declarations."

"What do you mean?" Sam asked, joining her. She downed half her glass and tilted her head.

"I never told you! She called all of us up to Peter's room before the wedding—me, Catherine, and Maya, and told us all where we could stick it, basically. She was going to formally adopt Hudson." She scoffed. "And she told Maya to take a hike, and something about Catherine's business . . . I don't even know. But it was crazy. The next day we all realized it was like she'd handed us each a motive for her own murder."

Leanne shuddered, thinking of Hudson. Tilly had handed him a motive, too, though she probably hadn't realized it at the time. Who would ever think an eleven-year-old could commit murder?

Sam slowly lowered her champagne glass. She looked like she'd just found out her beloved dog had died.

"What?" Leanne asked.

"That was Camilla's idea."

Leanne shook her head. "Sorry. What?"

"That meeting. Early that morning, I overheard Camilla when I was inspecting the grounds. She and Tilly were standing on the patio closest to the tent and Camilla told Tilly she had to find a way to get the three of you together and tell you how it was going to be. That her marriage would never be her own or something, unless she drew a line in the sand. Tilly was all over it—don't get me wrong—but Camilla was the one who planted the idea."

Leanne didn't know what to make of this. Why would Camilla do that? She'd always been supportive of Leanne's role in Hudson's life.

"Sorry, I would have told you. I figured she never went through with it."

"It's fine, I just . . . I don't get it."

"Maybe Camilla killed Tilly," Sam said jokingly. "Maybe she's one of those psycho moms who never want their kids to get married, but she planned ahead and made sure the cops would have plenty of suspects."

Leanne laughed. "She and Peter do have an almost disturbingly close relationship."

Suddenly she went cold. She and Samantha locked eyes.

"Maya."

———

Leanne tore through the hall and down the stairs, running as fast as she could to the first-floor deck where supposedly family photos were being taken, with Sam breathing down her neck. They skidded onto the deck, Leanne nearly tripping over one of the stupid cat statues. She was out of breath more from panic than from the exertion. There stood Maya and Camilla, smiling for the camera, posed with perfect posture, the bright blue sky as their backdrop.

Peter and his dad and brother stood nearby, sipping whiskey and laughing in their tuxedoes. Hudson was slouched on a lounge chair, playing on his Switch. Liam, the butler, stood nearby, watching the proceedings, and Farrah was pouring champagne. Everything was fine.

"Did you need something?" Peter said tersely, noticing her.

Leanne made a point of walking over to Hudson. He paused his game and looked up at her with a smile. She smoothed his hair and kissed his forehead.

"Just wanted to wish my little ringbearer good luck," she said, still feeling a bit shaky.

"Don't worry, Lee." He patted his breast pocket like a man three times his age. "I got this."

# CATHERINE

Catherine jogged up the steps to the Frank house, beyond late at this point. The police hadn't found anything of interest in her room, and the second they'd gone—telling her, once again, not to leave the state—she'd grabbed the bag out of the bushes, thrown it in her car, and hightailed it over here. She wasn't sure what her plan was, but she needed to talk to Peter and try figure out what the hell was going on—how could those sheets have ended up in her room? Yes, it was his wedding day and he most likely would not be psyched to talk about bloody sheets from the night of his *last* wedding, but this was her life, and someone was trying to fuck it all up.

To top it off, she was late for a job, which never happened. And she'd wanted to be her most professional self today, to prove to Peter and his family that she could rise above, that she didn't care. That he could marry whomever the hell he wanted and she would be just fine. Shaking, she tried the door, but it was of course locked, so she rang the bell just as her phone pinged.

A text from Cash.

*Our posts went live. Guess it's official.* Then a flat-mouthed emoji.

Catherine experienced a head-to-toe hot flash. She'd completely forgotten that today was the day her and Cash's breakup was going to hit social media. They'd both set up timed posts so that they could break the news at the same moment. She quickly opened Instagram to check her feed. There were already two hundred likes and comments on her post—and counting.

Beneath the smiling photo of her and Cash taken at a casual event promoting a new sports drink a couple months back, she'd written:

*Sad news to share. Cash and I have mutually decided to part ways but intend to remain friends and ardent mutual supporters.*

The front door opened. The butler, Liam, stood there in a full tuxedo.

"Miss Farr," he said, sounding surprised.

"Yes, I know. Sorry I'm late. Are they still on the deck taking photos?"

"Yes, I believe they are. Come in."

He looked out the front door behind her before closing it.

Catherine flicked over to Cash's feed as she followed Liam, at a snail's pace, through the house. They'd both posted the same picture. His message was similar to hers. She scrolled down his feed absently and paused on one of the shots from Peter and Tilly's wedding. She was laughing and clinging to his hand on the dance floor, and he was looking at her like he adored her.

Her eyes stung. What the hell was the matter with her? She was an emotional trainwreck. As soon as this day was over, she was going to book herself some spa time.

"Miss Farr?" Liam was standing, backlit by the sunlit picture windows in the great room, one big shadow to her still-adjusting eyes.

"Yes, sorry. I think I just . . . need the bathroom."

He gestured across the hallway, and she saw one open. She ducked inside and closed the door behind her. She needed to get a grip if she was going to survive yet another of Peter's weddings.

Her phone pinged again. This text was from Leanne, the latest of a dozen she'd sent that morning.

Are you okay? Are you still coming?

Catherine swiped it aside, ignoring it. There was Cash's feed again. He had tagged Tilly in the post. Catherine clicked on the link and landed on Tilly's page. There was only one photo from the wedding, of her and Peter taking their vows. In contrast to the shot of her and Cash, this one looked so staged. And Peter's smile was so forced. It was the last picture Tilly ever posted.

Absently, habitually, Catherine scrolled down. Tilly at a party. Tilly on the beach. Tilly at a fashion show. Tilly at another party. Tilly with friends. Tilly with Brandt. Tilly, Tilly, Tilly. She never posted photos she wasn't in. Then something caught Catherine's eye and she paused.

Tilly and a friend were posing at some crowded event, faces pressed together, looking sultrily at whoever was taking the picture, and Liam was standing in the background. While everyone around him was drinking, laughing, dancing, he was staring at Tilly.

Catherine stood up straighter. The photo was taken two months ago. At a music festival in Tahoe. Why would the Franks' butler be anywhere near Tilly two months ago?

She scrolled down farther, going more slowly this time. Tilly at a garden party. Tilly at a bridal shower. Tilly at a ribbon cutting. And there he was again. Tilly had taken a selfie, trying to get in the crowd behind her. Liam was off to the right, a sore thumb in the crowd of mostly young men and women, looking not at the camera, but at Tilly.

Shakily, Catherine took a screen shot, then scrolled back and took a screen shot of the first photo. Then she scrolled forward and found him in another picture, this one from way back before her parents had died. Another screenshot.

A cold realization settled over Catherine's shoulders. Liam had been stalking Tilly. Long before Peter had entered the picture.

"Please, please don't tell me the butler did it," Catherine whispered.

There was a knock at the door. She yelped.

"Miss Farr?"

Liam.

"Yeah! Yes, I'll be right out." She flushed the toilet and ran the water for a second, thinking. Then she quickly texted Leanne.

> What do we know about Liam the butler.

The response was immediate:

> ???

> Liam! How long has he worked for the Franks?

Three scrolling dots. Scrolling. Scrolling. Finally a reply popped up.

> He's new. A couple weeks? Peter said he's ex-military. Why?

Right! She had overheard that he was ex-military. And he'd come to work here right before the wedding. Catherine's pulse thrummed. She turned off the water and stared into her own eyes in the mirror.

Shit.

*Shit.*

This was it. This was the answer that had eluded everyone. Liam was in love with Tilly. He couldn't stand the idea of her marrying someone else. So he'd landed a job with the Franks. He'd gotten her down to the tent in the middle of the night and cut the rope. He was certainly strong enough to switch out the heavy cord for the lighter one.

She thought of the intruder who had been in her room the other night. The way that person had jumped over the side of the fire escape and landed like it was nothing. Military training could certainly account for that. And he'd had plenty of opportunities to both plant the fibers in her car and slip the ring into her jacket. Because she kept coming over here like some lovesick idiot, just hoping Peter would wake up and notice her.

Here they'd all been so focused on the motives Tilly had personally delivered to them, they hadn't thought that anyone else could have had a motive. They all hated Tilly so much they might have wanted her dead. But there was someone who had *loved* her so much, he had killed her because he couldn't have her.

"Miss Farr? Are you all right?"

She grabbed a tissue and blew her nose for show.

"Yes, fine."

Catherine put her phone in her purse and opened the door. Liam all but glared at her. She averted her eyes, her skin flushed.

"What is it?" he asked.

"Nothing!" she cleared her throat. "To the deck?"

"Yes. Follow me."

He turned wordlessly and led her there. Catherine tried to figure out a plausible way to get Peter alone, away from his family and Maya and the wedding party, so she could tell him what she'd just discovered. He would know what to do. He'd take care of it.

Liam held the door open for her and she stepped into the open air, gulping it in. It took her half a second to realize the deck was empty. There were half-drunk glasses of champagne on a few of the tables, but otherwise, nothing. No one.

"How much do you know?"

Catherine turned to look at Liam. He was standing squarely in front of the door, blocking the only way out. All the blood rushed to her head.

"What do you mean?"

"I know the police came to your room this morning. I know they had a warrant. And I know what they should have found there would have landed you in questioning, at the very least," he said, advancing a few steps toward her. "So I suppose my real question is, how are you even here?"

Catherine backed up instinctively. She was trapped. Her gaze cast around for something she could use as a weapon, but aside from a few potted plants and assorted furniture, there was nothing. Could she juke around him and get to the door? Not if he was lithe enough to land like a cat after vaulting off a fire escape. And certainly not in these heels.

She could scream, but if the wedding party had moved on to the next stop on their schedule, they were clear on the other side of the grounds by now. Between distance and the crashing of the surf, there was no way they would hear her.

She had to keep him talking while she figured out an escape plan.

"How did you know Tilly?"

"That hardly matters."

"It does if you killed her. It matters to the people who cared about her."

He screwed up his face and continued to advance on her. "You didn't care about her. You wanted her dead too. Don't deny it."

"Of course I deny it. I wanted her out of Peter's life, but that doesn't mean I wanted her dead."

"Unbelievable. All of you. You're unbelievable. Every last one of you knows what to do to get what you want and you're all just too chicken shit to do it."

"How did you know her? What, did you see her in the society pages and start stalking her?"

"Stalking her? Please. I was her bodyguard, for Christ's sake. Her parents hired me to look after her. And she was a spoiled, entitled, thankless bitch who didn't give two shits about anyone around her. She lied, she manipulated, she thought she was above all common decency."

Right. Well. That was all true to Catherine's recollection of her.

"She fired me a month ago, for no particular reason, and then after Mrs. Frank was kind enough to give me a job, she tried to fire me again. The night of her wedding. As if she had any say in the matter at that point. That's what she was doing when you broke it up."

"When I—"

Suddenly it all came flooding back. Someone manhandling Tilly in the tent. Catherine rushing to her aid. The torn dress. And Tilly's right hook. She'd cut her hand when she'd fallen on a piece of broken glass.

"Yeah, I've never seen a socialite with a shot like that," Liam said. "I was actually kind of impressed."

"So you killed her because she fired you?" Catherine asked.

"The world is better off without her." Liam reached over to one of the tables, whipped off the tablecloth and started winding it into a long cord. Catherine's vision pricked over. He was going to strangle her.

Then, the door behind him slowly, soundlessly opened. Catherine's heart leapt with hope as she tried not to react. She couldn't see who it was past Liam's massive frame, but she silently prayed they were here to help her.

"You know, when Peter sent me over to your hotel with that

bag of sheets, I told him I could just get rid of you. That it would be much easier. But did he listen to me? No. No more death, he said. I've really got to stop taking orders from people."

Catherine blinked. "Wait. *Peter* sent you?"

Liam lunged at Catherine. Now she did scream, leaning back over the railing of the deck, remembering, vividly, how Peter had said that if he'd wanted Tilly dead, he could have just shoved her over one of these railings. Down below, the water crashed against the rocky shoreline, and Catherine imagined her head split open, her body broken. Liam tossed the cord he'd made around her as if to tie her up and, at that moment, Farrah brought one of Camilla's iron cat statues down on the back of his head. Liam's eyes went wide and he slumped to the ground.

Gasping for air, Catherine threw her arms around Farrah. "How did you—"

"I saw your car pull up and we were all waiting for you down on the patio, so when you didn't show up, I figured you came out here. We were ahead of schedule."

*Since when has any wedding ever been ahead of schedule?* Catherine thought.

"I meant, how did you lift that thing?" Catherine asked, gesturing at the cat, now on the floor next to Liam.

Farrah shrugged and slapped her hands together. "I guess my years of lugging boxes around for my mother finally paid off."

They both looked down at Liam. He was still breathing. "I feel like we should call the police," Catherine said.

"On it." Farrah pulled out her phone. "What was he saying about Peter?"

Suddenly the adrenaline subsided and Catherine went cold. She hugged herself and sat down hard on the nearest chair.

"I think . . . I think Peter was setting me up to take the fall for Tilly's murder."

# LEANNE

Leanne stood with Hudson until it was his turn to walk down the aisle, then stepped aside and stood with Samantha near the rosebushes, trying to be as invisible as possible. Maya was radiant as she strode slowly toward Peter, on her own, head up, shoulders back, beaming. Whatever tension she'd seen in Maya earlier appeared to have melted away, and Peter, the jackass, had never looked this happy in his life—at least not as far as Leanne could recall. His father and mother stood off to the opposite side of the altar, smiling proudly.

She wondered if anyone other than her was even sparing a thought for Tilly.

Everything looked perfect. The white aisle, the little baskets of Gerber daisies hanging from the fencing. The arch of flowers Peter, his brother, and Hudson stood under, awaiting the bride. Catherine had even somehow secured a string trio, who played Pachelbel's Canon in D impeccably.

Why wasn't she here? Leanne hoped nothing horrible had happened. They'd had enough horrible around here lately to last a lifetime. She checked her phone again. Still no messages. Nothing since that weird question about the butler.

Where was the butler, anyway? And where had Farrah disappeared to?

The officiant, who had shown up about five minutes ago, stepped up to the center of the arch. He welcomed everyone, introducing himself as Pastor Paul from the local Reformed church, then began.

"We are here to witness the joining in matrimony of Maya Rose Romero and Peter Jeffrey Frank," he said in a deep rumble of a voice. "This is a blessed and joyful occasion, and a celebration of love, hope, and optimism for the future."

"I'm going to need you to stop right there, sir!"

Everyone froze as a half dozen police officers flooded in, followed by Catherine and Farrah. Catherine walked, head down, to Leanne's side, making eye contact with no one.

"Catherine?" Leanne said. "What the hell?"

"It was Peter," she whispered. "He was the one setting me up. Maybe he was protecting Hudson, too? I don't know, but it was all Peter."

Leanne stopped breathing. Peter knew? About Hudson? *How*?

"What is the meaning of this?" Camilla demanded, hand on the back of a chair as if for balance.

Detective Virgil stepped up. "My apologies, Mrs. Frank, but I need to speak to your son."

"But . . . this is our wedding," Maya said.

Leanne looked at Peter. Her heart didn't know what to do. That he had tried to set someone else up to take the fall in order to protect his son . . . Maybe he was a good father after all. He'd put his love for Hudson ahead of his long relationship with Catherine, his reputation, his own future.

But also, seriously? Trying to get his ex sent to jail for murder, even to protect his own son, was pretty cold.

Her eyes found Hudson. He stood frozen under the archway, next to his father, terror written all over his face. He was too far from Leanne for her to make a move for him without calling attention to them both, but she had to do something. She had to get him out of here. Now.

"What's the problem, Officer?" Peter said, walking up the aisle, confident and completely self-assured.

"Let's take this inside," Virgil said, matching Peter outthrust-chest to outthrust-chest.

"Take what inside? What in the hell has transpired that's so important you felt the need to interrupt my wedding?"

Catherine slowly edged behind Leanne and Samantha as if she was trying to stay out of Peter's line of vision. Leanne motioned to Hudson to come to her, but he didn't move. He shook his head—no more than a twitch from side to side—his eyes casting about for an exit.

*Don't. Run,* Leanne mouthed. *At least not without me,* she thought.

Virgil looked around, then cleared his throat. "Fine, you wanna do this here, we'll do this here. We just conducted a search of your room and—"

"You *what*? Where's the warrant?"

Magrin stepped up and handed a piece of paper to Peter, which he immediately handed to his brother, who had come over to stand beside him.

"And we found some bloody pieces of the chandelier stuffed in the bottom of a drawer in your closet. Messages on your computer between you and Tony Gladstone about cash payments made after the murder."

Leanne reached over and grabbed Samantha's hand. What the fuck?

"Plus a slew of text messages to Maya Romero detailing how you, quote 'never wanted to marry the bitch to begin with.'"

Peter tipped his head forward and shook it, smiling wryly as if everything Virgil was saying was beyond hilarious. "There are explanations for all of that."

"We also have Liam MacFarland in custody."

All the color drained from Peter's face.

"All in all, it's enough to arrest you for the murder of Tilly Dansforth-Frank." He pulled out a pair of handcuffs. "Turn around."

"No!" Hudson shouted.

He dropped the pillow with the rings on it and ran over to the officer. Leanne finally moved, lurching toward him, trying to stop him before things got truly out of hand. But it was too late. Hudson got right between the cop and his father, tears streaming down his face.

"You can't arrest him! He didn't do anything! My dad isn't a killer! He's not a killer!"

Leanne's heart rent into pieces. "Hudson, stop. Don't say anything else."

"I'm sorry, kid. I gotta do my job," Virgil said.

"No! No! No! He didn't kill anyone! It wasn't him!!"

"Hudson! Stop talking right now!" Leanne shouted, panicked.

"No! It wasn't him!" Then he whirled around to look back at the arch. "Tell them, Grandma! Tell them it wasn't him!"

Everyone turned toward Camilla, who somehow looked even paler in the sunlight than she had upstairs. She stepped over to a table where filled glasses of champagne were arranged, awaiting the declaration of Peter and Maya as man and wife. She plucked one up, drained the contents, and looked around at the assembled crowd.

"If you'll excuse me," she said.

Then she took one step and crumpled to the ground.

# CATHERINE

She found him sitting on a bench outside the hospital, alone. He was still wearing his tuxedo shirt and pants, but the jacket and tie were gone. His patent shoes shone in the bright sunlight. He was leaning forward, forearms braced on his thighs, pressing his hands together and pushing them back and forth. Part of her wondered where Maya was, why she wasn't there comforting him, but a bigger part of her didn't care.

"Peter."

He looked up at her, squinting one eye against the glare.

"Hey."

"I know what you did."

He straightened up and let out a half sigh, half groan. His elbows came to rest on the back of the bench, spread wide. "That's it? No *how's your mom?* or *are you okay?*"

"Are you kidding me?" she asked. "You tried to set me up for *murder.*"

"You have no proof of that," Peter said.

"That's all you have to say? I don't need proof. I *know* what you did. No one else could have planted that ring on me, and you were the only one who knew about the bloody sheets. You paid Liam to hide them in my closet. You wanted me to go to jail for something I had nothing to do with! For what? To save Mommy Dearest?"

"Don't call her that." Peter's eyes flashed. "She's up there, unconscious in a hospital bed, with the cops outside her doorway in case we try to make a run for it."

"Because she *murdered* someone! Someone she knew well. Someone you grew up with. Her friends' daughter! You were *married to her*. And you're indignant?"

Hudson had told Leanne the whole story after the ambulance had come for Camilla. How he'd been in his hideout in the middle of the night and heard yelling. That he'd come out to see what was going on and seen his grandmother use a pair of shears to cut the rope. The only way, in Catherine's mind, that this could have worked would have been if someone had weakened it already to the point that one last cut would do the job, and her money was on Liam. He hadn't denied that he'd murdered Tilly when Catherine had accused him, after all. Why Camilla had felt the need to make the final cut was curious, though. Was she protecting Liam—giving him a plausible out—or did she just hate Tilly so much she wanted to do the deed herself?

"Allegedly. She didn't confess. Innocent until proven guilty is still a thing, you know."

"Did you know?" Catherine asked, then lowered her voice. "Did you . . . help her do it?"

"What? No. Of course I didn't help her do it. I didn't know about it until after the fact."

"But you helped her cover it up. By trying to frame me."

Peter stared out across the parking lot. "She's not right in the head, Catherine. She's sick. Brain cancer. I don't even know if she understands how wrong this all is. But I know she thinks she was doing it to save me from a marriage I didn't want."

Catherine took a beat, absorbing this new information about Camilla. This whole thing was so complicated, so tragic. So entirely fucked-up. But it didn't change what he'd done to her. The lies, the deceit, the manipulation.

"You said you had never stopped loving me. How could you do this to me?" Catherine said, annoyed when her voice cracked.

Peter stood up. "If it makes you feel any better, you're not the only one I tried to put the blame on."

"I'm sorry, what?" Catherine's brain felt fuzzy and whirly at the same time.

"I'm the one who told the police about Tilly's ultimatums. I'm the one who anonymously tipped them off about my and Farrah's relationship. I *tried* to confuse them to the point that they didn't know which way was up, but nothing stuck! You were just the one with the most plausible motive."

Catherine had to sit down. She took the bench now that Peter was off it. "Wait a minute. You're the one who told us to keep those ultimatums a secret."

Peter rolled his eyes and shrugged. "Yeah, and?"

"Why would you do that if you were just going to tell the cops anyway?"

"What does it matter now?"

"It matters, Peter! It matters because you're a liar. You played us this whole time! Who the hell even are you?"

"Don't get all dramatic, Catherine. I was just trying to protect my family."

"At what expense? And what do you mean I had the most plausible motive? You gave the ring Maya picked out for herself to someone else and let her show up at your wedding! You didn't even warn her not to come. And you threatened to take Leanne's kid away. How am *I* the one with the most solid motive?"

"Because you're obsessed with me!" Peter shouted.

Catherine stared. She felt like she was going to throw up.

"What?" she breathed.

"You always, *always* come when I call you," Peter said venomously, as if he was accusing her of some crime. "Doesn't matter where you are. Doesn't matter what you're doing. Doesn't matter who you're with. You drop everything and come. Who does that? We broke up twelve years ago, Catherine. Twelve years! When are you going to wake up and realize this is never going to happen?" He gestured between the two of them.

"Oh my God." Catherine bent forward, head between her knees. Tears leaked from her eyes and splattered on the cobblestoned pathway. "Oh my God oh my God oh my God."

She was a fool. A complete and utter fool. He didn't love her. He'd never loved her. All this time he'd been using her. Consciously using her. And worse, she'd let him do it. She'd been a willing participant in a total farce. Twelve years. Twelve years of her life. Wasted.

He blew out a sigh and sat next to her. She sat up straight, face tight, barely holding it together, and slid farther away on the bench, staring straight ahead at the hospital parking lot.

"After everything I've done for you," she said slowly, her voice wet. "All the nights I was there for you when you were lonely or depressed or just didn't want to drink alone. I've risked everything for you," she added pointedly. "How could you ever speak to me like that?"

"Don't act like you didn't want to be there, Catherine," Peter said, dropping his arms. "Don't even try."

"You *murdered* Monica! And I helped you cover it up!"

He whirled and slapped a hand over her mouth, his eyes nearly bugging out of his head. Catherine stood up, shoving him away.

"Get off me!"

"What the fuck is the matter with you?" he whispered.

He glanced around and, finding that there was no one anywhere in the vicinity, stood up again.

"That was an accident and you know it."

"It was *manslaughter*," she said, shaking. "And you made me an accessory."

"I never made you do anything," Peter said. "You're a grown woman. You can make your own choices, Catherine."

"Stop saying my name like that. You're so condescending it makes me want to vomit."

He was so unattractive to her in that moment, she felt her entire worldview shift. The entitlement. The ego. The total obliviousness to anyone other than himself. It was written all over his face. How had she ignored it for this long?

"Whatever," he spat. "Let's just be clear on the fact that you've never done anything for me that you didn't *want* to do."

"Well, I didn't *want* to go to prison, but you were perfectly fine sending me there."

"My mother means everything to me, Cat. You know that," Peter said.

His use of her nickname at that very moment felt like a joke at her expense. "But what about me?" she said. "You could have ruined my entire life. Do you even understand that? Do you even care?"

She felt like she had ripped her own heart from her chest and was holding it out to him, bloody and beating, with both hands. What he did next would tell her everything she needed to know.

Peter sniffed. "Honestly, Cat? I thought you'd step up."

"Step up?"

"I figured, if push came to shove, and you thought I might go to jail for the rest of my life, you'd plead guilty."

Catherine flinched. She thought about doing what she'd promised herself she'd do when she heard he proposed to Maya.

She saw herself thrusting her knee up into his groin, imagined the shock and pain on his face as he doubled over.

"You're a sociopath," she said on a gasp.

"Oh yeah? Then what does that make you?"

Catherine picked up her bag from the bench and, steadying herself, looked him in the eye. "I think it makes me free."

And instead of resulting to violence, she turned around, walked away, and did not look back.

# LEANNE

The bakery doorbell chimed at 2:58. It had just started to rain, and Leanne was looking forward to a long afternoon of doing nothing with Hudson. He was leaving with Peter and Maya in two days, and she refused to waste a single minute of them. She was organizing receipts at the counter, hoping to make a quick exit. Everyone else had either gone home or was in the back, cleaning up.

Even with this deadline looming, she couldn't stop thinking about what Camilla had done. She'd told Tilly to call that pre-vows meeting so that Tilly would hand her and Maya and Catherine perfect motives. She'd known exactly what she was doing. She'd had her victim create suspects for her own impending death. It was diabolical. How did people like that even exist in the world, let alone in her own life?

"We're just about to close," she said, then looked up.

Catherine stood in the middle of the room, hands in her jacket pockets, droplets of water on her shoulders. Her mascara was smudged.

"Catherine?" Leanne asked, a thump of foreboding in her chest.

"I have something to tell you." Catherine's voice was hoarse. "It's about the night of the reunion."

# MAYA

"Maya! How does it feel to be married to someone whose mother was arrested for murder?"

"Maya! Maya! Do you really think this marriage will last?"

"Maya! Are you concerned for your safety?! Blink three times if you need help."

The chauffeur had driven his Lincoln SUV—more like a tank—all the way out onto the tarmac in an attempt to avoid the paparazzi, but they had just swarmed the security fence like hornets, hurling their stupid questions and flashing their cameras. Maya shoved her biggest, darkest sunglasses on and waited for Peter to come around the car with Hudson. The chauffeur pulled their bags out of the trunk.

"I don't want to go," Hudson stated obstinately, clutching a raggedy stuffed bunny Maya was pretty sure he was too old for. But then again, who was she to judge? She still had the American Girl doll her mother had given her the Christmas before she died. "All my friends are at soccer right now. We were gonna play World Cup today."

"They have soccer in Australia, buddy," Peter said, crouching down to his level. "Think of it as an adventure. You're going to make all new friends. And maybe we'll get to see some kangaroos."

"Maya! What's with the hasty exit? Do you two have something to hide?"

"We should get on the plane," Maya said.

She turned to walk toward the small jet, and Peter stood up, taking Hudson's hand. But when he started to follow Maya, Hudson didn't budge. She paused, her inner temperature rising. This was not the way she pictured her life with Peter. Hudson was supposed to be living with Leanne and Tony. That was the deal. That was what he'd always told her the arrangement would be. She had no idea why Peter had changed his mind—it was something she intended to talk to him about once they were settled in Melbourne—but she needed to get out of here and away from these psychotic reporters. Now.

Why didn't he just order Hudson onto the plane? Threaten to ground him? Why was he still crouched near the ground, coaxing the kid? The power dynamic here was all wrong. She never would have gotten away with this as a kid. Was there going to be a negotiation every time they wanted to go somewhere?

"Can I take your bag, Mrs. Frank?" A young, pretty, perfectly coiffed flight attendant asked, standing on the bottom stair.

Mrs. Frank. That was going to take some getting used to. She and Peter had been married yesterday morning in the hospital chapel. Better to make it legal before leaving the country. The police even allowed his mother to be wheeled in for the ceremony. They had officially arrested her right after they had said their vows. The woman was riddled with cancer now and not long for this world. From what Peter had told her, she'd greeted her arrest with a placid acceptance.

"It's Ms. Romero. And thanks." Maya handed over her leather tote and looked back at Peter. Maybe she should go over there. Show Hudson what was what. Never in her life had Maya thought about becoming a stepmom, or what sort of stepmom she'd want to be. But she was starting to think she might have to be an evil one.

Then her phone rang. It was Leanne.

"Hey," Maya said into the phone, turning her back to the flashing cameras. "We're just about to get on the plane."

"I'm here. Can you tell security it's okay to let me in?" Leanne sounded breathless. Frantic, almost.

"You're *here*? At the Atlantic City airport?"

"Yes! I'm actually right outside the gate. If you look toward the security booth, you'll see me." Maya looked. Leanne waved frantically from the small, window-walled booth, almost beaning the security guard next to her. Maya felt as if the cavalry had arrived. Leanne would be able to get Hudson onto the plane. Or better yet, maybe she could take him home with her.

"Give the guard the phone."

# LEANNE

"**L**ee!"

Hudson threw himself at Leanne when he saw her, Carrots the Bunny pressing into the side of her leg. She hugged him back, leaned down, and kissed the top of his head.

"What are you doing here?" he asked.

Leanne looked up at Peter, who looked about ready to throw down. "I just want to talk to your dad for a sec. Why don't you go ask Maya if she can introduce you to the pilot? I bet he'll let you check out the cockpit."

"I've seen like a million cockpits," said Hudson, rolling his eyes.

Leanne took a breath for patience. "Well, maybe this one is different. Go ahead!"

He walked over to Maya and spoke to her, then took the steps two at a time onto the plane. Maya took off her sunglasses and shot Leanne a quizzical look, but Leanne waved her off and she followed Hudson. The second Maya was inside the plane, the constant shouts of the paparazzi died down a bit, but some of them were still taking photos—of her and Peter now.

"Why are you here, Leanne?" Peter asked, crossing his arms over his chest.

"I know everything, Peter. I know you were driving the night Monica died."

She watched the color drain from his face and would have felt sorry for him if it wasn't so goddamned satisfying.

"I don't know what you're talking about," he said.

"Please, don't embarrass yourself," Leanne said. "I know you were driving drunk. I know you were speeding because the two of you were fighting. I know that Catherine found the car on the side of the road and found you in hysterics because you'd just murdered the mother of your only child. Oh, and because if you got another DUI you were definitely going to jail."

Peter turned and paced away, tenting his hands over his mouth.

"I know she helped you move Monica into the driver's seat and I know you paid the ME to cover up the discrepancies between her injuries and the state of the car."

"Jesus Christ," he said under his breath, staring off toward the runway, away from the reporters.

"I didn't want to do it this way, Peter. I don't think you're a bad father, and you can imagine how hard that is for me to say right now, knowing what I know about you and my sister."

She swallowed hard.

"But if you try to leave this country with that kid, I will go to the police. I will go to the press. I will find that medical examiner and I will make him talk. And Catherine is ready to back me up every step of the way."

Peter looked over at her, his eyes hard and rimmed in tears. Behind him, Hudson jumped down the last two steps.

"Are we going home?" he asked brightly.

———

Leanne clutched Hudson's hand, rolling his suitcase behind her as they crossed the parking lot to her car.

"Can we get back in time for practice?" he asked.

"I don't think so, buddy. Sorry. But you can go tomorrow."

"Dang it." He actually kicked the tire of her car. "I wanted to score on Caden."

Leanne smirked as she loaded his bag into her car. The worldview of an eleven-year-old. Did he really have any idea how close his entire world had just come to irrevocably changing?

"How about I take you to the diner and we get a waffle sundae for breakfast?" she asked, slamming the trunk.

His eyes widened. "Are you serious?"

"Dude, I've never been more serious about anything in my entire life."

Hudson cheered and jumped into the car. Leanne stood for a moment and took a deep breath as Peter's private jet picked up speed down the runway and took off. She had a feeling that nothing would ever be the same again—in the best possible way.

# MAYA

Maya held Peter's hand between them, leaning over the table as the speakerphone rang. An iPad was propped in front of them on the kitchen table of their modern, amenity-packed apartment in Melbourne, live streaming the scene at a Las Vegas coffee shop. Her father was in the back corner booth, a bodyguard lingering nearby. She watched as he picked up the phone.

"You're late," he said by way of greeting.

Maya glanced at Peter, who squeezed her hand, his expression bolstering. It was thanks to him and his creative neutralizing of Shawn that she'd come up with this idea in the first place, so it was only fitting he was here for this.

"I'm not coming." Maya pressed her eyes closed as she said it.

"The fuck? You called for this meeting."

"I did, because there's something you need to know."

"Oh, this I'm dying to hear," her father said, leaning back in his seat, then forward again.

"I've recorded ten hours of video. A tell-all, spilling every last thing I know about you and your business."

Silence. The color on the feed wasn't great, but she could still see his skin getting darker.

"I've sent the footage to a journalist I trust, with strict instructions that they are only to watch it if something happens to me, or Peter, or his son. And then they can use it to write an in-depth article about what it's like growing up as the daughter of a cold-blooded murderer and drug trafficker."

She had, in fact, also sent this tell-all to the FBI. But he didn't need to know that. Not yet. The bit about the strict instructions was also a lie. The reporter was currently writing an exclusive piece on Maya's life. But he also didn't need to know that.

Her father shook his head. "Maya, I don't know what you think you're doing, but—"

"I'm taking control of my life," she said, trembling with anger and fear. "I'm making it so that I never have to hear my phone ring again and have my heart drop, thinking it's you."

Her father laughed. "This is an empty threat."

Maya swallowed against a dry throat. "How do you figure?"

"Because you don't know jack shit about jack shit."

"Oh really?" Maya clenched her jaw and leaned even farther forward. "I know where you buried that FBI agent when I was ten. You thought I was asleep in the back of the car, but I was awake, and I saw *everything*. I know when you said you were going to Italy with Mom, you actually went out to Reno to execute some guy named Big Kenny for intercepting one of your shipments. I know—"

"Stop. Talking," he said through his teeth. He squirmed in his seat again, trying to compose himself. "How do I know you even did this? How do I know you're not bluffing?"

"Because the reporter, who happens to be not the least bit scared of you, is sitting across the café from you right now."

He looked up. It took him a couple of seconds, but he zeroed in on the camera. Maya imagined Nadine Force giving him a jaunty wave as she held her phone's camera trained at him. It had been almost shocking how quickly Nadine had jumped on board with her plan. It seemed that getting back into Maya's good graces and being guaranteed the first all-access profile on America's Sweetheart after her Wimbledon win and scandal-surrounded wedding, was worth a lot to a reporter. That and Maya was pretty sure Nadine had always been fascinated by Nico "The Nut."

"And just in case this wasn't clear, if anything happens to her, the trigger gets pulled as well."

"You ungrateful little—"

"I wouldn't finish that sentence," Maya said.

"What do you want?"

"I want you out of my life. I want you to never call me, never write me, never even think about me again." Maya's voice grew more confident with each word. She was starting to—not enjoy this—but not hate it. "Except for when Nadine approaches you after this call and asks you for a quote for the profile she's doing on me. You can tell her we're not in touch anymore, but you've been watching my meteoric rise proudly from afar."

"That it?" he said.

"That's it," Maya said. "I'd say it's been nice knowing you, but."

With that, she ended the call, knowing that, at that very moment, a squadron of heavily armed FBI agents was swarming the café.

# LEANNE

Sitting in the brightly lit office of her brand-new storefront, Leanne scrolled through the latest slew of internet orders, filing them away by date and size so she could determine whether she had to turn any of them down. She couldn't believe she might be in the position of having to refuse business, and wondered for the millionth time whether she should look at mass production. It wasn't her style, but it might come to that. Ever since Catherine had started posting photos of her cakes on her Instagram and website, Leanne's business had been steadily building. It had necessitated moving into this newer, larger space, with a kitchen twice the size of her old one, and now . . .

Tony had found a warehouse space a few towns over that could work, but so far she'd refused to go look at it. Maybe it was time.

"Ugh! I don't understand why we need to learn algebra! When am I ever going to have to solve for $x$ when I'm playing for Real Madrid?"

Leanne turned around in her swivel chair and looked at Hudson, who was doing his homework on one of the wooden worksurfaces.

"I use algebra every day," she said, just as Tony came in the back door with a pizza.

"You do not," said Hudson.

"She does. And so do I," Tony said, ruffling the kid's hair and dropping the pizza down next to him.

"Prove it," Hudson said, pulling out a slice of pepperoni.

"Okay." Leanne opened one of the new orders and said, "If I have to make sixty cupcakes and it takes roughly thirty minutes to make twelve cupcakes, how much time do I need to reserve to make the cupcakes?"

"That's easy." He leaned back and squinted. "Two and a half hours."

"You just did algebra," Tony said with a smile.

"In your head!" added Leanne, joining them at the table.

Hudson rolled his eyes but smiled. "Fine." He held his pizza slice in one hand and started to solve the next problem, gripping his pencil in the other. "But I still don't get how it'll apply to soccer."

"So listen," Leanne said, grabbing herself a slice and sitting down across from Tony. "I think maybe we should go check out that warehouse."

"Yeah?" Tony brightened. "I think it's a steal."

"Yeah," she said. "Let's do it."

He reached over and squeezed her hand, and Hudson rolled his eyes at them again. Leanne couldn't believe that this time last year, she was still terrified she might not wrest full custody from Peter. And now, here they were, a legal family unit with two booming businesses and a bright future.

Tilly Dansforth's bizarre five minutes in Leanne's life had been the best thing that had ever happened to her.

# CATHERINE

"**T**ell us the story, Catherine. Please, please, please!"

Catherine smiled as a round of catcalls and encouragements went up from around the fire. She was relaxing on the beach in Thailand with a dozen or so influencers—guests of another successfully planned event who had simply not wanted the party to end. Back in the day, if she'd stumbled upon this group at four a.m. after the wedding was well over, she would have let them be. But the line between herself and her clients had blurred quite a bit since her business had blown up, the happy confluence of Bea and Antonio's wedding being covered by TMZ, her involvement in the solving of the Tilly Dansforth murder going public, and her whirlwind reunion with, and eventual engagement to, Cash Blakely going viral.

No longer was she simply a B-list planner with a few hundred thousand followers. She was now a member of the A-list, with 1.2 million followers and counting.

"Fine! Fine, you heathens." Catherine laughed as she fell elegantly into one of the hammock-style chairs and looked around at her audience. "As it turned out, even though their families were *very old friends*, Camilla Talbot-Frank had never liked the Dansforths. And she'd always *detested* Tilly."

Catherine relished this bit of the story. God rest Tilly's soul and everything, but it gratified her that she and Camilla had always had the same opinion of the predatory, self-obsessed deceased. She smiled up as Farrah, now her trusted second-in-command, handed her a cold bottle of water, then went to settle among the group. Felicity had retired soon after the clambake, deciding party planning had gotten too stressful.

"So when she found Tilly was pregnant and blackmailing Peter, she decided to take matters into her own hands."

"Yeah, bitch!" one of the YouTubers cheered, lifting his forty up over his head. The rest of them hooted and hollered.

"Her original plan was to lure Tilly to the tent in the middle of the night and have her new butler, a man who equally detested Tilly, release the safety on the winch that held the chandelier in place. But the morning of the wedding, the winch died. The bride, of course, would not hear of having her wedding without the chandelier, so she threw a fit and the very savvy wedding planners had to improvise."

Catherine smiled across at Farrah, who rolled her eyes.

"So, like, if she hadn't thrown a fit, she wouldn't be dead right now," a makeup influencer by the name of Jessie Fab put in, leaning forward. She had become a good friend of Catherine's over the last six months and was a genius when it came to new trends. Her glitter eyeshadow was still on point even after ten hours.

"Probably not," Catherine conceded. "So the wedding planners called in a local fisherman and he and his crew used a ridiculously strong rope to hoist and secure the chandelier. Camilla's plan was back on, but it needed some tweaks."

Catherine went on to explain how Liam had used a chain saw to cut away most of the rope in the middle of the night, which took less than a minute, leaving just enough to be cut at the last second once Tilly arrived. How Camilla had called her down for "a chat," and Tilly had come willingly. How Camilla had cut what was left of the rope using a pair of shears from the garden shed, and the chandelier had come down on Tilly's head.

"Unfortunately, right in front of Hudson."

"Oh my God," someone muttered. "He saw the whole thing?"

Catherine nodded. Poor Hudson. He'd always maintained that he'd heard people yelling and that was why he'd come out of hiding, and Catherine still wondered who that had been. Obviously, Camilla hadn't even spoken to Tilly that night. Stray partiers on the beach, maybe? They'd never know.

"So while Camilla and the butler were disposing of the rope and switching it out for one that would appear frayed, he stole the shears in a bid to protect his grandmother."

"Wow. Some kid."

"Seriously."

Catherine took a breath. "Anyway, Camilla was supposed to stand trial for the murder, but by the time the trial started, her cancer had returned aggressively and she died the night before she was supposed to take the stand."

"So she went out like a boss," said Preston Party, a YouTuber who taught parents how to throw their kids elaborate birthday parties.

"I guess you could say that. The crazy bodyguard turned state's evidence, so it's not like her reputation is fully intact. But at least Hudson never had to testify against his grandmother and is living full-time with Leanne and her husband down at the shore."

"I hope he's in therapy," said Jessie.

"Oh, definitely," Catherine said. "And Peter and Maya visit him whenever they're in the States."

It still made her throat tighten a bit, saying Peter's and Maya's names together, like they were one unit, but it was getting better. She herself was in therapy, where they talked a lot about letting go of the past and standing in one's power.

"What a story," said another influencer, shaking his head in wonder. "Do you ever get tired of telling it?"

"Not really," Catherine said with a smile, as Cash walked up from behind, kissed her cheek, and handed over her favorite cozy sweater. "After all, you've gotta give the people what they want."

# MAYA

"Is that what you're wearing?"

Peter looked down at his polo shirt and cargo shorts ensemble and turned out his palms. "What? Too casual?"

"You might want to rethink the shorts," Maya said, pushing her sunglasses back up onto her nose and leaning back in her chaise. "And can you ask Etienne to send out something to nibble on? After that workout, there's no way I'm going to make it until dinner."

She and Peter were back in New York for the US Open, which was to begin in two days. Maya was ready. She'd been on a tear this summer, getting to the semis at Roland Garros, taking her second Wimbledon title in a row, and winning two of the biggest hard-court tournaments of the season. But she was most excited for this one, because Valentina had come out of retirement, and Maya was looking forward to wiping the court with her for the first time in her career.

"No problem." Peter leaned down and kissed her cheek. "I'll be back in no time."

Maya turned to watch him go, smiling to herself. It had been just over six months since his mother had passed, and he seemed to be handling it well. They kept busy, flying all over the world, courting new sponsors, building her brand. Sometimes she couldn't believe how close she'd been to losing it all. What would have happened if Camilla hadn't texted her that night?

COME BACK

THIS ISN'T OVER

Where would she be right now?

When Maya had received those texts, she hadn't immediately jumped up from the couch, but it hadn't taken her long. After all, Camilla was nothing if not intimidating, and Maya had been understandably curious. What did she mean, it wasn't over? Tilly and Peter had said their vows. She'd seen the photos on Instagram. There wasn't much more over than that.

But she'd gone back to Peter's apartment and gotten his Range Rover out of the garage and driven herself back to the Jersey Shore in the middle of the night, where Camilla had been waiting. Shawn hadn't been lying when he'd said they'd spent hours on the phone, but she'd been driving at the time. And he'd known it. A secret that not even Peter had known about when he'd tricked Shawn into that new job and that NDA.

"My son wants you," Camilla had said. "He only wants you. And if that conniving little harlot thinks I'm going to allow her to trap my son into a loveless marriage he never asked for, then she's sorely mistaken."

Maya hadn't asked for details. She'd found those out later from Peter himself. But she did say she'd do what she could to help.

There was already a plan. It was already in motion. All Maya had to do was get Tilly down to the tent at three a.m., and Camilla would do the rest. She didn't say exactly what she was going to do, which was the detail Maya had been reminding herself of for the last year in her darker moments. She hadn't *known* Camilla was going to murder Tilly. Maybe Camilla was going to talk her into an annulment, or pay her off, or have her kidnapped. She never said she was going to crush her under a chandelier. She'd simply asked Maya to get her to the tent.

"Why me?" Maya had asked. "Why don't you just ask her to meet you down there yourself?"

Camilla had laughed. "She has no interest in what I have to say. But if there's one thing I know about Tilly, she's always up for a fight."

She'd given Maya Tilly's number and a burner phone, and Maya had called her.

"I'm not going to just go away," Maya had said. "Why don't you come down here and tell me again that I'm out of Peter's life? See what happens when he's not around."

She'd felt like an actress in a bad play saying it, but apparently it was enough. Tilly had instantly taken the bait.

And that was all she'd needed to do. She could have simply gone home after that. But she'd kind of wanted to see what would happen next. After all, she was her father's daughter.

Maya had hidden outside the tent. She'd watched as Tilly stormed down the stairs and across the many patios and down more stairs and eventually, inside. Then she'd gone to one of the tent's windows and peeked inside.

Liam had been standing in the center of the dance floor.

"What the fuck are you still doing here?" Tilly demanded.

"I just wanted to be here to see this through," he told her.

"See what through? How many fucking times do I have to fire you?" Tilly shouted.

Liam had simply smiled.

"What is that? Get the hell out of here, you psycho. I'm meeting someone."

"Or so you think," Liam said.

It was then that Tilly's face registered fear, but it was already too late.

A shout from outside. Camilla yelled, "Now!"

Liam dove out of the way and Maya watched, frozen, as the chandelier came crashing down, and Tilly was silenced forever.

And then she'd run, and she'd never looked back.

Over the next few hours, she had formulated a plan. She would let Peter apologize to her. She would let him explain. She would play hard to get. Because that was what she would have done if she knew nothing about this murder. If she hadn't participated in it. If Tilly's death had been as big a shock to her as it was to everyone else.

She hadn't counted on Camilla *believing* her act. The woman had actually thought she had no intention of getting back together with Peter. Which had led to the unfortunate incident with her father. That Camilla had felt the need to call in guns that big only proved how well Maya had played it. If she'd known her acting job was going to force her to see her father, she would have clued Camilla in earlier. But really, in the end, seeing the old man that day had been a good thing. It had helped her find the snakes in her nest and slaughter them. No more Shawn. No more Christopher. If her dear old dad hadn't come to the country club that day, she might never have known.

She shuddered at the thought and picked up her ice water, taking a long, satisfying sip.

Her new hitting partner, Oona, had signed the most ironclad NDA ever written by man. And she hadn't hired a new life coach. She hadn't had an "incident" in months. She had Peter. She had her career. She would be number one in the world before the end of the US Open.

Maya was, as always, in control.

# ACKNOWLEDGMENTS

This book would not exist without the tireless work of my amazing agent, Holly Root, and my insightful editor, Abby Zidle. Special thanks also to Alyssa Maltese and Frankie Yackel, and to the team at Gallery Books, including Jen Bergstrom, Aimee Bell, Lauren Truskowski, Bianca Ducasse, and the entire sales team. I'd also like to give a special shout out to the book's cover designer, Sandra Chiu, for the incredible, eye-catching cover. Thank you so much to all the indie bookstore owners, librarians, book clubbers, and bookstagrammers who support my work! I definitely wouldn't still be doing this without you.

I would never be able to pursue my writing dreams without the support of my family—Matt, Brady, and William—who have all kinds of patience for the hours I spend in front of the computer and even bring me coffee when needed. And I would never finish a manuscript without my constant cheerleaders, Jen Calonita & Britt Rubiano.

Finally, thanks to my mom, who always made me believe I could do anything, and all the teachers and professors who helped me figure out how to prove her right.